Friendshipping

A NOVEL WITH AN ECLECTIC SOUNDTRACK

GARY S. LACHMAN

PAGE PUBLISHING, INC.
Conneaut Lake, PA

First originally published by Page Publishing 2020

ISBN 978-1-6624-1809-9 (pbk)
ISBN 978-1-6624-1810-5 (digital)

Printed in the United States of America

It seems no wonder if our ancestors regarded Friendship as something that raised us almost above humanity. This love, free from instinct, free from all duties but those which love has freely assumed, almost wholly free from jealousy, and free without qualification from the need to be needed, is eminently spiritual. It is the sort of love one can imagine between angels.

—C. S. Lewis

Prologue

January, 1997, Faisabad, Tajikistan

BEN LAY FACEDOWN in the cold mud. He had just regained consciousness and understood that he had been abandoned by the others, presumed dead from the mortar attack less than fifteen minutes ago. He felt like he had been blown into the very earth. His chest was constricted, and he was experiencing the same difficulty breathing as he had witnessed in a friend who suffered with chronic asthma. His ears weren't functioning properly. Sounds came in fragments and were unnaturally muffled. As he lay facedown with his arms bent at the elbows beneath him, the cold ground felt brittle against his skin. Although he couldn't see very much due to the position of his head and the intense pain in his neck, he knew that there were bodies nearby. He could smell them or, more accurately, he could smell the defecation that often accompanies violent death.

He wasn't afraid, only sad—deeply sad that men he had worked with for months had died, men who weren't necessarily his friends but were nevertheless more than passing acquaintances. He had imparted both knowledge and technology to them. He could feel their hands and arms as he had guided them in training and the rough, sweat-starched texture of the sleeves of their shirts.

But even so, there was a vast difference between supporting these Tajik freedom fighters and serving with conventional US military forces. His countrymen would never leave another American behind. For these Tajiks, Ben meant only one thing. They considered him a mere quartermaster, a source of military hardware, electronics, and logistics, not to mention cash and information about their common enemy. They were hunting an unholy alliance of renegade former Soviets, Iranian intelligence officers, and Chechen freedom fighters who had been conducting lethal strikes against the new government of Tajikistan. Once he could no longer provide what they wanted, he was just a body—an innocuous corpse. They left him to rot along with the other casualties. He had deluded himself into thinking that his dedication and support of their cause for the past eighteen months had elevated his status to brother-in-arms.

Ben closed his eyes and hoped that the EPIRB signal he had triggered a few minutes ago would summon an American medevac helicopter. He slowed his respiration, refocused his attention on the sole of a fake Converse All-Star basketball sneaker that was still on the detached foot of a fighter he had known as Omer Felaket, and waited for the concussive downdraft of chopper blades coming from above. He would not let himself believe that he had survived cancer only to die in the mud among people who apparently neither cared about nor appreciated him.

CHAPTER 1

Ben

Present, Istanbul

BRUCE WILLIS HAS a perfectly shaped head for being bald.

This idea was typical of the random thoughts and observations that routinely entered the easily distracted mind of Ben Jacobson. The other thing he often thought about, and this wasn't random at all, was how unusual it was that you could establish a terrific relationship—wait a minute, let's back that down to a *rapport*—with someone in a nonvisual manner, say by e-mail or telephone, but if you met them face-to-face and the face wasn't attractive to you, all those beautiful words went right out the window. The face didn't have to possess any classic beauty in the artistic sense or exotic beauty in a Hollywood/Bollywood way or even Barbie doll prettiness. For Ben, the minor imperfections were what really attracted him. If there wasn't that certain something, a sexy little defect, then whatever intimacy that had been earned over the intellectual part of the relationship was worth frightfully little. In fact, more often than not, it simply evaporated.

Currently, Ben often wondered what the hell he was doing in Istanbul of all places. Even before he was finished with university, he had always loved to travel and took advantage of every opportunity to experience new places and people. In fact, while a student and soccer player at Duke, he had become friends with kids from the Middle East, the UK, South and Central America and made it a point to visit them all at their homes after graduation. Later, as a diplomatic officer with the State Department, Ben had spent extended tours of duty in many countries, but never for more than several months at a time. He simply chalked it up to geographical ADHD, perhaps due to a psychic running away from the death of his sister and the subsequent abandonment by his parents. He had always felt a little damaged. Unwanted. He knew this was an unrealistically egocentric feeling, but why else would those he loved always leave him?

Pelin Pamircan, the assistant *du jour* provided by his employer, brought him a small tea glass of apple tea. "I hope it is sweet enough for you, Mister Ben. I was told that you love sweet things," she said with a saccharine inflection that was lost on Ben. She stood across from him, modeling her tight black jeans, the sole of her right foot pressed against the inside of her left thigh in a ballet pirouette position. Seeing that he wasn't interested, she completed the rotation and glided quietly out of his office, feeling that she had failed to interest a man for the first time in her life. She could not fathom this American.

Ben gazed out the dirty window overlooking Inönü Caddesi in the Gümüşsuyu neighborhood near Taksim Square in Istanbul. The building in which he officed had been constructed in the early 1800s and sported the kind of fanciful details usually associated with Baroque architecture. Ornate moldings, turrets, oversized window boxes, and black wrought iron festooned the exterior while the interior of the space he occupied provided twelve-foot ceilings with large crown moldings and divided light windows. He had just overcome a temporary writer's block that had stymied his work on a biography of a prominent Turkish man and his family. It had been commissioned by one of Turkey's most celebrated lawyers, a woman known locally by only her first name, Lale. The tulip. It was Lale who had selected Pelin to assist Ben break through his writer's block. Pelin, petite and shapely, with dark hair and eyes, had seemed perfect for the most exquisite seduction and inspiration any writer could want. However, Ben was far beyond that. Pelin was wasted on him. Her face was of no interest to Ben, and despite her physically delicate and precise movements, her attempts at seducing him were clumsy and obvious. Out of politeness, he ignored her.

Ben was now fully engaged in his favorite cerebral activity break of people watching. His perch on the second floor above the Bin Hong Lo restaurant afforded him an excellent view—not too high, but high enough to remain out of sight of the pedestrians passing below, unaware of his scrutiny. Occasionally, like at the present moment, a woman would walk by who looked eerily familiar. He had been thinking of her off and on for years. Ben was not quick to forget the first girl to break his heart, and in such an incredibly embarrassing way. But rather than dwell on his humiliation, being a generally positive kind of guy with a resilient ego, he preferred to think back on the tall, lithe Southern belle as a benign mystery. After learning that he had been unceremoniously replaced by a scrawny, pencil-necked hippie who was suddenly living with her at the house where Ben had spent so many nights, he never saw her again. Literally. Not once. Ben returned to New York for the rest of the summer. Rachel stayed at Duke University to finish her degree and then, presumably, returned to Colliersville, Mississippi, to do whatever Southern belles do in little towns founded by their forebears.

Thinking back on it all, nearly thirty-five years later, sitting in his eclectically furnished office in Istanbul, he doubted that he had really thought that much about her during the intervening time until about ten years ago when his brief marriage fell apart. An interesting set of circumstances followed that breakup. First, he noticed that his circle of friends had gone from local to global, and overall, the quality of the relationships, both at home and abroad, had vastly improved. The second thing he noticed was that he became tremendously curious about friends from his past. Occasionally, he would surf the web looking for references to them, information about them.

When he couldn't write, such as during the past few days, he would often sit at his desk, surfing the web, Googling old friends. Ben rarely gave much thought to why he was interested in finding people. He passed it off as idle curiosity and experimenting with internet sleuthing. He clicked over to Facebook.

Facebook helped this personal quest considerably. As everyone knows, Facebook is an enormously powerful tool for reconnecting, but with the benefit of a filter. He found that finding someone on Facebook provided access to entire webs of others. These interconnecting webs of individuals sometimes led to undesirable encounters with people he would have as soon deleted with a keystroke from the planet, but in the absence of such violent measures, they could be successfully blocked. More often than not, his searches for old friends on this social networking site yielded positive results. But of all the people he became committed to finding from his personal history, Rachel eluded him.

He imagined what Rachel must look like now. He wondered what she would think of his own appearance. Actually, he thought he looked okay. Not great, but better than not bad. A small but nasty scar ran from the left side of his nose toward his ear, a reminder of a gift of shrapnel from a mortar round in Tajikistan. He was of average height and still had most of his hair although it was thinning rapidly and getting very gray these past few years. Self-conscious about balding, he kept it short, eschewing the artifice of a comb-over and hair dye. In reasonably good physical condition for someone in his mid-fifties, he had obviously been hard on his body over the years with the aching knees and shoulders to prove it. His eyes were an unusual shade of dark blue, a trait that came predominantly from his father's side of the family but could also be found scattered throughout his mother's lineage. All in all, he was reasonably comfortable in his skin.

He assumed that Rachel had changed her name, appropriately married, had children, and become a serious academician who shunned the frivolities of tweeting, chatting, and the narcissism of posting one's life for all to see on the internet. Ben always felt ambivalent about how much information about his life should be shared with the world. He maintained fairly rigid security settings but knew that anyone determined enough could gain access to his photos and personal information. He, therefore, adhered to the old *Washington Post* test that he and his colleagues at the State Department used to follow: if it isn't what you'd be happy to see printed on the front page of the *Post*, don't write it; do it, film it, or talk about it.

His thoughts would return to Rachel at the oddest moments. During a summer rain when the air smelled a certain way and the mist was warm and moist on his neck and face. Walking along the residential streets of Washington in the early spring when lilacs and hibiscus would broadcast their scents from window boxes and planters in the still mornings. Random temperatures and dew points could initiate a memory of a girl with long brown hair and a very short skirt, a cut in her sandaled foot from broken window glass along Franklin Street in Chapel Hill.

More often than not, Ben was more fascinated by how an extraneous condition could trigger a memory than by the memory itself. He wondered if others occasionally experienced the same sensations. He accepted as normal that he was particularly attuned to his senses, a natural master at embodied cognition. Perhaps that's why he particularly enjoyed James Lee Burke's novels. Like Ben, Burke's character Dave Robicheaux always noticed the smells of his Louisiana environs. Before rain, during rain, and after rain were the most commonly mentioned. A pity, thought Ben, that most writers ignored the sense of smell. They painted great pictures with words, often punctuated with sound, the occasional sensual touch, but it was as if their characters inhabited deodorized worlds where smell had been antiseptically removed.

Burke's character Robicheaux lived in a pungent Southern world: the bayous of New Iberia Parish and occasionally the raucous streets of New Orleans. Ben also lived in a world of unique smells. New Iberia was obviously different from Turkey, but still similar to the non-touristic streets of Istanbul in subtle, sensual ways—not visually, but rather with respect to the variety and power of their sounds and smells. Ben thought this through more carefully. He decided that it wasn't the similarity of the sounds and smells; it was the fact that whatever sound and smell presented itself at any given moment was not merely *there* but was intrusive. At least intrusive to him. Ben didn't consider such intrusions onerous, just obvious and strong. Noticeable.

It was time for a late lunch. As he rarely had dinner before 8:30 or 9:00 p.m., a 2:30 lunch seemed reasonable to him. Ben descended the stairs—the building was of an early nineteenth-century Western European style—stepped outside, and walked down the hill.

Ben glanced through the window of a modest little *pastane*. Attracted by the scent of *baklava* and *lokma* from the bakery, he slowed his pace. He briefly considered sending some of the delicious pastries back to his office but changed his mind when he realized that this might be misunderstood by Pelin as an expression of his amorous intent. Inside the pastry shop, he saw a small group of friends who worked in the area drinking *Türk kahvesi* while engaged in a heated discussion. No doubt their never-ending debate over the relative prospects of the Beşiktaş, Fenerbahçe, and Galatasaray football teams. A young lawyer in the group he was acquainted with, Cemo Yanaras, gave him a wink while tugging the narrow lapels of his European-cut suit. Ben smiled and made the universal sign of a pistol with his thumb and index finger, pulled the trigger, exited the shop, and continued on his way. Fifteen minutes later, he couldn't shake the feeling that he was being followed. Practicing some basic tradecraft he had learned while at the State Department, he crossed and recrossed the street and ducked into a succession of other shops with varying lines of sight. Surreptitiously peering out at the sidewalk from behind their display tables and seeing no one dogging him, he relaxed and chalked it up to some kind of residual anxiety from the days when he actually had to worry about that sort of thing.

He passed through the sloping park and crossed the busy street to the sidewalk along the Bosporus. Being a fisherman, he never failed to notice the smell of fish. Whether schooling in the shallow water of the Golden Horn, reclining on the ice beds of the fishmongers at the Kumkapı market, or dangling in groups of five or six from the multi-hooked lines of the *balıkçılar* (fishermen) along the Bosporus, the scent could not be ignored. It had variations, of course. Some might dismiss them all as simply malodourous, but Ben appreciated the difference, much as a horticulturist delighted in the varieties of floral perfumes—not that he was equating those fish odors to those released by flowers.

These are sensations that are difficult, if not impossible, to write about. They are experiential. Whether you have smelled spawning bream along a Louisiana bayou or the Zambezi River that flows between Zambia and Zimbabwe, you will never forget that odor. It is different from the oily fish smell emanating from the *sardalya* (sardines) and *hamsi* (anchovies) dangling from the monofilament sabiki lines of comically long poles extending from the Galata Bridge and easily distinguished from the strong smell of the market fish, lying on their beds of ice in parallel rows like sleeping children in a dormitory.

Earlier in the day, he had passed the bakery that engaged in the passive-aggressive advertising of allowing the aroma from its kitchen to waft onto the sidewalk. Now using the same advertising tactic, the odor of grilled meat from a *kebabçi* assaulted Ben. Curiously, the smell brought Ben a flashback of walking down Franklin Street with Rachel and passing in front of a barbecue joint whose large plate-glass windows revealed orange plastic booths and blond faux wood tables. The irony of any aromatic similarity between Chapel Hill, North Carolina, and Istanbul didn't fail to strike him.

Last night, Ben had been checking on the sales of his latest book when he noticed a reader's comment posted to Amazon. The extremely flattering review had been signed R. Colliers and contained some references that only *the* R. Colliers, as in Rachel Colliers, could know. To say that this had struck him like a thunderbolt would not be an exaggeration. It took him more than an hour to regain the control necessary to attempt to find her again using the Duke alumni website, yet no e-mail address was provided—only a PO box to which he resolved to write to when he was in the States in the upcoming weeks.

CHAPTER 2

Rachel

Present, Mississippi

SHE WATCHED THE small brown bird hop along the branch outside the window of the house her great-grandfather had built almost 170 years ago. It was covered in the water stains of a recent storm that had kicked up the dry soil, adhering to the glass in its aftermath. As the sun was temporarily blocked by a passing cloud, she could see her reflection. She was fifty-seven years old and still attractive in a natural sort of way. Hours spent in the gym at the university where she taught in Hattiesburg, Mississippi, helped, of course. Not much to do in the little town of Colliersville where she currently lived. Founded by and named after her forebears, this timeless land was as lush and spiritual as she.

Rachel, standing with her arms firmly crossed over her chest, was palpably frustrated. She was addicted to the university life—so many years gathering degrees like a Girl Scout collecting merit badges. She had known a brief marriage and subsequently a parade of overeducated men with inflated egos and insecurities to match. The average life span of her relationships was six months and could be predictably divided into thirds: two months of flirtation and court-ship, two months of intensive sexual activity, two months of either the man or herself trying to exit gracefully. She was searching. They were searching. None found what they sought in the other.

Some of the men loved the fact that her inherited home was like a museum. They fussed over the antiques and old family photos yellowed with age: men with facial hair and women who, although considered good-looking in their day, now fell into the matronly category, uniformly overweight, and overserious. For many years, she kept enlargements of pictures of herself with an old college sweetheart hung in contemporary black-lacquered frames against the vine-adorned wallpaper. In one, they were at the beach with his burgundy Corvette and his chocolate Labrador, Buffalo Gal. In another, she wore her yellow and purple minidress with him in front of Studio 54 in New York. And farther along the wall, they were with his younger friend Jimmy, fly-fishing at their country house on a lake.

But now those photos were down from the wall and relegated to a box somewhere on the musty third floor where she never ventured for fear of cobwebs and spiders. She lived with Annie, her maiden aunt from her mother's side, who, even well north of eighty years old, was still tidying up and putting everything in its proper place. Annie had spent nearly twenty-five years *supervising* Rachel and acting as majordomo of the household. Whether this was out of habit or some deeper psychological connection with either her or the house, Rachel never understood.

Nor did Rachel ever fully understand why Annie had never married as she appeared to have been quite attractive and popular in her day from old photographs Rachel had seen of Annie and her friends. Whenever Rachel brought up the subject, Annie deflected with some anecdote about a college adventure that had a good laugh at the conclusion. Not that it mattered. Rachel was the first to admit that a woman didn't need a man to be happy. Well educated for a woman of her age with both undergraduate and master's degrees in English, Annie had literally read every book in their substantial library and, on occasion, even assisted Rachel as a proofreader of her academic manuscripts.

Annie was frugal and had invested wisely, buying foreclosure properties during each economic downturn suffered in the South.

GARY S. LACHMAN

Her income from rentals was spent educating poor children from Colliersville, many attending prestigious universities like Davidson, Clemson, Tulane, and, of course, Rachel's alma mater, Duke. Despite the twenty-five-year age difference, not to mention the enormous educational divide, at times they acted like characters from *The Odd Couple*, Annie the cantankerous Walter Matthau and Rachel the manic Jack Lemmon. At other times, the age and experience difference emerged strongly, Annie clearly assuming the role of an improved version of Rachel's mother, better equipped to deal with her moods and concerns. Annie was also far more protective and loving of Rachel than her mother had ever been as manifested by her constant reminders for Rachel to make appointments for everything from hair coloring to colonoscopies.

"Rachel, honey, can I bring you another tea? Something else? Perhaps a coffee this time, with a shot of Old No. 7?" Annie called from the kitchen.

Annie, anticipating Rachel's wish for the fortified coffee instead of tea, shuffled into the study, balancing herself on the tea trolley she pushed before her like a walker. "I'm getting tired of this routine, Rachel. You need a new life. When this fall semester at the university is over, I think you should wave goodbye to those worthless students of yours. I'd love to see you getting on a plane for somewhere, anywhere, so long as it's out of Colliersville before you follow in my piteous footsteps and become more furniture than human."

"I know, Aunt Annie. I know," Rachel agreed, inhaling the scent of Tennessee sour mash whiskey mixed with the freshly ground Columbian coffee. "And it will be done before thy kingdom come. I was just thinking about redecorating the old place. I mean just to have a quick change of appearance. Maybe it would lift our spirits. Some new rugs, curtains, pictures, lamps, paint, maybe even tear off that atrocious vineyard wallpaper that Daddy put up when I came home from college." Yet despite the aged carpets, threadbare lampshades, and faded wallpaper, the house still carried its dignity, so this facelift had to have more to do with Rachel's current state of mind than any real desire to change a superficial status quo. Her aunt's reaction was visceral and her response incredulous.

Annie's eyes bugged out more than usual. "What now? If you got that kind of money, you'd be better off on a European journey, not wasting it on frivolities like curtains!" Her voice sounded like a chair being scraped across a hardwood floor.

As Rachel couldn't understand Annie, likewise Annie couldn't understand Rachel: caring for her mother and father all alone, paying the taxes, keeping everyone on the payroll until they died or quit. The divorce stripped her of half of everything, and all that was left, for all intents and purposes, was the big old dusty house. As Annie looked at the attractive fiftyish woman who had grown from the carefree young girl she had known since birth, she knew it was time to push this bird out of the nest for a second time. It was one thing for an old woman of her kind to be married to a house but quite another for someone with the upbringing of Rachel. It offended her sensibilities, such a fine woman afraid to break free of her roots. Afraid to leave the comfort and security of some university. Afraid to take a chance. Why was this? What had happened that she missed? For the life of her, she couldn't figure it out. Such a beautiful girl, even in those hippie days, she was always the freshest flower among the flower children. Her Rachel. She had been beautiful as a young bride, too, but such a cruel man she had married back then.

Annie was well aware that Rachel didn't fully comprehend her adherence to what was of no more significance than her sister's house. She didn't mind that Rachel failed to appreciate the rich life she enjoyed during the long hours of solitude spent in the home's vast library. Annie was a different kind of soul, not content to make small talk with the pastor at her church on Sundays or waste time with the idle gossip of the other elderly people, who were simply waiting to die at the Colliersville Nursing Home. Annie thrived by using her imagination to maintain the rich history and lives of the generations who had lived here, black and white alike.

As Annie was pondering Rachel, Rachel gazed back at the woman she had never known life without. How could she explain that she could never leave her alone here in the house? She felt weighed down with stones, sinking below the surface of a warm farm pond covered in green algae that blotted out the sun as it closed over her head, the smell and feel of the summer heat, the pungent breath of the water, the chirping sounds of crickets fading, muffled by the depths of the pond. She was drowning in this house, in this life. But try as she might, she couldn't manage escaping to the surface. She couldn't regain the light. This primal need to get back into the light was kabbalistic, irresistible. She knew she was a good person and an old soul. Rachel had convinced herself that teaching was the only way she could fulfill her purpose in life. Yet all she was doing was teaching how to read, what to read, and how to write to a bunch of kids who were more interested in satisfying a foundation course requirement than truly appreciating the uniquely sweet flavor of Southern litera-ture. Yes, she had to follow Annie's advice. She had to make a break for it before she was broken herself—irreparably. The faint itching of an idea entered her mind. She would begin a quest.

Rachel decided to brave the ascent to the third floor and find those photos of her and Ben. She had decided to find him and, if she could pry Annie away from this crypt, bring her along to keep her from embarrassing herself. Whether he would ever give her a second chance…Well, that she didn't know.

CHAPTER 3

Ben

Present, Istanbul and past/high school

BEN HAD RECENTLY returned to Istanbul from his thirtieth high school reunion. In some ways, it made him feel good and fed his mercurial ego, which had been in a rather negative place lately. He had aged better than some of his former classmates, even looking like he had graduated more than ten years after they had. Some were easily recognizable, just with the addition of some wrinkles, gray (and less) hair, and a few extra pounds. Others were like strangers until he saw their name badges.

High school had been a memorable time for Ben. He had finally emerged from a long dark period that enveloped him and his twin sister, Laura, after she was diagnosed with Ewing's sarcoma, a particularly virulent cancer that preys upon children and adolescents. They shared her fear and pain for three long years between sixth and eighth grade, enjoying manic periods of fun during a few brief remissions. Ben and Laura spent virtually all their time together then, not wanting to share a moment with friends.

A cloud of grief hung over him as he ascended the great stone steps leading into the high school's fortresslike building. The other kids in his grade, of course, knew his name, but they certainly didn't know him, except as the kid whose twin sister had died of cancer. He was very much alone without Laura. He tried to imagine her walking along next to him in the hallways, between classes. But he couldn't seem to conjure her up and was frightened that she would completely disappear from his mind. He felt like every day he was in school, he was betraying her in some indefinable way. He dressed in blacks and olive drab greens, starting out in ninth grade as a wannabe hippie-political leftist-antiwar-stoner because he thought that it would be easier to disappear into that seemingly less-judgmental crowd. But it wasn't. In fact, his twin sister's death became an unwanted emblem of his identity. During the first week of classes, a hulking senior with black leather pants and long, dirty hair grabbed his arm and pushed him against the wall outside of the cafeteria. "Hey, you're the kid with the dead twin sister, huh?"

Ben just stared back, at a loss for words.

"Answer me, dickhead. I asked if you're the kid with the dead—"

"My sister, Laura, died of cancer this summer," Ben replied quietly.

"That's so cool, man. I wish my sister would die like that. Fucking bitch." A crowd of other students entering the cafeteria had started to hang around, listening to the bizarre exchange. A short, skinny girl with raucous acne across her forehead started giggling inanely, and another, dressed in her cheerleader uniform, stared dumbly at Ben, as if expecting some revelation. Two young teachers were leaning against the opposite wall, apparently not taking notice of the steadily enlarging group of students.

"So tell me, did you lose like half your brains when your twin died? Did you have some secret language that they say twins have? I'm just wonderin', you little shit."

The skinny girl laughed nervously and shuffled her platform shoes as he said that. "C'mon, Brian, leave him alone," she said in a squeaky voice.

"Shut the fuck up, Marcy. I'm askin' him somethin'." He looked menacingly at Ben.

Ben didn't know what to do or what was expected of him. He wished Laura was there. They always discussed things before taking action. Ben suddenly felt Laura beside him, then saw her in his mind turning away and boarding a train, the doors closing and it leaving the station with a hiss and screech. He turned and faced the brown brick wall and fought back tears. He was fourteen years old but felt like only four. He could smell the disinfectant that had been sprayed throughout the hallway the night before and vaguely hear the snickers of the senior and his pals. The skinny girl was doing something that was making some of the other kids laugh. He slowly turned around and faced the boy. The two teachers had walked away, so it was just Ben with a brick wall behind him and the kid, with the stairs to his back and about fifteen students flanking him.

"What's your name?" Ben asked him.

"None of your fuckin' business, dipshit" the older boy responded with a smirk.

The interesting thing was that Ben wasn't taking any of this personally. To him, it seemed rather like a direct assault on his sister. Ben slowly advanced toward him and quietly said, "Well, dipshit, this was our secret language," and lowered his head and charged, butting the larger boy in his gut and driving him backward toward the stairs. Losing his balance, the kid went down hard, tumbling downward until he came to rest at the first-floor landing, motionless. The small crowd of students that had assembled to watch the drama disappeared just as quickly as they had assembled, leaving only Ben and the quiet cheerleader alone.

"That was like totally awesome!" she breathed and trotted away, blowing him a kiss.

After that, Ben gained some confidence in his ability to exist as an individual and eventually metamorphosed into a relatively conservative jock during the summer between sophomore and junior years, joining the football team and radically changing his circle of friends, even wanting to enlist in the Marines after graduation.

It was during this time that he came to understand the transitory nature of most friendships. After suffering betrayal by certain kids he had grown to trust and realizing that it was strange that new friends appeared only after he changed his style of clothing and joined a team sport, his eyes were opened to the superficiality of most people.

To those he considered superficial, he allowed himself to be superficial, which was easy for him at the time because he was, for the most part, superficial. To those with a little depth, he provided a little substance. With them, he dove deeper and opened himself to vulnerability in exchange for the excitement and inspiration they provided. His soundtrack at this time included a song by Frank Zappa, "*Plastic People! Oh baby now you're such a drag.*" Nevertheless, Ben included many of those plastic people within his circle and, in some way, had become a social chameleon, if not a karma chameleon like Boy George since he had certainly learned "how to sell a contradiction."

What always brought a smile to Ben were his mother's words, "None of these people will matter to you at all in ten years." He hated to admit it, but by and large, she was right. Nevertheless, it was beyond the comprehension of a seventeen-year-old that the crowd around which his life centered would eventually scatter to the four winds, some never to be heard from again.

CHAPTER 4

Ben

Present, Istanbul and 1995, Washington, DC

WEEKS PASSED WITHOUT anything remarkable occurring in Ben's life, and considerable progress was made on the family biography he was writing for Lale. One early afternoon, having finished their daily power walk and accompanying Lale back to her law office, a thought came to him. As often happened to Ben, it was a thought triggered by a smell. This time, it was the smell of burning rubber from a *Fast and Furious*-type street racer that had just peeled away from the curb as he approached. It was as if the driver had been waiting for him. It brought him back to his personally dark days of 1995.

Ben was a different person after February of 1995. Throughout the ordeal that followed, many people asked him if he felt he had changed at all. At first, he wondered what they were talking about. Later, in the deepest darkness of his despair, he suspected that he had undergone some fundamental psychological and spiritual changes. Many of these turned out to be nothing more than the offspring of temporary depression. But now he truly knew. Although he didn't fully understand the actual metamorphosis of spirit, he knew he'd somehow changed. He imagined it was akin to a when a tadpole loses its tail and sprouts arms and legs. It certainly doesn't know that it's a frog, but somehow it must feel that it isn't a tadpole anymore. There was something different about Ben—his thinking, feelings, and values. Sometimes, with a clue just beyond the horizon, he almost thought he understood the changes.

There is both a physical and a psychological dimension to cancer. Both of these dimensions of the disease have their own distinct cycles. From the misfortune of receiving a diagnosis of cancer, Ben experienced firsthand the circle of his own life, a circle that doesn't quite complete itself at the same place it started. For example, from a cerebral standpoint, it began with denial. After all, it shouldn't be surprising that the human brain simply can't immediately process the entire weight of the thought that it may imminently cease to exist. Not on all levels, anyway.

Many years had passed from the date he heard those unreal words from the gastroenterologist: "We found a moderate-sized lesion in the wall of your colon." How many times a day, in how many places around the world are words to this effect spoken? And how could he offer hope, encouragement, and advice to those who are hearing them? Perhaps it is by opening some windows on the experience for those who are afflicted as well as those who are along for the ride. The first window that should be opened is labeled *Anger*.

It's typical for a cancer patient to experience the highs and lows from hope to despair or fear. But for Ben, the more significant emotional pendulum swung between joy and anger. Joy at receiving good news, joy at the return of his appetite, being able to take a shower and not freezing when he emerged, watching a good movie that completely distracted him from his pain, pleasure at receiving love from concerned family and friends. All these experiences were taken for granted when he was healthy, but they were welcome gifts when he was suffering. This basis of joy was also the launching platform for his anger.

The first seeds of anger were sown at the moment of understanding that he had a life-threatening disease. There was anger turned inward at his body for betraying him. He was far too young to get colon cancer. The childlike belief that he was, indeed, invulnerable was suddenly shattered when mortality was confronted. Then a more generalized feeling of anger was experienced. It was directed outward, nonspecifically at external influences and conditions.

"Why me?" he asked. "Was it my diet? My genes? My environment? My destiny?" But no one could provide the answers he sought. The doctors simply didn't know. The precipitating factors were unclear, yet the prognosis was expressed in unsettling percentages.

Ben asked each of the doctors he consulted, "Was it because I don't eat many vegetables? Or because I put a lot of Equal and powdered nondairy creamer in my coffee? Maybe the result of a high-stress job?" Nobody knew. No one had any answers.

The possibility of a genetic basis for his cancer was a very real concern for Ben. Cancer had a history in his family. He preferred to think of it that way. That is, cancer had its own history in that it had intruded and stolen from him the person he had loved most in the world—Laura, his twin. Laura had been thirteen years old when she died. Ben and she had been best friends, confidants, and jolly but nefarious coconspirators against their parents. Despite years of psychotherapy after her death, the family had virtually disintegrated. Ben ultimately had made peace and grown closer with his parents after he finished university, but his parents, original members of the Beat Generation, had drifted apart, taken new partners, and seemingly forgotten about their son.

Now Ben felt like he was the victim of the ultimate irony. Ben had never forgotten the tortuous death suffered by his sister, and although he knew from the doctors that the chances were against his being struck down by the same disease, he had always tried to take extremely good care of his body. Despite the fact that he had been relatively hard on the old corpus, subjecting it to many insults and injuries from self-destructive sports and dangerous pastimes, he was in excellent shape. Ben had been working out with a personal trainer for years and had put countless miles on the treadmill and exercise bike. He had broken his shoulder, ruptured his spleen, broken his nose on numerous occasions, shattered his jaw, taken a few 9 mm bullets, and torn up his knees, but Ben considered those painful experiences as the price paid for fun and adventure. So what was this cancer all about? He hadn't asked for trouble here. This couldn't be right.

What he couldn't come to grips with was the fact that maybe he wasn't as invulnerable as he had always felt. In retrospect, he supposed he always saw himself as larger than life. He played football in high school on an undefeated team. Even though he wasn't any star, he did his best. He was an accomplished skier. He had conquered many of the fourteen-thousand-foot peaks in the Colorado Rockies and climbed the Mont Blanc in the Alps. He earned his Pincks with two foxhunts and played high-goal polo at several clubs in the US as well as in Mexico, Argentina, and South Africa. He was the proverbial legend in his own mind. Colorectal cancer. It was like one of those brainteasers: "What's wrong with this picture?" Living legends just didn't get such an unglamorous disease, especially not in their forties. He couldn't accept it. He didn't want to accept it. It didn't make any sense to him. He couldn't figure out what had happened to the person his sister had always referred to sarcastically as the Golden Boy.

Unfortunately, the tumor hadn't just been resting on its laurels. It had grown completely through the wall of the colon and was dangerously close (if not actually into) the surrounding lymph nodes. Ben was told that this was an advanced stage two, or most probably a stage three, lesion. It was inconceivable that two internists had failed to notice it during the prior year.

The punch line came a few months later when Ben found out the possible reason the first internist had missed the polyp/tumor. The doctor was practicing medicine while suffering from Alzheimer's disease. It was the opinion of another in his field that he should have retired from his practice long before this missed diagnosis. If a polyp had been detected from a properly performed sigmoidoscopy, it could have been removed with a simple wire snare—an outpatient procedure.

Was this cause for Ben's anger? Damn straight it was.

So there he was—angry with his body for betraying him, angry with one doctor who thought it was just a case of pesky hemorrhoids and another with Alzheimer's who gave an incorrect diagnosis, angry at the hand fate had dealt him, angry that he might follow his sister to a painful, slow death—yet he didn't know he was angry. Go figure. After the first waves of anger washed over him, a new phase began. This was a period when it seemed like everything he did was solely related to his diagnosis. This had the collateral benefit of keeping him focused away from the depressing aspects of it. This ensuing denial phase just acted to provide an incubation period for the feelings of anger to further germinate. When Ben learned that he had cancer, it was like being presented with a new challenge. At least that was the way he apparently chose to hear it. This reaction was probably the result of his being an inveterate problem solver. It became an opportunity to phone and fly around the country seeking the best surgeon and the optimal hospital care.

Donald, a close family friend, had offered to put one of his planes at Ben's disposal for visiting far-flung cancer centers. So on a brilliantly clear winter's day, he and his good friend Howman Steinblitz, a.k.a. the Blitz, flew out to the Mayo Clinic to meet with a renowned colorectal surgeon. Although he was a "white knuckle" flyer, Howman wasn't about to let Ben take that journey alone. Ben always remembered Howman's nervous grip on his shoulder when they hit some turbulence on a commercial airliner several years before, so flying in Donald's fast but noisy Merlin took an extreme act of friendship.

In the midst of the initial period of radiation, Ben lost his appetite for normal food. A craving for Little Debbie Strawberry Shortcake rolls took hold. He'd go through nearly a dozen a day, driving his pals crazy with requests to bring along boxes of this sweet treat whenever they came to visit so that he would never face the desperation of running on empty. This was really bizarre. Ben had never particularly had a sweet tooth. No hot fudge sundaes, white frosted birthday cake, Krispy Kreme donuts, or strawberry milkshakes for this boy. But thank God for those Little Debbies. He would have starved without them.

Ben had heard that such cravings apparently are not all that unusual when one is under the influence of chemo and radiation. He was repeatedly told that these treatments make you a little crazy.

Not only do weird things happen to your appetite, but your taste in many other things also undergoes a change. Movies, books, TV shows, colors, and attitudes—all are subject to the influence of the rays and chemicals. And your dreams get strange as well. That was certainly Ben's experience.

During this period of cancer treatment, Ben was comfortable being alone in the house with his German shepherd, Berta. Whenever he was home, Berta followed him from room to room. It was like they were attached at the hip. At night, she would crawl up into the bed with him, her ears pricking up every time the infusion pump made its little cycling noise. Ben didn't know if she was just distressed by the incessant pump noise and lack of sleep, or she somehow perceived that Ben was the walking wounded. Either way, it was a great comfort having her around. Lately, there had been many articles and television newscasts on the subject of the value of pet therapy. Ben believed that there was a lot of truth to this. There was something comforting about having this beautiful big dog padding along behind him, watching every move he made with eyes filled with canine compassion. Some people are comfortable being alone. Ben was not one of them. He liked a full house.

Since he didn't really have a family, his time with Berta was elevated to almost human significance. Ben also began to perceive that his friends fell into three categories. The first category included all the people that were more acquaintances than friends. Some of those acquaintances actually became elevated to friend status by virtue of their reaching out to him and offering support. The second category was comprised of those friends who, for some reason, were uncomfortable with his being sick. Ben got the feeling that his having cancer reminded them of their own mortality. As a consequence, he didn't hear much from them while he was fighting the disease. After he regained his health, some made their way back into his life. Some didn't, and that was okay. No hard feelings. There were enough people that fell into the third category to make up for their lapse of attention.

This third category was comprised of people that Ben called the true friends. He hoped that anybody who must suffer through the indignation of cancer had at least a few of these people around. True friends fill in the gap that family cannot be expected to fill, either by reason of geographic remoteness, personal time constraints, or, on the other hand, simply being too close to the situation. In addition to providing love and support, true friends supply a sense of objectivity and humor. The true friend is able to do this effortlessly, so Ben never felt that they were even trying.

Sometimes Ben found these people performing acts of kindness that were way above and beyond the call of duty. Sometimes they were just there. Whatever the case, Ben was wise enough to accept everything they had to offer. He knew that it was doubtful that at any other time in his life he would be so rewarded and indulged. During the course of his battle with cancer, Ben learned that he was a very fortunate man. He had initially thought that he had been blessed with a wonderful family, but after his sister's death, he had witnessed that steadily fall apart. Now he knew that he was rich in true friends. Not as comforting as a supportive family, but really quite extraordinary considering that it was all voluntary.

So when Ben looked back on this period from the vantage point of more than twenty years later, it was interesting for him to note that some of those true friends were temporal. Whether this condition of *true friends of the moment* was due to the normal attrition of people who pass through one's life naturally, due to reasons of geography or common interest, or some deeper individual psychological reason is perplexing. A few of those true friends from that period were still very much in his life. Others had vanished. Were they only around because they felt a need to feed off his weakness from the disease, or were they, by virtue of personality, Florence Nightingale types? How would those he currently called close friends react if this had happened now instead of a decade ago?

In some ways, he was glad that there wasn't a wife or children in the picture to watch him suffer, and at other times, he longed for a woman's familiar and comforting caress. Several psychologist friends had advised him that he had intimacy issues with women that were undoubtedly connected to the loss of his sister at such a young age. The fact that they were twins made it even more traumatic and emotionally indelible. But rather than put the work in with therapists to address this condition, Ben preferred to play the role of the confirmed bachelor. He had enjoyed the companionship of several extraordinary women over the years, but the relationships usually ended when the subjects of marriage and children arose. The man who wasn't afraid of anything was apparently afraid of a commitment to love and the responsibility and vulnerability that having children brings. The one time he had placed all his trust and love in a woman, she had betrayed him. Although over the years he came to see that as nothing more than a college romance that couldn't survive a long-distance summer, it still had a profound effect on Ben.

The night before his surgery at Duke University Medical Center, Ben's old college pal, Peter (who had consistently remained in the true friend category until his own death from cancer), called to see how he was holding up. Peter was one of Ben's closest friends during the four years he lived in the Durham area. Since their graduation from Duke, Peter had remained in North Carolina, acquiring a small agricultural tract, which he named Moonshadow Farm after the old Cat Stevens song. He restored the century-old farmhouse and built several outbuildings, including a large music hall. He and his wife raised five fine daughters, countless sheep, horses, dogs, and chickens and developed the farm into a refuge for writers, artists, and musicians to focus on their crafts.

Peter was also a psychiatric social worker and drug counselor, employed by the county to aid the less fortunate members of this newly affluent area. His natural talent for connecting with anyone and communicating calm, realistic, and appropriate advice was prodigious. He had known Ben as a brash, materialistic, spoiled kid, then as an aggressive, ambitious professional. Always the ego had been strong, large, out there. Ben was pretty sure that even now, so many years later, Peter would probably still think of him as a relatively superficial person. Sometimes Ben couldn't understand why Peter was such a close friend.

Peter appeared at Ben's hospital room in the same manner in which Kramer always slid dramatically into Seinfeld's apartment. "You look positively alluring in that sexy gown, Ben."

"So would you like to introduce yourself to my tumor up close and personal?" Ben said, starting to roll over.

"Stifle that thought. I left my anal probe back at the farm although it was quite effective extracting a length of cord that one of the dogs managed to ingest earlier this evening. So I wouldn't even have to sterilize it for you." Peter rarely exercised the same sensitivity he used with his patients on Ben. In fact, he was more like a steel wool Brillo pad scrubbing at Ben's ego.

Ben winced at the thought. "I imagine…No, *I hope*, my surgeon will be more precise with his…uh… *extraction*."

"He knows you're an asshole, so I imagine he will treat you accordingly." Peter kissed Ben on the cheek and ducked out the door, the words, "Good luck, brother!" trailing behind him.

That night before the surgery, after Peter's visit, Ben had one of those frustration dreams. Ben was calling endless lists of ads in the papers for Morgan cars, finally giving up and going from dealership to dealership. (That alone was a joke since you could probably count all the places Morgans are sold in the US on one hand.) Each time he arrived to see a car, it would be gone for one reason or another. Finally, just before he was ready to give up, a gorgeous strawberry blond drove up in a red Morgan, parked, and handed him the keys. He slid behind the wheel as she walked away. He noticed she was wearing a nurse's uniform. Ben turned the key in the ignition, shifted into first, and woke up.

Even though all the terrors of surgery and post-op were literally only hours away, at least subconsciously, Ben was steadfastly trying to maintain his bravado. He was obviously trying to convince himself that he still held the keys to the car. That he was driving this baby, he was in control, and he was confidently driving away from the nurse and the hospitalization she represented despite how attractive she was. Like all coins, this one had two sides. One was his denial of the cancer by nonchalantly driving away from it in the sexy red sports car. The other was that he was not laughing in the face of adversity, but fleeing from it with all possible speed.

The following evening, Ben slowly but surely began to emerge from the haze of general anesthesia. The epidural helped a lot since he didn't have to keep hitting a morphine button and getting drugged out. He remembered watching a lot of television during the late-evening hours before drifting off to sleep. He had no recollection of any specific shows, but he was sure he saw the movie *Mystery, Alaska*. He remembered something about hockey in that film.

On Saturday, Ben answered the phone to find his friend Donald on the line. A noted Washington plastic surgeon who had become wealthy investing in the aircraft industry and biomedical companies, Ben knew him from their fox-hunting days when they would spend long hours dashing across the open fields of western Montgomery County and hiking leisurely back to the trailer. Ben had also been Donald's patient after a polo accident left him with a badly broken face. Donald was one of those peripatetic folks who was either riding a bike or a horse, surgically turning sows' ears into silk purses, investing in biomedical start-ups, heli-skiing, elk hunting, giving lectures on the benefits of cosmetic surgery, or flying about the mid-Atlantic to consult with young entrepreneurs or visit patients in far-flung locales.

Anyway, there was Donald on the line, asking how he was doing and inquiring about the weather. Ben didn't know how the hell he was supposed to know what was happening with the weather. After all, he was laid up in a hospital room—a virtually hermetically sealed environment. He did have a small view out the window, and he was able to relate that it looked cloudy, but that was about it.

"How cloudy?" Donald asked.

"Christ, I don't know. Cloudy. Ya know, gray sky cloudy," Ben replied.

"Is it raining?"

"I don't think so. But I can only see *up* from here. I can't see the pathways below to tell if they are dark and wet. But it doesn't look like it's pouring or anything."

"Have you heard a weather report?"

"Donald, give me a break. Why would I pay any attention to a weather report? It's not like I'm going anywhere today."

Donald finally gave up on this line of questioning. After a few more minutes of generalized banter, he said goodbye. Ben drifted off to sleep.

An indeterminate time later, Ben heard a gentle knocking on the door. He opened one eye.

Donald's grinning face was peering around the corner at him. He had flown the Merlin down to Raleigh-Durham airport and taken a taxi over to the hospital. He brought a huge history-of-the-world-type book as a gift (big enough to put legs on and use as a coffee table) and a bottle of Casa Herradura Seleccion Suprema tequila *for the visitors*. Now this is what Ben considered an effort that qualified Donald as a true friend. It blew his mind, his showing up like that. Donald ended up having to make an instrument landing to boot. The weather had been worse than he had thought.

* * *

By the time he returned home in the second week of June, Washington was in the viselike grip of summer. He had a slate patio behind the house that during the early-morning and late-afternoon hours received partial shade from an ancient black oak. The backyard ran several hundred feet out to a white three-board fence that defined the boundary with Hunt View Farm, 160 acres of pasture that about thirty horses called home.

Ben had an old vinyl-clad metal chaise longue that was slowly melting into the patio. A hunter-green cloth-covered mattress stretched across it, and it was really pretty comfortable, except for the ragged end of the left armrest where a young Berta had once chewed on it. There was a certain angle that he could place the chaise at that afforded Ben a particularly pastoral view through a pair of oak trees to the horse pasture and red barns beyond. Berta would often sit outside with him, stationed beneath the shade of the black oak, staring out at the lackadaisical movements of the horses in the fields nearby. Ben had obtained Berta at the age of ten months from the German Shepherd Rescue of Washington, DC. She was the best hundred-dollar dog he had ever known. She seemed to sense that he was in this waiting mode, and she was perfectly happy to be his patient sentry.

Every few hours, Ben would rise from his chair and do his circuit training. Unlike the exercise regimen that term implies in a modern gym, his circuit was along the flagstone path that ran widely around the outside of his house. Four hundred and twenty feet, more or less, approximately two hundred abbreviated paces, Berta always at his side. They would occasionally stop to inspect the flower beds, rhododendron bushes, and random malodorous weeds or to allow Berta to playfully jump at a meandering butterfly. If a car drove down the little dirt lane, she would fiercely bark and charge, stopping just short of the invisible fence that ran around the perimeter of the property. Every day, this scene was repeated, Ben counting his steps, Berta playing the part of the palace guard.

Ben would hold court back there on the patio. Although those June weeks were basically long stretches of boredom, the visit of a friend would serve to dispel any accumulated gloom. Ben would rise to the occasion, believing the friends who told him how good he looked despite having lost nearly 30 percent of his body weight and almost all of his muscle mass. Ben never had that much excess weight to spare, so he looked like a refugee from a horrific war or catastrophe. His butt had literally disappeared. He couldn't even stand to sit on the thatch seat of his kitchen chair without a cushion under him.

Ben was quite different from the self-conceived legend that roamed the planet a year before. He was not only vulnerable to a life-threatening disease that wasn't a result of his typically reckless behavior, he was also feeling fear that was initiated by the anxiety from not knowing what lay just around the corner. Being completely inexperienced with fear, this was extraordinarily disturbing for him.

At this point in time, Ben had survived the major surgery with the cancerous lesion having been completely removed. He was receiving weekly doses of cancer-killing chemo. Other than the sword of Damocles in the form of a lingering concern about a reoccurrence for the next five years, he had nothing to be worried about in the immediate future. He was, however, seriously underweight. The thirty-eight pounds he had lost within a few weeks after the surgery were stubbornly refusing to return. His butt consisted of some sharp bones with skin stretched over them. No matter how padded the seat, it was uncomfortable to sit in one position for more than a few minutes. In fact, he was generally uncomfortable most of the time. This discomfort was probably 20 percent psychological, but that didn't make it any less real, the result being that he was still waiting. Waiting to feel better. And waiting for his fear to abate.

The fear he was experiencing was nonspecific. Sure, there is always the possibility that the cancer could mysteriously reappear sometime, either in the next few years (some possibility) or much later in life (as it could with anyone), but Ben didn't think that was it. He was afraid in general, like a seriously wimpy type of person—a *panphobic*. Ben remembered that from a book he had read in a psych course at Duke. A term first coined by Théodule-Armand Ribot in his 1911 work *The Psychology of the Emotions*. This unaccustomed fear included panic at the thought of everyone leaving him high and dry.

At the height of this anxiety, his good friend Jimmy Jason arrived. For the first time in their lives, he came to Ben's rescue as sure as any hero of yore. Jimmy was a few years junior to Ben. They were very different people. Jimmy was always more sensitive to other people. Although he was often brash, outrageous, and materialistic, he was always sensitive to how others felt. Without having to question him or say a word, Jimmy understood what was going on inside of Ben. And he knew how to deal with it.

Jimmy became really worried about his friend. Ben was acting even more sensitive than even Jimmy could be at his most absurd. Jimmy was witnessing a role reversal that he was unprepared for. During their entire history as best friends, Ben had been the one to defend him, both physically and verbally. When they were little kids, Ben came upon an older boy repeatedly hitting Jimmy in the face. He threw the boy down a steep hill near the playground. Miraculously, despite hitting his head on a rock at the bottom, the kid didn't die. Another time, when they were riding the school bus together, a bigger kid had pounded on Jimmy and threatened to throw his shoes out the window. Ben pushed the kid's head out the window and ratcheted it closed, trapping his neck. The unfortunate bully had to ride all the way to school with his head stuck outside the bus.

When they lived in Colorado, Ben had joined Jimmy in climbing some of the most challenging fourteen-thousand-foot mountains. Ben often climbed in the lead and then protectively belayed Jimmy on the technical pitches until Jimmy became more proficient. So imagine his shock at finding his older brother from another mother so out of character. Now it was Ben's turn to reach for the rope.

Jimmy had telephoned their mutual friend Howman, the Blitz, the fellow who had flown out to the Mayo Clinic with Ben, and arranged for him to come over for dinner. Howman's wife and daughters were at the beach for the summer, and he spent the week in Washington running his advertising agency. This would be a cancer patient's version of boys' night out.

The combination of Jimmy and the Blitz did much for Ben's sagging spirits. They grilled a medley of fish and meat on the patio and swapped lies, the two of them sampling a vast array of beers Jimmy had bought at the local liquor store and wine the Blitz had brought from his cellar. It was such a success in improving his mood that Jimmy also lined up other dinner-joint ventures with the Blitz and other friends. These dinners were of much greater significance to Ben than one might imagine. Ben was plagued with the constant oppression of waiting. Usually, he would just be waiting to feel better. The dinners gave him a positive goal to wait for. Being together with good friends who had known him BC (before cancer) was important because he didn't have to be "on stage." These were people that knew what he was all about; there was no need to try to impress them. If he felt like curling up for thirty minutes on a couch and not participating in the discussion, that was all right. If he felt like complaining about something, that was all right too. Since he didn't have an appetite, the dinners were not about food. They were about being with friends.

Although it was difficult for some of his friends to understand, he believed that their suffering together with him was like gravy on the mashed potatoes of the pain he alone was actually experiencing. Other friends, not the truest of the true, the best of the best, may love you and sincerely care about how you are getting along. They may even be shocked and distressed at how awful you look. But generally, they will try to make the best of a bad situation and, after giving you all the opportunity you need to tell them how you are feeling, attempt to move things on to more positive subjects. They know how to distract you and help you have a good time to the extent that's possible. Then unlike with immediate family and the inner circle of friends, everyone else goes back to their respective homes and they can feel that the pressure is off them.

Ben clearly understood that he needed his true friends to help with the daily grind—all the little chores that he couldn't do by himself and would feel uncomfortable imposing upon friends, no matter how close. And the next concentric circle of friends to help him escape from the ugly circumstances—to hear what's going on in the non-cancer world and let him feel like he was participating in his old life. Even if it was just a few hours every week, this escape became really important.

Ben recovered completely just over a year after the initial diagnosis. In time, he regained the weight, rebuilt the muscle strength and tone he had lost, and rediscovered his old confidence hidden under a Colorado crystal blue sky on the face of a massive rock wall known as El Muerto de Miedo.

He saw all his friends in a whole new light—his true friends who gave so much of themselves and were along for this gruesome roller-coaster ride, his colleagues at work who were so supportive, and his worldwide array of acquaintances who checked in to provide encouragement and laughs. They had done much to teach him much about what it means to be a friend. Yet Ben was intimidated about friendship requiring some level of constant attention and responsibility. Although these aspects can be ratcheted up or down depending on the circumstances surrounding the relationship at any given stage, he had difficulty coming to grips with the fact that friends should always be sensitive to the needs of each other as they move through their respective lives. He couldn't be a true friend to everyone with whom he was acquainted; the commitment was simply too great. Given his fear of loss, he preferred to think of himself merely as a kind of a personal SWAT team to any level of friend, ready to mobilize if and when the need arose. He could always tailor the response to the degree of intimacy he was comfortable with under the circumstances.

Despite this newfound understanding, Ben's ability to be a truly selfless friend and supremely responsible man had never really been tested. However, on some subliminal level, he knew that one day it would.

CHAPTER 5

Ben

Present, Istanbul

WHEN HE FIRST came to the city straddling the Bosporus to live,
he was interviewed by one of the larger newspapers and asked that
question.

"Why are you living in Istanbul of all places?" the reporter
queried.

"I needed something more Byzantine," Ben responded simply.

"You left your life in the States, all your friends for...Byzantine?"
she asked.

"Yep." Ben was occasionally a man of few words.

However, after a couple of glasses of wine, he opened up and
told the full story. Mustafa Koçeli, a good friend Ben had made in
Turkey while working for the State Department, had gotten a bee
in his bonnet about having a book written about his famous father,
Mehmet Ali Koçeli. Knowing that Ben had recently left his life of
public service in the US government to pursue a career as a writer,
Mustafa had sent his sister Lale and her son as envoys to persuade
Ben to leave the States for a year to write this biography. They would
pay Ben handsomely for the book and provide him with an excellent
home and work space while he was in Istanbul. Mustafa had called

Ben and asked him to meet with his sister and nephew at a hotel in Washington where they were attending an international conference.

A young man about twenty-four, looking like Tom Cruise's younger brother, met him at the bar of the Ritz Hotel and introduced himself as Kaan. "My mother will be down in a minute. She's just taking a phone call."

This was to be his first experience with a Lale minute. The woman had no sense of time, which was unusual for an attorney who billed by the hour. Ben supposed that this could work either for or against her clients, depending on her mood and level of distraction. Lale had found a niche legal market in representing upscale European and American fashion brands that, over the past ten years, had come to understand that there were thousands of Turkish people who would prefer to shop locally than travel to London, Dubai, Paris, or New York. She not only represented the companies that were disinclined to franchise but also local Turkish businessmen and women who were eager to license the more risk-averse big names in fashion. Lale became a legend when it came to negotiating leases for impressive stores in the newly developed shopping malls throughout Istanbul.

Ben was pleased to learn that Lale's son, Kaan, was educated at Wharton, well traveled, and interesting. They quickly established their mutual passion for NBA basketball, and when Kaan told Ben he had been trying to buy a good seat to watch Michael Jordan play in one of his last games with the Wizards, Ben took out his cell phone and called the Blitz, the most well-connected close friend he had.

Howman "the Blitz" Steinblitz was still one of Ben's best true-blue friends, one of the few he really missed living in Istanbul. With a Jewish father from Eastern Europe and an African American mother, the blue-eyed, mocha-complexioned Blitz looked like an older version of Lenny Kravitz. Despite his fear of flying, as one of America's foremost sports marketers, the Blitz frequently had to travel to sports events throughout the US.

"I can set you up," the Howman told Ben. "Two for tomorrow night's game against the Magic."

Ben noticed a fashionably dressed blond demurely making her way to their table. In the low lighting of the lounge, he assumed this was Kaan's date for the night. When she kissed the young man on both cheeks and then extended her hand to Ben, saying, "Hi, I'm Lale, Mustafa's sister," his jaw dropped.

"Uh...you and your brother had different parents?" he stammered. "I mean which one of you was adopted?"

"I got the beauty and my brother Mustafa got the brains," she laughed, adding, "I'm just a simple girl." Ben was to later learn how short she sold herself. An hour of consulting at her law office went for $1,000, and there was no shortage of international clients willing to pay the freight.

The next night at what was then known as the MCI Center, Kaan and Ben picked up their tickets at the will call window. They were immediately accosted by a uniformed young woman who said that she would be escorting them to their seats. Although Ben said he didn't think he needed an escort, she insisted, saying that they would never get to their seats without her assistance. She guided them into an elevator reserved for VIPs and stood at attention like a guard until the doors opened. It was only then that Ben and Kaan fully appreciated where they were headed.

The woman showed the way to two seats on the floor. Literally *on the floor*. They could have made three-pointers from their seats. Well, maybe Kaan could have made three-pointers, but Ben sucked at basketball. By sheer dumb luck and the gift of the Blitz, Ben had inadvertently won the hearts and minds of Kaan and, indirectly, his mother, Lale. It was a disconcerting experience for Ben. Having spent a number of years literally trying to stay in the shadows, here he was under bright lights and on national television with terrific-looking cheerleaders bouncing up and down, back and forth, directly in front of him. He couldn't fail to notice that these cheerleaders were spending an inordinate amount of time flashing and dashing in the immediate location of Kaan and him. Or more accurately, Kaan.

As the first half ended, Ben made his way to the little corner corral where the cheerleaders were clustered, chatting away with typical inanity. "Excuse me," he asked, "would it be possible for my young friend and me to have our photographs taken with y'all?" He tilted his head slightly in an avuncular fashion.

These goddesses of the sidelines apparently didn't make the connection between Ben and Kaan at first, thinking he had some snot-nosed kid who wanted a titty shot. They were giving out strong "Oh, puhleeez" vibes. "You see over there? We're sitting in the front row of courtside chairs. The guy with the dark hair? That's Tom Cruise's younger brother, Max."

"Max Cruise!" they shrieked in unison, nearly trampling Ben in their stampede to reach the ersatz Cruise. The resulting photo still hangs in Kaan's house. It's a classic. And if there ever was a Max Cruise, Kaan would be a dead ringer for him.

CHAPTER 6

Rachel

Present, Mississippi

SHE REMEMBERED THAT he was left-handed despite the curious fact that she couldn't always remember the difference between left and right. This sometimes led to confusion when they were together. Her memories of some of the chaos that resulted from her lack of left/right sense and his left physical orientation brought a smile to her face. She began to key in on what constituted *left* by observing which hand he was writing with or doing some other task that required manual dexterity. Consequently, she was directionally lost for many years after their breakup. Perhaps in some kind of unconscious deference to Ben, this memory brought her left hand to her brow.

Once, many years ago, Rachel had consulted with a psychologist regarding why she, obviously no fool with her master's degree from Duke and her BA from Princeton, didn't know her right from her left. To her, her hands were just her hands. She couldn't perceive them as either left or right. When she was walking or driving and made a turn, it didn't register in her brain as turning right or left. She just turned in the direction she knew she was supposed to go. She differentiated the sides of the car as the driver's side and the passenger side or what side of the street she was walking as the side she was walking on and not the other side. This or that, here or there, windward or leeward, sunny or shady, correct or incorrect. These were concepts that mattered, not arbitrary (in Rachel's mind) terms of right and left.

The psychologist wanted to write a scholarly essay about Rachel. He thought that Rachel had a variation on Gerstmann's syndrome, albeit without the inability to express thoughts in writing, the difficulty in performing simple arithmetical calculations, or inability to recognize her own or another's fingers. In any event, once she was able to understand that she wasn't suffering from any degenerative disease or other life-threatening condition, she came to accept it as just a quirky part of her nature.

When she was in bed with Ben, there was her side of the bed and his side of the bed. She never saw it as "right side when facing the headboard" or "left side when her head was on the pillow looking down the length of the bed toward her feet." She appreciated it, unconsciously perhaps, when she was trying on shoes at a store on Madison Avenue she frequented, when the saleslady asked, "Would you like to try on the other shoe?" as opposed to asking if she wanted to try on the left shoe or the right shoe. To Rachel, the fork didn't go on the left side of the plate; it went on the fork side of the plate. She learned to navigate life without right or left.

She also had the unique ability to visualize musical lyrics. However, she couldn't fathom the song, "Sex on the Radio" by the Five Fingers:

> *Can you see sex on the radio? If you so how does it look?*
> *Let's try just like in the book.*
> *I'll bend you over a chair.*
> *I will pull back your blond hair*
> *As we ride like in the rodeo,*
> *The rodeo, the radio, the rodeo.*

She rarely understood euphemisms, and although it was difficult for her to imagine sex on the radio, with a grin she thought about how Ben could certainly see sex on the radio or anywhere else for that matter. And he wouldn't want to stare at her butt or her boobs because she remembered he was more of a face guy. More than just looking into her eyes, it was as if while she talked, he was enchanted by her entire visage and fascinated by the miniscule facial expressions that accompanied her voice and words as well. It was a totally visceral practice for him when they had a conversation. In that, they were alike. Communication was a multidimensional experience with him, and she had never encountered that with any man since. His intensity might make other women self-conscious, but not her. His rapt intellectual attention and equally matched physical attentiveness captured her heart.

To be sure, they had a normal quota of trivial chats and meaningless commentary between them, such as insignificant observations on superficial subjects, stupid comments about other people's appearance, the weather, health, or physical conditions. But when talking about their strong feelings on something of substance, their exchanges always verged on telepathic as he focused on the myriad of tics, grimaces, and color changes of her skin. She knew that she had anything but a poker face. In fact, when she became sexually aroused, the skin on her neck became frightfully red. But that was obvious. Ben could perceive even the minutest twitch of a cheek muscle or contraction of her nostrils. And somehow, he knew what that meant. He was a different kind of man.

The only thing that scared her about Ben was his ability to change in an instant from passive and calm to brutally violent. She remembered an afternoon in Chapel Hill when she had injured her foot on a piece of glass from a newly broken window on Franklin Street. Recent small riots of local youths had resulted in sporadic vandalism of the establishments along that busy commercial strip in an otherwise quiet college town. Wearing only hippie sandals, she hadn't seen the shard of glass until she had stepped on it with her full weight. It had penetrated the thin leather of her sandal and painfully sliced open her foot. She immediately sat down on the curb, not conscious of the way her miniskirt had slid all the way up her thighs, fully exposing her little floral-print thong. She was probably the only woman in North Carolina at that time to prefer that kind of underwear, years before Victoria's Secret would make it the standard for young women.

Suddenly, out of nowhere, a group of three young men had surrounded them, taunting and staring at her long legs without any care or concern for her injury. Ignoring Ben, who was standing just behind her, one man made the mistake of reaching his hand between her legs, boasting, "I'm gonna get me some of this." Despite her intense pain, she immediately tried to pull herself away but was stopped by Ben's legs. The man leaned forward and started to shove his hand in further.

That was a big mistake. Like the strike of a rattlesnake, Ben had grabbed the man's wrist and broken it in one powerful twist, mashing the man's nose with his other hand and sending him tumbling down to the asphalt. Impressed with Ben's reaction, the other two pulled up their friend and ran away down the sidewalk.

And that was only one of several such occurrences that she knew were probably her fault. She liked to shock and tantalize the locals with her short skirts, see-through blouses, and braless chest. She loved the way Ben always seemed to be there as her personal bodyguard. He had smashed beer steins over rednecks' heads, slammed faces into tables, and flattened tires with his buck knife, all on her behalf. In fact, one way or another, perhaps perversely, she had provoked these extreme circumstances because she loved his reaction.

So when Ben caught her living with another guy during a surprise summer visit, she was afraid that he would kill that boy. But he hadn't. Just looking sad and surprised, he had simply walked away, never to speak to her again. She learned more about Ben in that moment than during any other single event, perhaps more than all the other events combined. Ben wasn't a macho man. He wasn't about proving himself or bravado. After all, he wasn't such a big guy. It had all been about protecting her from harm. In the forty years since, she had never met another man quite like him.

CHAPTER 7

Ben

Present, Istanbul

ODD ENCOUNTERS WITH *yabancılar* (foreigners/non-Turks) had been occurring for Ben on a steadily escalating basis. For the most part, they were friendly; however, Ben thought it odd that nearly all of them were Russian. He had become accustomed to the tour buses packed with Chinese that stopped on a daily basis for lunch at the Bin Hong Lo restaurant beneath his office, but Russians had never seemed to visit the Russian tearoom that was just around the corner until quite recently. It was always the same five or six men—always keeping Ben in sight whenever he entered or left the building, always overdressed for the season with long, bulky coats that were perfect for hiding weapons. Ben was undeniably concerned about them. He believed in intuition. It kept you alive. It was the most primordial of senses, giving our predecessors an unusual psychic edge over other predators who might wish to turn early hominids into prey themselves. His sixth sense for danger was on high alert.

This third-party-induced anxiety conflicted with his naturally casual friendly nature. Under most circumstances, he welcomed the attention of people. Yet he never understood why people liked him. Even though many of his friends would take issue with this belief, he felt incapable of seeing deeply into the heart of someone else, and as a result, he often made mistakes when it came to responding appropriately to another human being. His natural tendency was to make a joke when things got stressful or uncomfortable with a friend. He was often embarrassed when he said something that was perceived as insensitive. He felt that he had evolved a little bit but had a long way to go.

Lately he had been suffering from the angst of a revised self-analysis on this subject. Perhaps the truth was that people didn't really like him unless he worked really hard at appearing likable to them. This originated with the sense of disconnect he felt when he transitioned from being top dog in middle school to being a freshman nobody at high school. Ben experienced this again during the transition from high school to university. He obsessed about wanting to be popular, but due to his immaturity and naivete, he confused popularity and its concomitant large social group with being a good person with good friends. In other words, quantity over quality. He therefore continued to reinvent himself until he found an incarnation that resulted in being surrounded by the most popular people.

It wasn't until about ten years after that once-popular group of cheerleaders, partyers, rich kids with hot cars, and all-state star athletes began to disassemble due to the realties and pressures of life that Ben had his first epiphany about those friends. Their natural popularity was only supported by the most superficial core values. Out of the core group of perhaps fifty people, ten of whom were real social organizer types, five had died from drug overdoses, two from alcohol-related car accidents, four were in jail for a variety of offenses including securities fraud, domestic violence, and check-kiting, and one of the guys he had considered his closest friend for many years in high school and college died of AIDS. David had become a porn star, unfortunately at the very genesis of the epidemic when actors in the adult film industry eschewed condoms and HIV testing was rare. As for the girls Ben had known in high school, the majority had married young to guys like those described above, cheated on their husbands because their husbands were cheating on them, and completely failed at parenting whatever unfortunate progeny they had produced for the wrong reasons.

In all fairness, not all the popular kids had strayed so far off the path. Some were happily married to stable people with good careers and admirable goals, but it was almost like they had to make a compromise. It seemed to Ben that they had uniformly exchanged excitement and fun for constancy and stability. He didn't understand why fun and responsibility had to necessarily be mutually exclusive. He had committed himself to having as much fun as possible while also being reasonably responsible. The only problem with this game plan was that Ben's idea of being responsible didn't necessarily fit the generally accepted definition of responsibility. Lately, some of the people closest to him had been making little observations and suggestions to him. As most of them were Turkish, these comments were camouflaged with several layers of politeness. This *kibar* (polite) tendency of Turks was often lost on Americans like Ben, who basically wore his heart on his sleeve and said exactly what he meant. But after so many years in Istanbul, he was slowly beginning to understand that he had some work to do with respect to the way he navigated through life and treated people who mattered to him. He had to learn why people were there and close to him. There usually was a reason, and he very much wanted to understand it. He just didn't know where to start.

Ben was sitting at his desk in the Gümüşsuyu district of Istanbul. He had just finished lunch with Ipek Elmayiyen, one of his younger and newer friends, who, at twenty-eight, couldn't have been his friend for that long. Despite this age canyon, he knew that this was a friend for life and was fairly sure that she felt the same. Although chronologically short on years, Ipek was a girl with a very old soul. They were never at a loss for things to talk about, and he studiously avoided dispensing advice to her, except when he thought it necessary to push her in a direction that a twenty-eight-year-old Turkish woman could never be expected to discover herself. So in a sense, he considered himself more of a catalyst for her than a mentor or some other such traditional older figure in her life. She didn't need a father figure. She had a perfectly sound relationship with her dad, a solid, accomplished, and sophisticated former military guy who years ago had survived mass arrests of senior officers suspected of plotting a coup against the Turkish government.

It's just that fathers and daughters have certain walls that are both appropriate and restrictive. Fathers rarely want to learn from their daughters and usually don't have the patience it takes to listen to them anyway. Fathers, at least good fathers, also have this irresistible tendency to always be trying to fix things for their daughters. Whether the breakage is in their heart or their car, Daddy can't seem to help himself from trying to ride to the rescue.

Ipek still lived with her parents, a fairly typical condition for unmarried Turkish people without high-paying jobs. Mothers with sons and fathers with daughters liked this situation as it fulfilled several different but synchronous needs. First and foremost, it allowed the parents to maintain some degree of control over their offspring even at such an age where most American kids were long gone from the home with their own lives and personal issues that they would never want their parents to know about.

Secondly, having your kids at home virtually guaranteed that the parents would have more interesting companionship than the spouse they had been married to for over twenty years. In Ipek's case, this was a good thing for all since she had an extremely dysfunctional relationship with her mother (they would go weeks without saying more than two or three words a day to each other) and a father who doted on her and treated her like a best friend as well as a child. Sometimes this would get a little claustrophobic for Ipek, but all in all, it made her feel special and powerful within the family.

She'd had a few relationships with men that had lasted approximately four to six months each but inevitably ended in her disappointment. Bad manners, bad sex where the boy was only interested in his own selfish pleasure, over-possessive behavior, and overly *ala Turka* attitudes were generally to blame. Other than Ben, her father, and her little brother, Ipek just couldn't communicate satisfactorily with men. She rarely felt any chemistry or romance with those she had met, which resulted in disappointing, perfunctory sex and a taxi ride home as the agenda of a typical date.

A Freudian psychologist could have had a field day with Ipek, her overly protective father, and her fifty-year-old best friend, but neither she nor Ben cared much for psychological theories. Their friendship worked. They trusted each other. They were so unlike in the obvious ways yet cut from the same cloth in subtler ways. They must have had some kind of profound relationship in another spiritual existence.

Fortunately for Ben, Ipek's father had exposed her to the best music of the sixties, seventies, and the Beach Boys, Dylan to Dire Straits and Credence Clearwater to Cat Stevens, not to mention Pink Floyd, one of her favorites. Just as Ipek had such an unquenchable thirst for learning of things beyond her everyday pale, Ben had a desire to share his legacy of strange adventures, unique geopolitical philosophy, and highly sophisticated/semi-aristocratic lifestyle. You'd think that would be a lot for a twenty-eight-year-old Turkish maiden to assimilate, but Ipek soaked it all in, filtered out the bullshit, and retained the añejo of his wisdom.

Ben and Ipek often discussed how different their lives were. She was the sole English-speaking employee in the local branch of a bank where he opened an account when he moved his office to Gümüşsuyu. Ipek was extremely helpful, in fact virtually indispensable for Ben with his complicated cross-border banking relationships. Over a period of time, she demonstrated her loyalty and attention to detail, and one day, months later, over an accidental but serendipitous lunch at a nearby café, a great friendship was forged.

She had also recently become engaged to a guy she had known only a month. A very skeptical Ben was listening to Ipek relate how she had met Bekir Barlin.

"He is so easy to be with. Not pushing me to have sex and then sending me home. We don't really sleep together. I mean, we have slept together but just a few times and always a lot of *sarılma*."

"What's that?" Ben asked. "This is beyond my Turkish vocabulary."

"Buddling? Cuppling? You know like hugging while you are lying down."

"Cuddling."

"Yes, cuddling. Good word for me to have. He's just so sweet and understands me better than my friends and doesn't always talk about *futbol* and never compares me to other women."

"How did you meet this guy? Bekir?"

"*Evet*, yes, Bekir. My friend Guneş and I were having dinner and drinking *rakı* at a fish restaurant near my house. We were…you know…girl talking. We didn't even see the two guys sitting at the next table."

The licorice flavor and mind-numbing effect of the *rakı*, the succulent sea bass, the unintelligible irrelevant chatter of the surrounding diners, and the ambient lighting had made it easy for them to tune out everything but their own conversation. Ipek said she had to pee and got up to make her way to the WC while Guneş checked her Facebook and Instagram for new postings. She failed to notice the man sitting barely a meter away from Ipek's chair surreptitiously place a paper napkin on the now-empty seat, then get up with his friend and leave the restaurant.

"When I got back from peeing, I saw this napkin on my chair seat. I didn't remember leaving my *peçete* on the chair, and I was about to toss it aside when I saw that it contained a long note someone had written. Here, look, Ben. I kept it. You can read it. I can translate for you if you need."

> *Sorry, but I couldn't help watching and listening to you. I've never seen such a beautiful woman who thinks exactly like me. You're funny and liberal and free-spirited and obviously a wise and loyal friend. I think you would like me because I am the same kind of person. I didn't want to interrupt you while you and your friend were talking and drinking rakı. Please call me at 0532 549 18 03 if you are brave.*
> BB

Not sharing the note with Guneş, she again was ready to crumple it up and throw it away. After all, she hadn't even noticed the guy, so obviously he was no Shia LaBeouf. Maybe he was a creep. A loser. Or worse, a predator picking on young women who've had too much to drink. But she hadn't had too much to drink as she was a copious and experienced *rakı* drinker from many a late-night drinking session with her dad. In short, she was a tough, hard-drinkin', hard-fisted wench. She recently coldcocked one of her best male friends when he had drunkenly and painfully squeezed her boob in a taxi on the way home from a bar. Her father had taught her well.

When they'd had enough of fish, *rakı*, and gossip, Guneş paid the check in exchange for Ipek taking her home. Dropping her friend off, she noticed that it was still relatively early, 11:45 p.m. to be exact, and she took out the note and read it again. Of particular significance to her was the challenge with which it concluded: *if you are brave.*

What the hell, she thought and took out her cell phone and dialed Bekir's number.

Bekir, on the other hand, had just put on his pajamas and was about to climb into bed. He'd had a long day at work as an auditor with a large accounting firm. He faced the uncomfortable situation of having found a discrepancy of approximately 250,000 Turkish lira in the cash reports of one of the corporate branches he was auditing that week. It was one of the largest deficiencies he had ever uncovered, and all signs of culpability pointed to the assistant manager. His mind was on overdrive, his thoughts bouncing between how to break the news to his boss and whether he would ever hear from the black-haired girl from the next table. He highly doubted it, but it made for a great fantasy. And then his phone blared out the cash-register opening sounds of Pink Floyd's "Money."

"So that is how I met Bekir, a very kind man who I think I am dating now. But it is a little strange, and I don't know if we are in a relationship because I'm not in passionate love and I'm not super attracted to him, but he is definitely more than just a guy friend but somehow less than a boyfriend. He is very smart which I like, but he is not big macho physical which I also kind of like so, as usual…I'm a little confused. But happy. So it's okay for now. Good cuddling." With that, she stood up, grabbed the check before Ben could, gave him a hug, and, after leaving some cash at the register, disappeared out the door with a little wave.

So it was from this particular lunch with Ipek that Ben had returned to think about who still mattered to him and who had vanished, who he still loved and whom he had forgotten. And most of all, why?

His problem was that he continued to experience people as complex, unfathomable, and independent organisms with whom he would occasionally connect and then disconnect. Even after a terrible year with a close brush with death from cancer, learning to appreciate the difference between acquaintances and true friends, he still didn't feel that the people closest to him were real. It was partly a matter of the delicate balance of the priority of the self versus the priorities of others. People were, for the most part, free to do what they liked. In fact, he had gained a basic tenet of his personal philosophy regarding humans during that time: *people do what they want to do.* Sure, sometimes people would go out of their way for one another, especially in times of need, but usually the need was bilateral. Sharing suffering, or sharing a hazardous condition, often provided something intrinsic for those who weren't the actual victims. Ben thought of it as the hero effect. Most people loved to be perceived as heroes, riding to the rescue of those, at best, less fortunate and, at worst, truly in danger.

It reminded him of the David Bowie song "Heroes." Perhaps the most profound lyrics of that song came at the end:

> *We're nothing, and nothing will help us*
> *Maybe we're lying,*
> *then you better not stay*
> *But we could be safer,*
> *just for one day.*

Yes, people loved to be heroes, if just for one day.

But where were they after the danger passed? It was as if once you were strong again, they didn't think that they were still needed or, along a darker train of thought, that they were superior and stronger than you. Ben didn't think he was like that. He genuinely enjoyed helping people in need and was all the more pleased when they regained their power, be that health, confidence, or financial status. He also enjoyed teaching, as well as mentoring. However, in his current evolutionary mental state, he was beginning to suspect that there were ulterior motives for that, such as creating a basis for people to need him. But why? He didn't have to go through such a strenuous exercise to attract people. He was starting to stress from all this introspection. He wasn't good at it. Except when he was sick, for most of his life he had avoided introspection.

There was a slightly sociopathic side of Ben. Good sociopathy, if there was such a thing. Except when he was asleep and having a nightmare, Ben never experienced fear. Anxiety and apprehension on occasion, to be sure, but never the cold sweat, quaking, or paralysis most people associate with terror. Others could sense this attribute in Ben and were often drawn to him in difficult times.

The upshot of all this was that Ben never quite felt the essence of deep friendship. He had evolved to the point where he could discern true friends from false, but then his development arrested. He knew this about himself but couldn't seem to do anything about it. Maybe it was simply a trust issue, something a few sessions with a good shrink could cure. He would give of himself, perhaps even too much, too often, with little in the way of expectations in return. He had learned the hard way that the best way not to be disappointed was not to expect anything from people.

He also cared deeply about just a few people. He couldn't really understand why he cared so much about those he felt that way about. Harking back to the hero issue, he supposed that it was because he somehow felt they were more vulnerable than him. Even though they had never called and asked for help, or even actually needed it, Ben felt that their peril was just around the corner. So he remained vigilant, and that was his version of caring and loving. Only two people fell into that category—his Ukrainian friends from Kiev, Kateryna, and her young son, Vlady. Many others he really liked, but only those two required his vigilance.

CHAPTER 8

Rachel, Ross, and Annie

Present, Mississippi

HER HEADACHE BEGAN simultaneously behind her eyes and at the temples and spread aggressively into her sinuses and up to her forehead. Before she could seriously think about Ben with any clarity, she had to get rid of Ross. A total disaster as a boyfriend and complete failure as a man, she had met Ross at a particularly low point of her life that followed the death of an ex-husband with whom she had still been on friendly terms. Very friendly terms. How could she have gotten involved with someone so fundamentally different from her? To begin with, the first thing she noticed about Ross when they found themselves in bed together was that the cologne that she thought was so alluring on his cheeks and neck—a smile broke across her face at the choice of that word, *alluring*, because he wore Chanel Allure— unfortunately didn't extend its attractive scent to the rest of his body. True, he had nice muscle definition for a man in his mid-forties, and she liked the fact that he was more than ten years younger than she, but he was too hairless in that Scandinavian sort of way. Frequently, she would wake up in the middle of the night with him and, with a quick caress across his back or chest, awake with a start afraid that a young woman had somehow crawled into her bed.

Ross was like an infected appendix in her otherwise placid life. He was so secure and embedded in this situation that he needed physical excision. In fact, the comparison to an appendix was ironically appropriate. He was vestigial to her existence. He provided little in the way of intellectual stimulation, had the emotional maturity of a seven-year-old, and the sexual appetite of a radish. Over the past three months, he had become little more than a bed warmer, an escort for boring social events of the local landed gentry, and someone she felt safe jogging with at night during the hot summer months when daytime running was out of the question. Meanwhile, a nice Rottweiler could provide virtually all the same services on a much lower budget. She was also getting tired of Ross's endless promises to find a job. Trained as a computer programmer, the only thing he had engaged in that resembled programming was channel surfing with the remote of the sixty-five-inch Samsung that he had talked her into buying in a moment of weakness. She had to end this relationship quickly.

"Ross, I want to take a trip out of Mississippi sometime soon."

"Sure, where should we go? So long as the beer's cold and the music's loud, I'm game," he quipped, searching the channel guide for a bass fishing show he wanted to watch. Finding it, he turned up the volume to dance around to the corny banjo music that accompanied the announcer.

"I said '*I* want to take a trip,' not '*We* should take a trip,'" Rachel corrected him. "If you would kindly turn down that volume to a level at which we could effectively communicate, you would have heard me. In fact, I want to take one last voyage with Aunt Annie before she's too old to travel out of the country."

Earlier that day, she had decided to enlist Aunt Annie's help. She knew it was unfair of her to ask the old woman to be involved with this, but she also knew that Annie suffered under Ross's presence in the house. Her plan was simple. Ross had an obnoxiously derisive attitude when it came to Aunt Annie. He couldn't understand why Rachel allowed this ancient woman to ramble about the house, making what he deemed a feeble pretense at dusting and straightening up. He embraced every opportunity to ask her for things he knew she couldn't provide or to do things he knew she couldn't perform. In a pitiful sort of way, it was like he felt competitive with Annie for Rachel's affections because she was true family and he knew deep down that he'd never qualify. There was no way that Ross would want to accompany them for anything like a cruise to England and Western Europe.

Rachel knew how to socially engineer the right situation where he would force her to choose between her aunt Annie and himself. The choice would be a foregone conclusion. As if on cue, Ross blurted, "No way I'm going on a cruise with your aunt. Unless it's a cruise to the cemetery," he chuckled derisively.

Rachel dropped the coffee cup she was holding. It shattered with a sharp crash, flinging brown liquid all over the oriental rug and white floor boards. "That's it, you shiftless piece of crap!" she screamed at him. At the moment, her biggest regret was that she had dropped the Wedgwood cup before she had a chance to fling its contents at him and save the precious gift from her father. "Really, Ross. Enough of you. I want you out of this house…out of my life now! Pack up your junk, take this damn TV if you want, and just get out of my house before I…before I…" She wasn't going to make empty threats about calling the police or shooting him with her daddy's ancient 12 gauge. He had insulted her and her aunt for the last time, and it just felt so good telling him to piss off.

"Fine, you boring old bitch! I'm outa here. This house *is* the cemetery as far as I'm concerned. And you and your aunt are the walking dead," he railed after her as she ascended the stairs to her bedroom.

Rachel went to the mid-nineteenth-century writing desk that occupied a nook with natural light from a dormer in her room. The burled walnut desk was an heirloom from her great-grandfather who had accepted it in trade from a skilled cabinetmaker. The young man, down on his luck, had worked rent-free in one of the family's outbuildings for several years. When he got back on his feet, he insisted that the elder Collier accept this remarkable piece of fine furniture. He later became a partner of Duncan Phyfe in his New York custom furniture business in 1847.

Rachel, fearing one of Ross's drunken stumbling dashes to the toilet in the middle of the night, had surrounded it with a few over-stuffed chairs for protection. Now she pulled the chairs back to their appropriate locations and sat herself down at the desk. She could hear Ross banging around downstairs and screaming at Annie that he was going to break her arms. Grabbing as many of his clothes as she could hold, she started flinging them over the railing down to the first floor.

"Do not come upstairs, or I will shoot you, I swear to Christ," she announced firmly to his back at the bottom of the stairs. She had grabbed the old Browning 12 gauge and loudly racked a shell into the chamber. It was scratched and marred from decades of use in the scrub and swamps of Mississippi, but she had always kept it clean and well-oiled. In fact, with her senses heightened from anger, she could detect the faint petroleum smell of the Rem-Oil she had recently sprayed in the action and forestock of the long gun.

Ross glanced upward at the *chick chack* sound of the chamber being loaded. "There's a better chance of me being struck by lightning in here than you shooting me with that antique," he said as he started up the stairs.

The deafening sound of the shotgun's discharge and over four hundred pellets of birdshot splintering the steps just above his feet were enough to convince Ross to abruptly halt his ascent. The air was permeated by two new smells, sulfur and shit, as Ross fled out the front door, his arms draped with his meager wardrobe. Rachel smiled sardonically at the widening stain at the backside of his jeans.

After a few moments of relative quiet, Aunt Annie peeked around the wall that separated the entry hall from the dining room and kitchen. "My goodness!" Annie remarked. "When you said that you wanted to get that poor excuse for a boyfriend out of the house, you weren't kidding around."

"You always said that we Colliers don't kid around, Aunt Annie. I hadn't planned on shooting up the house to run him off, but as they say, whatever works."

CHAPTER 9

Ben

1976, Iran

MORE THAN FORTY years ago, in keeping with his goal of visiting every one of his friends in their home countries after graduation, Ben and his Persian pal Bamkiz were dancing to the songs of the Beach Boys through the high desert at the foot of the Zagroz Mountains in central Iran. They especially liked "I Get Around" as it seemed apropos of their present circumstances. To their *tiryak*-influenced eyes, the desert floor sparkled nearly as bright as the star-encrusted heavens above, with the lingering snowfields on the mountain peaks luminescent in the glow from the full moon.

The two Merry Pranksters performed their Beach Boys routine in the most unlikely of places although, for sure, Dennis Wilson would have heartily approved. That was true fame, Ben thought, when your music echoes in the mountains halfway around the world from where it was written in a countryside that has remained virtually unchanged for thousands of years. Converse All Stars in a land of leather sandals. Faded Levi's and Grateful Dead T-shirts among white robes and brown wool vests. Bamkiz had become a belated fan of the Beach Boys when they had performed at Duke for a Joe College Weekend.

Earlier in the evening, a domestic comedy unfolded as Ben was introduced to the classic method for smoking the drug known locally as *tiryak*. A brass brazier filled with glowing coals, brass tongs, and a long pipe with a ceramic egg-shaped bulb at the end were the requisite tools. A small wad of opium was stuck just behind a small hole in the bulb, and holding an olive-sized briquette of coal above and behind the drug with the tongs, the user steadily drew in air. The coal heated the opium, which began to smoke, the intake of breath drew the smoke into the pipe and, thus, into the lungs where it was held for a few seconds until…bliss.

They were sitting around casually, reclining on large pillows piled at various heights about the artistically tiled room. Blues and reds predominated with a patchwork of magnificent locally produced rugs haphazardly scattered about the floor. As was typical of culturally oblivious Americans at the time, Ben failed to notice that there was a subtle pecking order to the way everyone was positioned.

As the pipe was passed from man to man, perhaps ten of them including Ben and Bamkiz, the feeling of relaxation became almost overpowering for the American. With every passing toke, Ben began to slide lower, farther down from his stack of pillows on which he was perched, a dreamy smile spreading across his face—not asleep, just a profound feeling of comfort and release of tension permeating his body: solipsistically indeterminate. He sank lower and lower until he was almost laid out flat on the richly carpeted floor.

Bamkiz's foot shot out and caught Ben in the thigh. "Sit up, Ben!" Bamkiz commanded in a harsh whisper.

"Huh…what…why? What's the matter?"

"Haven't you noticed that there's a social hierarchy in place here? We have been honored with these high pillows and cushions because these men revere us as superior in social stature to themselves. They feel they must always be below you. As you've been sliding down, it's gotten rather hard for them to remain lower than you. I mean, if you get any closer to the floor, they will have to start digging foxholes for themselves!"

It was true. With an embarrassed, nervous chuckle, Ben realized that this was, indeed, occurring. As soon as he remounted his cushions, the men all relaxed.

"I think that's enough *tiryak* for now," Bamkiz chided. "We can have some more later, after we eat."

All the men proceeded into a covered esplanade adorned with hanging flowers and plants, wind chimes tinkling melodiously beneath the eaves, and a long wooden table with plates piled high with roasted lamb, brown rice with raisins and apricots, chicken kebab, sliced apples, dates, and pears, and a formidable jungle of vegetables and salad greens. Their host, a dead ringer for the old comic actor Dean Martin, emerged clad in his original Abercrombie and Fitch hunting jacket and slacks. He looked right out of a novel by Ernest Hemingway. If only he could have known how A&F would come to change in the next thirty years. He was a first cousin of Bamkiz who went by the name of Rudy Reza.

Bamkiz asked Ben, "Do you mind if I make a Persian toast and welcome you to our table?"

"No problem," said Ben.

Bamkiz turned to the local men, and Reza and spoke about ten words of Farsi to which they responded with hysterical laughter.

"What the hell did you say that was so funny?" asked Ben.

"Oh, I just asked them if they wanted you to lick their dogs' assholes before or *after* dinner." He smiled. "I thought it an appropriate price for you to pay after nearly requiring their self-entombment."

"*Bes salaam a ti,*" Ben responded in perfectly accented Farsi, raising his glass to the clearly shocked men. "To your health."

In the intervening years between then and the present, both Ben and Bamkiz had related that story innumerable times. Traveling between Australia and America, rendezvousing in Africa and Asia, the two friends had invested the time and energy necessary to maintain their deep friendship. Ben had always felt inferior to the big Persian. He wasn't as athletic, as exotically handsome, as brilliant, or nearly as charming as this man with a thousand-plus years of breeding and culture in his genes. They both traveled through life relatively alone without family but both relying on a widely distributed network of friends they had developed independently of each other. While vastly different in terms of backgrounds, they were cut from the same cloth of character and treasured each other's company above all else.

They also shared a peripatetic nature, although for different reasons—Bamkiz because he didn't want any of his more fanatical countrymen to become too familiar with his whereabouts and Ben because he was reluctant to gather any moss. Therefore, it worked for them that Bamkiz continually traveled to avoid his foes while Ben joined the foreign service and stayed in perpetual motion to avoid confronting himself.

CHAPTER 10

Rachel

Present, Mississippi

"SELF-ANALYSIS IS A critical component of personal growth and maintenance of mental health." Rachel had written these words while a grad student and regularly practiced what she preached. Sitting at the Duncan Phyfe-style desk in her bedroom, Rachel wondered why she hadn't traveled more. Other than overpriced, overorganized trips to Europe and the Caribbean with ex-husbands, New York, Atlanta, and Washington, DC, for academic conferences, and a memorable road trip with Ben from Jackson, Mississippi, to New Orleans, she hadn't ventured more than about 150 miles from the place where she now sat. As a fully tenured professor at the university, she couldn't remember how long she had stood before students whose faces all merged into a blur and faculty she rarely could relate to on anything more than an academic level.

Rachel understood that this wasn't unusual. She had heard that many Americans have never traveled more than 100 miles from where they live. Whether this was due to fear of flying or lack of financial resources, or probably both, Rachel believed the real problem was a combination of laziness and disinterest. Most people didn't want to experience anything truly different in their lives. She was seriously considering whether she wanted change or consistency in her life. As she was beginning to think that change would be positive in her case, she had recently hired a contractor to paint the house, install new kitchen appliances, and refinish the floors.

Rachel knew that this was all quite superficial, but she likened it to dipping your toes in the water of a swimming pool to see if the water temperature was acceptable. Hearing voices downstairs, she left her bedroom and went out to the hall to see what the commotion was all about.

"Put that back! You put that right back where you got it, young man. There's nothing wrong with that stove."

Experiencing no small degree of angst at the change Rachel was inflicting upon their domestic lives, Aunt Annie was challenging one of the young men handling the appliance installation in the kitchen. The poor guy was balancing a fifty-year-old avocado-green General Electric range on the steel toe of his work boot.

"Ma'am, with all due respect, this ole boy might have value for the Smithsonian Museum, but what I'm about to replace it with is like the difference between a ceiling fan and central air-conditioning."

"Aunt Annie, please, "Rachel implored. "Just give it a chance. I promise you'll like this new Wolf. We've had gas to the house for decades, and it's time we caught up with the times."

"Looks like something from an industrial kitchen if you ask me. That GE is such a pretty color green."

Rachel and the installer both rolled their eyes at that last comment by Annie, and Rachel tenderly moved her aunt out of the way to allow the fellow to pass with the obsolete stove. The two women continued along the hall to the study.

"I know what you're doing, Rachel. You are trying to make us both feel better by giving this old house a makeover. But I think the money would be better spent if the two of us went to Houston and got makeovers at Neiman Marcus!" Annie cackled. Little did she know that she would outlive that department store chain.

"Aunt Annie," Rachel began, "I know you know. But it's not the time for me to be picking up and leaving you with this albatross of a house while I gallivant around the world. Some people are perfectly comfortable with living their lives within a small geographical radius.

And for now, that's the way I feel. I have the money to fix this place up, and it's time to do it. In fact, it's been rather fun. More fun than grading work written by barely literate freshmen and sophomores where I have to waste so much time ensuring that they aren't plagiarizing or buying their papers from ghost writers on the internet."

"They do that?" Annie was incredulous. "That's another reason why I hate that internet. It's a tool for cheaters. And I don't mean just your students. The other day, my hairdresser was telling me how she caught her husband on some website called Zipless.com for folks that want to have affairs. Good lord! He was stepping out with a crossing guard from the elementary school. Must have thought that would qualify as safe sex!" Annie laughed.

Rachel joined her laughter. "Well, it's rather hard to get away with an extramarital affair in a town with less than 1,600 people. Should have gone to Foxworth or Mount Hermon, at least."

"Oh sure, Rachel. Those towns have an oversupply of bad-behaving women. I bet they do," Annie commented sarcastically.

The two women sat quietly, enjoying each other's company as workmen moved appliances, cabinets, paint cans, and drop cloths into the house. Annie was wondering when they would commence sanding and staining the floors. She'd have to ask the men to carefully move all the rugs and furniture from room to room and cover everything to protect from dust. Rachel was off in another direction entirely. She was wondering where her old lover Ben was at the moment and why he could never be happy staying in one place.

The truth was Rachel wasn't sure if she would like all that freedom of movement. She wondered how people who are constantly relocating maintain friendships and contact with their families. It was so much easier knowing literally everyone within a five-mile radius of where you sat. Yet it was also stultifying, and she understood that if she was to advance as a person, she would have to break this geographical equilibrium she had become so accustomed to. Ever since she had moved back to Collierville after the breakup of her last marriage, she had read travel magazines and dreamt of one day packing a bag for parts unknown. Maybe Morroco, Marrakesh, Casablanca, and Fes. Or Turkey Istanbul, Cappadocia, and Ephesus.

But why was she even thinking of Istanbul and Marrakesh and Ben Jacobson? Her academic brain was screaming that this was absurd. Those cities were unquestionably the opposites of Colliersville and a good diversion from life as a university professor in the American South. But Ben Jacobson? What was that all about?

CHAPTER 11

Ben and Johan

1999, Ghana, Africa

IN THE WINTER of 1999, Ben was sent to Ghana on a particularly time-sensitive mission. Not only had the American embassies in Dar es Salaam and Nairobi been bombed with devastating effect, but intelligence also revealed that the US embassy in Accra was particularly vulnerable as well. In his typical systematic approach to such an assignment, Ben did his homework carefully. He investigated not only the political and business climate but also the broader social, recreational, entertainment, and cultural features of the country. He believed that the wider he cast his net of research, the richer the bounty the local sea would yield.

It was during the course of one of these web searches that he ran across the name Johan Niedermann. The name struck him as curious for a professional fishing guide in, of all places, Ada Foah, Ghana. His colleagues in the intelligence community revealed that Niedermann had been South Africa's youngest accredited ambassador from the Mandela government, opening new diplomatic facilities in half a dozen African nations between 1993 and 1998 before accidentally discovering one of the world's best and closest-to-shore blue marlin fishing grounds. Between the months of January and April 1998, he had caught and released nine behemoth fish weighing in excess of one thousand pounds, huge pelagic creatures that were called "granders." When the marlin weren't biting, giant yellowfin tuna weighing in excess of three hundred pounds took his bait. Johan thought he had died and gone to heaven. He respectfully tendered his resignation from the South African Foreign Service and started his high-end sportfishing charter service.

Ben also learned that Johan had recently obtained government approval to construct a massive shopping mall, hotel, and office complex along the Government Highway, an unusual concession to be granted to a non-Ghanaian native. This revealed a closer degree of political ties with local government than a fishing guide would be expected to have. A deeper background search revealed a pending liquor license and gambling casino application that would certainly be approved in the upcoming months. Ben decided that it was time for a little marlin fishing in West Africa.

The Labadi Beach Hotel was to be Ben's home for the next several months. Located along a sparsely populated beach where the riptides and crosscurrents made it too hazardous to swim, the hotel was arranged as a collection of eight-room buildings around a central courtyard and restaurant facilities. The other guests were primarily Africans from neighboring countries on a variety of diplomatic, business, and cultural engagements. The day Ben arrived, a wedding party was in evidence, judging from the exaggeratedly bright smiles and colorful clothing. The women were tittering. *Yes*, thought Ben. *That's what they were doing, tittering.*

A funny word, *tittering. Maybe it's related to some kind of bird*, thought Ben. He followed behind the waistcoated bellman, his mind lost in a fog of jet lag and the aftereffects of too much cheap airline wine. The sun was unnaturally bright, he observed. He could see a shore break, sending sheets of foamy water up onto the beach. It smelled faintly of brine. A large sign warning of deadly rip currents was posted conspicuously at the beginning of a path that led to the beach.

"What good's a beach if you can't swim?" he asked the bellman.

"It's nice for the families," replied the porter. "I take the wife and kids to the beach on the days off. The kids like to make shit in the sand and watch the water wash it away."

"Lovely," said Ben. "Remind me to stay away on your day off." *Great place I've come to,* he mused. *Sun's too hot, too bright, can't swim in the sea, can't chill at the beach because of kid crap.* He definitely needed a boat here to survive. To escape.

The bellman opened the door to a spacious white-painted suite that unfortunately reeked of someone's body odor mixed with mold and musty carpets. Even though there was only a tile floor, that old carpet smell predominated. After tipping the man, he flipped on the overhead fan and collapsed onto the bed, which promptly swallowed him up like a giant Venus flytrap. The room may have smelled musty, but the mattress smelled like ass and was as soft as a fat one too. He fell asleep and dreamed disgusting dreams.

At 5:00 p.m., what looked like an animated Fernando Botero woman noisily entered his room and stood directly over what little of his body remained in view from the engulfment of the Third World mattress.

"You want turn down service?"

"I want excavation and rescue service."

"I don't do nunna that."

Ben literally had to claw his way out from the bed and stagger into the shower, leaving Botero woman to her own devices. The cold water blasted him into consciousness.

Johan picked him up fifteen minutes later in something that looked like it had been spawned from the movie *Mad Max*. "It's a retired Dakar racing machine," Johan advised Ben in his uniquely South African drawl.

In true rally racer form, Ben and Johan hurtled along pot-holed roads with interminable construction delays that Johan finally began ignoring, taking advantage of the car's beefy suspension to blast through the partially cleared and graded shoulders until asphalt returned. It was during that four-hour bone-jarring, eye-searing journey through dust and mayhem the two forged an everlasting friendship. Ben also gained a new respect for those guys you see riding shotgun during off-road rallies and offshore powerboat races. Unlike the drivers, who, at least, had their steering wheels to hang on to, the navigators or copilots or whatever you called them had no such convenience nor did they have much control, except for the possibility of reaching such a point of discomfort and fear that they literally threw their drivers out the door or overboard or whatever, and continued at a more leisurely pace. However, as darkness descended, Ben had no wish to assume the not inconsequential risk of running over the random animals and people who constantly wandered in front of them or the abandoned construction vehicles left along the side of the road down which they were traveling at speeds ranging from fifty to ninety miles per hour.

Eventually, Ben relaxed and grew accustomed to the reckless abandon with which Johan drove. He actually began to enjoy the concept of traveling at breakneck speed with Johan. He came to fully appreciate the adjective *breakneck* because, indubitably, if they had hit anything, either their necks would be broken or whatever they hit would suffer a similar fate or, perhaps, even both. They shared more of their personal histories, especially fishing related.

"I have literally circumnavigated Africa in search of big fish on my boat, *Karma*," Johan boasted.

"Without knowing that about you, I've nearly accomplished the same geographic distribution. But I bet I've spent more time than you off the salt, fly-fishing in South Africa and Zambia." Ben regaled Johan with tales of tiger fish on the Zambezi River and rainbow trout in the Barkly East and Rhodes area of the Southern Drakensberg Mountains. It gradually devolved into a "can you top this?" competition.

Ben: "A hundred and thirty peacock bass weighing over 5 pounds in a single morning in Panama."

Johan: "Just one 1,140-pound black marlin off the Cape."

Ben: "Three brown trout in excess of 20 pounds in the River Itchen in County Hampshire in England, where Isaac Walton used to fish."

Johan: "Four elephant yellowfin tuna over 350 pounds just twenty minutes from my dock here in Ada Foah."

Ben: "Accidently killed a 125-pound Pacific sailfish that got tail wrapped in Fiji that fed an entire village."

Johan: "In 1999 caught and released twelve grander blue marlin in one week."

Ben: "Forty-six rainbow trout over 4 pounds each in two hours on the fly from Steamboat Lake in Colorado."

Johan: "Boated and released a young great white over 3,500 pounds near Durban on 100-pound test line."

Ben: "Boated and released an 850-plus-pound blue marlin off Lomé, Togo, on 60-pound test."

Johan: "Ha! That's just a rat!"

And so forth. Ben couldn't win. They pulled into the grassy yard of Johan's fishing villa in Ada Foah to find four characters out of Alice in Wonderland barbecuing an enormous wahoo. It must have been at least 95 pounds. He didn't know that there even were wahoo in these waters.

The fishing villa belonging to Johan, although not luxurious, was more than adequate for Ben. In fact, it exceeded his expectations by having air-conditioning, a *sine qua non* as far as he was concerned. The fridge was well stocked with Castle Lager, burgers, salad greens, and cheeses from France and Italy. The pantry revealed the colorful labels of Jiff peanut butter, Heinz ketchup, Campbell's soup, Tomco baked beans and peas, All Gold strawberry jam, numerous boxes of (no doubt sugar-enhanced) cereal, Vesuvius hot sauce, and an infinite variety of other condiments and cookies, candies, and canned goods. A gallery of photographs worthy of the Metropolitan Museum of Art depicting Johan and various anglers with enormous marlins, tuna, and other game fish also served as a salon for the rare days of inclement weather that would keep one inside. Rattan and well-worn furniture was the decor, complemented by plantation shutters and hanging baskets of tropical plants. The house smelled of fresh fish and men who bathed in the brackish waters of the Volta River.

Outside, a tall, spindly, and lugubrious man in his fifties was relating a tale in a sepulchral voice that no one appeared to be listening to. Another, more ebullient fellow who worked on one of the oil rigs just to the north was talking about a large school of juvenile tuna he saw being chased by a pack of tiger-striped wahoo while he was conducting stress tests on the underwater pylons. He said that he had radioed a sitrep to the guys topside who immediately joined him below the surface with spearguns and scuba gear. A fresh tuna steak dinner was his reward for the tip.

Without having to go through the usual biographical protocol, Ben found himself subtly insinuated, assimilated, and virtually marinated (after a few tall glasses of Volta Voltage) into the conversation, as if he had been there all along. And that wahoo was so good he resolved to never release another from his line.

He awoke the next day to gray gold light as dawn broke across the alluvial plain of southeastern Ghana and the Volta River estuary. He could hear the muffled chatter of the mates, Abeeko and Kobeena, through the unadorned window as they loaded ice and fuel onto *Karma*. The morning coffee clutch of whistling ducks, terns, avocets, and greenshanks were already well along with the day's avian gossip. The air in the room was less hot than it was humid, and Ben stumbled over to the window and wrenched it up a few inches to let in a riverine breeze. Without bothering to remove his SpongeBob SquarePants boxers, he ran outside and down the dock and plunged in the tepid waters of the Volta, then used the boat's freshwater showerhead to rinse himself off. He joined Johan at the chrome-edged gray Formica kitchen table for a mug of strong coffee and a bowl of Kellogg's cornflakes.

Johan was aggressively masticating an unknown species of salted dried meat and stirring more sugar into a dainty glass of English tea. "I figger we'll head out to about 250 feet of water and wet some lines," he managed between chews that accentuated his jaw muscles. "Unless, of course, we see some birds overhead somewhere else."

Ben just nodded.

"For the past couple of weeks, the granders have been riding the water columns between 150 and 300 feet," Johan commented once they were in the boat.

Pellucid sky, mild humidity but searing sun burning at thirty degrees to the marine horizon with the hypnotic, lazy baritone drone of the engines was putting them all back to sleep. A big marlin hit the right long lure so hard and fast Abeeko almost missed it.

"Boss, we got a grander!" he yelled over his shoulder as Johan threw the engines into reverse and backed down on the fish before the screaming reel could dump its entire 300 meters of eighty-pound test monofilament. Ben clipped himself into the fighting chair as together Abeeko and Kobeena slammed the butt of the short, stocky tuna stick into the cup between his legs. "All yours, Mister Ben," Kobeena beamed. Then the two men quickly reeled in the other three rods: one long and one short left and the remaining short right-side line. The next 190 minutes were excruciating, exhilarating, frustrating, and invigorating as Ben and Johan, working in tandem, gained inches on the behemoth marlin, only to lose meters, then regain them, then see them slip away as the fish sounded, then charged the stern. It exploded into the air in a series of acrobatic jumps, worthy of the most gymnastic freestyle skiers, then tail walked as gracefully as a ballet dancer, only to crash back into the sea with the heavy crush of over a thousand pounds of muscle and bone. Throughout the battle, Ben and Johan worked together as a choreographed team. When the marlin charged the boat, Johan slipped into forward gear as Ben furiously cranked the reel, attempting to maintain pressure on the line so the fish couldn't flip the hook from its mouth while it was slack. When it sounded, Ben sensitively increased the pressure of the drag to slow its descent as Johan hovered the boat overhead.

Sometimes both man and beast would, by some gladiatorial telepathy, just take a break, the marlin apparently hanging suspended, spear downward, letting the deep current carry it away from the boat. During these brief respites, Ben would give his cramped right arm a stretch and his weary left a rest by switching hands and bearing the enormous weight of the fish with his right pulled straight along the shaft of the rod. It was during these breaks in the action that Abeeko would offer him a cold bottle of water while Kobeena sprayed him down with the freshwater showerhead. After an hour and a half, Ben swallowed two salt tablets and a quinine pill to fight the cramps that were beginning to cripple his shoulders and stab his lower back. Throughout the ordeal, Johan and Ben had maintained a dialogue that was remarkable not only for the degree of eloquence and lucidity but also its relative joviality considering the stressful circumstances. To Ben, this seemed like Johan was either trying to distract him from the pain of trying to coax over a thousand pounds of desperately fighting fish to the *Karma*, or this was so quotidian for him as to be the equivalent of two joggers discussing city politics as they circumnavigated the Central Park Lake in Manhattan.

Their conversation was well beyond phatic. "Should we slightly increase the drag?" Ben asked.

"Bad idea," Johan responded. "That's how you lost that big marlin off of Lomé, wasn't it?"

The marlin started yanking on the line with a series of powerful jerks as if to remind Ben that this was no day at the beach for it, either, and increasing the drag of the reel was not a friendly thing to do. But for the clips and steel lines between rod and fighting chair, these repeated tugs would have pulled Ben right out of the chair and possibly over the stern of the *Karma*. He remembered seeing an incredible video of a man being pulled overboard by an enormous bluefin tuna while attached to his fishing rod and reading about a captain being pulled over and down by a large shark off Ocean City, Maryland. The tuna fisherman had lived, but the shark boat captain had not.

Ben pushed such funereal thoughts from his mind and returned to the task at hand. After two hours in the heat and no real progress having been made, he began to entertain thoughts of surreptitiously cranking up the drag, letting the fish break the line, then quickly backing off the drag so that Johan wouldn't know he had wimped out. But then the cruelty of knowing that he had condemned a magnificent animal to weeks of hunger and the discomfort of swimming around with a hundred meters of translucent fishing line trailing from its bill (thus making hunting and feeding impossible) discouraged such an idea.

It seemed that *Karma* had taken on the tropism properties of a chlorophyll-structured organism as it maneuvered to align itself with the marlin. This was the source of considerable suffering for Ben as the sun remained in his eyes for most of the duration of the contest.

He may have been anthropomorphizing the marlin as he pictured this huge fish smiling with the knowledge that its tormentor was paying for his troubles with an egregious sunburn. A vile marine mountebank was how Ben began to characterize the marlin as the two-hour mark passed. His left forearm muscle was cramping badly at the point where it met his elbow, and a sharp pain stabbed at his right forearm every time he had to maniacally wind the reel handle if the fish began to surface or approach the boat. Johan, long a student of the human condition, thankfully interrupted his mordant thoughts, "On a Dasein scale, who do you think is at a higher level at this point in time? You or that fish?"

"You've got to be kidding," Ben said. "My arms are being pulled out of their sockets and you are asking for some irrelevant Heidegger-inspired philosophical argument? Just help me, will you? Jig this boat around on him a little." Ben was definitely feeling inferior to the fish by this time and didn't want Johan reminding him of that, by coincidence or otherwise.

As if the marlin heard Ben's suggestion about using the boat more as a tool than a platform, he began slowly swimming toward them. Ben was forced to furiously start reeling in to take up the slack. After seventy-five meters, it abruptly veered off at a ninety-degree angle and accelerated. The line screamed off the reel at an alarming rate. The four men watched as the great fish launched itself skyward well to the west of the boat, descended to fifty meters below the surface, and waited, as if to see what the boat would do. In response, Johan did what Ben least expected: he put the throttle in forward and, at a speed of about five knots, cruised away from where Ben imagined the fish to be.

But he was wrong. The fish had taken advantage of the weight of the water on the line and had looped back toward *Karma*, intuiting that Ben wouldn't realize that he was going to come up almost under the boat while Ben still thought he was 150 meters behind. Fortunately, Johan had experienced the same uncannily intelligent behavior before. By slowly moving away, Johan was taking up the slack and robbing the marlin of its stealthy strategy. After three or four minutes of this, Johan shifted the *Karma* to starboard and told

Ben to start reeling in quickly. They were turning the fish on its weak side before making a fast charge and regaining virtually all the line it had stripped from the reel only a few moments before.

A school of flying fish erupted from the surface in a small cloud of movement as marine birds dived at them, occasionally snaring a hapless meal. Several small tunas followed, chasing the Exocoetidae and creating pandemonium around *Karma* as the great fish began to rise, oblivious of the havoc on the surface. Abeeko, the wireman, put on his oily leather gloves and approached the stern. "She's coming home, boss," he murmured to Johan.

Without having to be told, Kobeena grabbed the tagging stick and joined the other mate. As Ben feverishly cranked in line, the two men tensed, and suddenly the bill, as thick as a man's leg, and a softball-sized eye breached the surface. Kobeena extended his body toward the marlin and, with one fluid motion, implanted the tag while Abeeko snared the circle hook with his gaff and flipped it out of the fish's mouth with a violent turn of his wrist. Ben unclipped himself and the rod from the chair and stumbled forward to look at his adversary of over two hours. Bending deep over the gunwale, he grasped the bill and planted a kiss on the fish's cheek, just below the huge eye, and held tight as Johan gently eased the throttle forward. They continued on like that for nearly five minutes until the great fish was fully resuscitated. Finally, with a shake of its mammoth head, the marlin pulled free and slowly swam down into the sea.

CHAPTER 12

Rachel

AUNT ANNIE DIED suddenly of a heart attack just shy of two months after Ross left her, and Rachel had never been so alone. She never had *felt* so alone. In a town where she knew virtually every one of the 1,562 residents, she began to think that she had become invisible. She understood two things. No one in Colliersville had liked Ross, much less even acknowledged him as her man. They were too polite to say anything to her face but had let her know in other not so subtle ways. Invitations to dinner and picnics had ceased, favors were never asked, and long afternoons discussing politics and literature at the homes of other local academics and writers had dwindled to virtually never.

She had spent the last four days sitting by herself at Founders Cemetery. As a family member, Annie was entitled to the one in which she now rested. Even though she came from her mother's Tennessee side of the family, Annie had established herself as Colliersville incarnate at some point over the past few decades—Rachel didn't know which. Annie was embraced by the small community, and her funeral had been widely attended. She'd lost someone who defied categorization: substitute mother, philosopher, humorist, font of country wisdom. Rachel wandered back and forth between the modest headstones of her parents and Aunt Annie, not acknowledging time or weather. She wrote poems in her head. Sonnets about loss. She forgot them within minutes.

In the evenings, she would walk back home and sit with her feet in Colliers Lake, looking at the headlights of the cars parked across from her little weathered dock. The water, so green and opaque during the day, turned black as obsidian at night, its cloudy surface not reflecting the moon even when full. She knew well what was going on inside those cars, the newest no less than ten years old, Fords and Chevys, the odd International Harvester Scout four by four from the mid-1970s. People connecting, physically and emotionally—perhaps even more spiritually—while she had closed herself in an artifact, an old house built by her forebears that she felt some kind of filial duty to maintain, voluntarily becoming its prisoner. Maybe she should have been thinking about Annie as her warden or, at a lower level, her guard. Or maybe, she mused, Aunt Annie was just another prisoner like herself but elevated to the status of trusty. Certainly not like the armed trusties of Parchman Farm, the huge old prison not too far away from where she now sat, who were expected to take a shot at any inmate who attempted escape or harm to a guard. More like the second tier of trusties, those who were free to roam so long as they cleaned, repaired, and performed other menial tasks for the guards. That was exactly what Annie had become, a trusty in that old house, roaming its halls, inefficiently dusting and straightening, occupying the furniture so, speaking, it wouldn't feel forgotten. A relic in charge of relics. Now that she was gone, Rachel was a prisoner without chains. She could, rather should, escape.

This thought was depressing for her. To even think of starting to live her life again as a *free* woman was stupid. She knew intrinsically that she had always been free. So why had she imprisoned herself along with Aunt Annie? Because she was afraid? Because it was easier? Or because, at least before the arrival of Ross, she had an eternally rotating parade of visitors and supporters, admirers, and sycophants, locals who considered themselves inferior and beholden to her birthright and the local status that came from it? Everything in life is about the choices one makes, she told herself. It didn't matter why.

She had chosen that life for the past God knows how many years, and now it was time for her to choose to make a change. Perhaps this was Aunt Annie's last gift to her.

On this particular evening, after dusk had surrendered to night, she gathered her tools and small wicker stool (she had been doing a little gardening and maintenance around the dock) and began walking back up the slight incline leading to the house. The porch lights illuminated the countless flying insects that appeared like thousands of randomly circling stars, grand and miniscule, all somehow managing to avoid crashing into one another, as if possessing some kind of innate radar.

The smell of eutrophication wafted off the lake behind her and followed her progress into the empty house. As night came over the landscape, a resolve to choose a different life began to grow in her.

She entered the brightly lit and still-tidy kitchen, brewed herself a mug of strong black tea, and poured a shot of Southern Comfort into its steaming maw. Carrying her traditional predinner concoction to the long, knotty oak kitchen table, she paused to pick up a notepad and pen. She would make a list. Rachel was a big believer in lists.

Taking a tentative sip of the hot, aromatic tea, Rachel drew two vertical lines down the center of the page. On the left column, she wrote *Ideas*, on the middle column *Positives*, on the right column, *Negatives*. She dedicated the rest of the night to filling the page. And then another page.

Ideas	*Positives*	*Negatives*
Sell the house.	Immediate cash, less responsibility, lower monthly expenses, downsize, freedom to travel.	Weak real estate market, loss of sentimental value, what to do with all the family heirlooms and furniture, guilt feelings/ betrayal of six generations of Colliers.
Write a book, leave the university.	I have a recognized name in academic publishing, I could write about the house and Colliers family influence in Mississippi.	Who the hell would want to read it? Sounds boring, even to me.
Change my field and teach another subject(s) at the community college.	Always wanted to teach contemporary art.	Would have to go back and get at least a masters. I don't paint or sculpt, collect, etc. Where are my credentials?
Adopt a child.	Social responsibility, receive and give love, support, etc.	Lots of responsibility, loss of personal freedom, new expenses.
Start an NGO to promote education somewhere in West Africa, like Gambia.	Put my teaching experience to better use, make a difference, change the world, etc.	Rising incidence of religious extremism and feuds between Muslims and Christians. Dangerous.

Take an *Eat, Pray, Love* trip like in the Julia Roberts movie.	Might help me with reawakening, get in touch with my core values, find love like Javier Bardem.	Just saw Javier Bardem in movie *The Counselor*, and it grossed me out. And the trip looked like it would get boring after a while. In any event, I already know myself.
Get involved in local politics.	Help bring some positive change to this stagnant community. I could easily win a seat on the town council as a start.	I'm probably not tough enough, and I usually avoid confrontation.
Learn about/experiment with digital art.	I can't draw, sculpt, or paint, but I've got a great visual imagination and I'm good with a computer.	I would have to spend some time at a fine arts school, expensive without a scholarship. I would be forty years older than the other students.

She hadn't thought of Ben for the past few weeks, but that was about to change. Perhaps she should have added a column about taking a trip to find him, just for kicks. Just not yet. It was too soon for her to abandon her grief. For the moment, she was comfortable with it.

CHAPTER 13

Ben

January, several weeks ago. Kiev and Istanbul

JANUARY TWENTY-THIRD—SALVADOR DALI died on this day in 1989. Also on this day, grandchildren celebrate their grandmothers in Bulgaria, Richard Nixon announced the end of the war in Vietnam (two years too early as it turned out), and some Catholics some- where observe the feast of St. Ildefonsus. Ben was sitting in a Turkish Airlines jet flying back to Istanbul from Kiev, Ukraine, after a three- day weekend visiting his good friend Kateryna and his godson, Vlady. He spent an hour reading the English-language Turkish newspaper *Sunday Yildiz* and then the English-language Ukrainian paper, *Kyiv Post*. He didn't understand why Turkish Airlines distributed that par- ticular English-language newspaper to its fliers as it was generally known to be a mouthpiece for the ruling party's sworn enemies. The Turkish paper was drawing a parallel between the Ukrainian and Turkish approaches to leadership and democracy, an interesting and bold position to take, despite not being particularly accurate.

Every day he read the other newspaper in Turkey directed at expats and tourists, the *Hürriyet Daily News*, an English-language version of *Hürriyet*, one of the most prominent of the Turkish dailies. In a country where journalists could be imprisoned, the op-ed writ- ers of *Hürriyet Daily News* were, like those at *Yildiz*, quite outspoken, perhaps even downright bold in their assessments of the current state of affairs.

As an American and former government official with a stratospherically high security clearance, Ben had not participated in any of the recent protests in either Ukraine or Turkey. He hadn't written any articles in the local or international newspapers, and he didn't have a blog. He kept his head down as his father had tried to teach him to do in times of difficulty. It never occurred to him that simply because of his lifestyle, his friends, his contacts in Istanbul, Washington, and Kiev that he had become very interesting to a number of deeply covert organizations.

Ben had spent the past seventy-two hours living the life of an average, educated, well-employed person in Kiev. Kateryna and Vlady lived in an eighty-square-meter, fully renovated flat located on the top floor of a Soviet-era midrise apartment block surrounded by un-landscaped land, derelict cars parked alongside new compacts, and patches of dirty snow under a cold, gray sky. The difference between inside and outside was dramatic. Inside it was brightly lit, with warm radiant heating, perfectly clean floors, windows, countertops, bathroom fixtures, and colorful contemporary art, books, toys, and sports equipment nestled in every available nook and cranny. Outside it was…well…cold, barren, and steel gray.

The view out Kateryna's windows was toward the Dnieper River, partially blocked by new residential buildings with neo-Ukrainian architecture complete with domes, turrets, and spires. Their ground floors were occupied by expensive children's stores like Chicco and international gourmet markets like De-Light where a small jar of Dijon mustard sold for over $25. Most of the cars in the parking lots were of the Mercedes and Porsche flavor while most of those in Kateryna's complex where Ladas and other less identifiable brands.

Although by nature Ben was a rescuer (of people, animals, and lost causes), Kateryna and Vlady certainly didn't need rescuing. Yet he was fully focused on how he could help them have the life they deserved. Kateryna was one of the most uniquely successful and impressive people he had ever met. Born into a land of six-foot-tall skinny blond fashion models, she was five feet four on a good day.

Pretty, actually beautiful in the long-lasting kind of way typical of Slavic brunettes, she was one of the few people Ben had ever met who could say that literally everything she had, she had provided for herself—education, possessions, job, kid, social network. No family to contribute or support her. Hadn't won the lottery unless you count having given birth to the most beautiful blond son in all of Ukraine, with the happiest outlook on life and already demonstrating high intelligence by his prodigious vocabulary and incessant questioning.

Ben met Kateryna through an attorney he was working with on a major US government project in Kiev approximately ten years before. He required the services of an interpreter and research assistant who was appropriate looking to bring to high-level dinners and business lunches and pose as any one of a number of persons: lawyer, assistant, interpreter, girlfriend, wife, student, or relative. Their professional relationship evolved into the classic handler-asset duo until their personal feelings got in the way and they became the truest of friends. All who knew them marveled at how protective they were of each other.

He had been in many dangerous situations, yet he found it curious that even in the most perilous places he never felt like he was in danger. Even when he was being fired at, Ben never stopped to think, "Hey, I could get hurt very badly here." Yet just a few days before, late at night in a perfectly safe part of the city, he was walking up a steep sidewalk out of a parking garage, and he felt vulnerable. Was this his intuition trying to tell him something?

Ben had certainly felt hunted before. This feeling, he recognized, was instinctive and intuitive. But in him, it didn't instill fear. His ability to feel safe and secure when he shouldn't was unusual, especially if it was an accurate feeling at that particular time. In fact, it could be quite hazardous if he wasn't prepared as his flight reaction was completely missing. The absence of feeling hunted or in danger when a dangerous hunter was just around the corner. Now that was something to be afraid of even though what you were afraid of was yourself or, more accurately, a failing or flaw in yourself. Successfully dealing with a hunter in an effective manner was something he could control. But *not* knowing if he was someone's intended victim, a predator's prey, now that was seriously scary.

He knew that this was a dangerous game. He had been in a number of situations where he was simultaneously hunter and hunted, and often it hadn't ended well for him. While facedown in the mud with a combination of shrapnel and other men's bone fragments embedded in his skin, he thought he had an epiphany regarding his mortality only to find himself six months later standing in an embassy kitchen frozen from PTSD-induced paralysis with the crack of bullets breaking the sound barrier next to his head. Only the comic relief from a bottle of Heinz ketchup shattering behind him and spraying red sauce across his back and neck triggered the survival action of dropping to the floor while a US Marine security guard returned fire from an adjacent room.

Ben knew he was overintellectualizing when he emerged from the shadows of the stairwell and into the gray light of the city. The damp smell of cold concrete blocks and the dismal glow from energy-saving lamps gave way to automobile exhaust mixed with wet asphalt and fashionable women with liberally applied perfume and winter sun reflecting from plate-glass windows.

CHAPTER 14

Kateryna

January, several weeks ago. Kiev

SHE THOUGHT THAT she was probably the only woman in Kiev whose favorite book was *The Art of War* by Sun Tzu. She had committed the five essential elements for achieving victory to memory albeit it modifying them a bit to suit her sex:

1. She who knows when not to fight and runs away lives to fight another day.
2. She who understands how to deal effectively with both superior and lesser forces (exploiting their relative size against them) will always prevail.
3. She will win who is able to instill in her forces the same ideals, goals, and *esprit de corps* as her own beliefs will have an undefeatable army.
4. She will win if she has the patience and preparation to wait to catch her adversary unprepared.
5. She will win if she doesn't have to be distracted or countermanded by an inept boss.

She remembered Sun Tzu's conclusion that "if you know the enemy and know yourself, you need not fear the result of a hundred battles. If you know yourself and not the enemy, for every victory gained, you will also suffer a defeat. If you know neither the enemy nor yourself, you will succumb in every battle."

Ben hadn't mentioned anything more about any surveillance over the past few weeks to Kateryna. If anything, he seemed oblivious to everything these days. She wondered what happens when you know your strengths and weaknesses, know your enemy, but don't know whether it's your originally anticipated enemy out there or a new enemy. She only knew that there was a definite threat nearby, and that threat stood somewhere between her and Ben.

During the days prior to his visit to Kiev, she had used her considerable research skills and access to Interpol and several intelligence agencies' databases to look for correlations. Anything that might indicate what was up that could possibly involve Ben and their former activities. Nothing even remotely relevant was revealed. But then he came around the corner of the hotel's parking structure, his unique and slightly hunched-over posture and loping gate giving him away. Upon seeing that he was alone and safe, an incongruously large smile spread across her relatively small face.

Ben flashed his luminescent white teeth in a return grin, and both immediately forgot their respective fears of the moment. "Where's Vlady?" he asked Kateryna.

"Right behind you."

Two little arms reached around Ben's waist from behind and squeezed, and two legs swung up so that the attached feet were suddenly in his face. Ben grabbed Vlady's ankles and swung him round and round until both man and boy were overcome with dizziness. "We are going to the park now!" Vlady commanded.

Ben now understood his intuition that he was being followed. He just hadn't suspected that it was his little protégé. Ever since he could communicate with the boy, Ben had tried to equip him with the rudimentary skills for surviving in a big city and neutralizing threats by stealth rather than strength. Obviously, Vlady had learned his lessons well. Ben had just been a victim of his own success with his godson. They drove to the park that meandered along the banks of the Dnieper River, not far from Kateryna's apartment. Vlady removed his scooter from the back of his mother's Volkswagen Golf and took off in the direction of the wide asphalt-paved river path. Faint smells of fresh coffee, roasting chestnuts, river waste, and charcoal fires with spits of small chickens competed for attention with the sounds of families arranging their picnic lunches and dogs of indeterminate breed challenging one another with timorous barks and threatening growls. Ben and Kateryna jogged to keep up with Vlady and his scooter, Ben wondering whether it had been such a good idea to buy the damn thing for the boy.

Behind them, a man in a long, dark coat and black watch cap casually strolled, occasionally speaking into a cell phone. Anyone listening to him would not hear anything remarkable. Just soft commands and innocuous comments. He maintained a rather considerable distance from the couple with the young boy on the scooter but always kept them in sight.

Kateryna was telling Ben about a new friend she had made, an Australian doctor who had joined her cousin's medical practice in Kiev. Her name was Megan, and she was treating Kateryna's stepfather for severe vision loss from macular degeneration, a condition that had grown substantially worse over the past year. Kateryna was teasing Ben that Megan was just his type—a triple B: brilliant, brunette, and beautiful—when they heard a shriek.

Swerving his scooter to avoid a collision with a toddler, Vlady had crashed into the low wall that ran along the side of the pathway and been catapulted over the wall into the water. His clothes quickly became heavy, and Vlady was sinking into the deep, dark river and screaming that he couldn't swim. Without hesitation, Ben sprinted forward, jumped into the river, grabbed Vlady's jacket, and pulled him to shore. He boosted the boy over the wall into his mother's arms and then climbed up himself. The water had been very cold, and both boy and man clung to each other, shivering uncontrollably, while bystanders offered coats and picnic blankets to cover them. Vlady was crying and Ben was trying to console him, but he was shivering so hard that his words were barely intelligible. They sat close to someone's propane grill and tried to warm themselves while Kateryna brought the car. People were trying to communicate with Ben, but neither speaking Russian nor Ukrainian, he could only speculate on what they were saying. In any event, he didn't care. He just continued to hold his godson and reassure the boy that everything was okay, that he, Vlady, had actually done such a good unselfish thing, putting himself in danger to avoid hurting the little child. That he, Vlady, was really a hero and had protected the toddler. This had the desired result of distracting Vlady from his fear and shock, and the crying stopped, replaced by a confident calm. Kateryna came, and all three got into the car and drove the short distance to her apartment, where Ben and Vlady jumped into the hot shower and laughed and laughed.

The tall man with the long coat had sat down at a bench about fifty yards from where the excitement had occurred and thought about Ben's virtually instantaneous and automatic reaction to save the boy. This was good. A very good attribute for a man to possess, he believed.

CHAPTER 15

Rachel

Present, Mississippi

RACHEL SAT IN her car waiting for the rain to slacken. The sudden downpour had found her pulling into the only available parking space within one hundred yards of the shopping mall with its vast expanse of asphalt designed to accommodate the minivans, SUVs, and SAVs of Jackson's middle and upper-middle classes on a Saturday afternoon. On her Pandora music channel, Emmylou Harris was lamenting about winning someone's love. This was a concept she hadn't much respect for. Love had always seemed to be in pursuit of her despite her habit of wearing what had recently become an inordinately tight T-shirt that said, "It will always be unrequited."

Rachel wondered how far she would go for love, or friendship, for that matter. What were her individual bounds for friendship and love? She made a mental chart with two columns, one for love and one for friendship.

ACTION	LOVE	FRIENDSHIP
Big lie, with evidence of the untruth, fraud	Yes	Maybe
Steal an inanimate object of substantial value	Yes	No
Steal a person's heart from another person	Yes	Never

Cheat for the benefit of another	Yes	No
Self-efface, embarrass herself, subject herself to public humiliation	Yes	Yes
Kill	Yes	Maybe
Engage in potentially dangerous behavior	Yes	Probably

Rachel realized she was more equivocal when it came to friendship than in love. She was also equivocal when it came to getting wet while wearing nice shoes and clothes. It was still pouring, and she abandoned the idea of making a dash into the mall. This couldn't keep up forever, could it?

She thought about which of these things on her list she had done and why she had done them. The potentially dangerous behavior had generally involved sex, drugs, and very fast cars. She hadn't really done any of her crazy things for anyone's benefit, certainly not out of love or friendship. They were simply done in a series of blind attempts at proclaiming her existence and freedom from the stultifying Southern conservatism of her family. During that one year at Duke, it was no doubt as a result of Ben's being a bad influence. She smiled at the thought of the night she stood naked on the passenger seat of his red Corvette, roaring along the two-lane blacktop between the towering pines of the Duke Forest at fifty miles per hour on a hot spring night in late May. She was drunk on Jim Beam and stoned on some Michoacán weed that a football player had brought back to school from a Mexican holiday. She remembered with a grin the exquisite feeling of the wind in her long hair, tangling it so irrevocably that she resembled a tripped-out Methuselah for days afterward. That was such a great night, at least until the campus police pulled them over.

She remembered the time when as a little girl she was stumped over what to get her mother for her fortieth birthday present. She had been playing dress-up at a friend's house, pulling long gowns from her friend's mother's closet and accessories from drawers in the bedroom. *Damn! What was that girl's name? Linda Fellman or something like that.* A jewelry box had fallen from the dresser top, and its contents spilled on the floor. As the girls gathered everything up, a pair of gold earrings with little diamonds had caught her eye, and while Linda looked under the dresser for other pieces, Rachel had quickly pocketed the earrings. Later that night, she felt so guilty she couldn't sleep.

For several days, the earrings had remained hidden in a small metal box that had originally contained Band-Aids while she experienced a crisis of confidence. How could she, a nine-year-old girl, explain where she got the money to buy such expensive jewelry? Her father would immediately know and ask how she got them. She never lied to him. She was physically, emotionally, and, well, whatever. She couldn't lie to her father. She started to cry.

Later that day, she went over to Linda's house to play and surreptitiously returned them to the jewelry box. Upon returning home, she wrote a story about a little girl who couldn't decide what to get her mother for her birthday and robbed a jewelry store for a huge diamond ring. The little girl's father, a bank robber, asked what she had got for her mother's birthday present, and she showed him the ring. As he was obviously shocked, the girl told him the truth. This created a great moral dilemma for the father because although he was a thief by profession, this was a secret from the mother. She thought he drove a taxi for a living. Then the little girl had a great idea.

They would tell the mother that someone had left it in his taxi by accident, but she went to the airport and flew to Brazil and her father never knew her name. So they were giving it to her mother as a present. This was the inauspicious but nevertheless profound start of Rachel's creative writing career.

Her thoughts wandered to another item on her list—stealing a heart from another. In a sense, that's how she hooked up with Ben. She had heard him playing guitar at an after-party for folk-rock singers Loggins and Messina given at a friend's house following a concert at Duke University. She had seen this guy around campus, driving a sports car with a handsome Labrador retriever sitting on the lap of his blond cheerleader girlfriend in the passenger seat. She had a flash fantasy of being able to erase that girl from the picture and replacing her. She had completely forgotten that brief thought when she had seen him at the party. His girlfriend was not there. She was cheer-leading at an away football game. Rachel was not one to forgo an opportunity. When the cheerleader had returned to campus later the next day, she had been replaced just like in the fantasy. Pandora came to the next song from Emmylou.

I would rock my soul in the bosom of Abraham.
I would hold my life in his saving grace.
I would walk all the way from Boulder to Birmingham
If I thought I could see, I could see your face.

And would she walk 1,350 miles (she once looked it up) to see anyone's face? The rain stopped, and she realized with a shock that she would. For Ben.

CHAPTER 16

Ben

1996, Colorado

As HE HUNG suspended about nine hundred meters above the trail-head, taking a brief respite from the nearly vertical crawl up the face of El Muerto de Miedo, it occurred to him that despite what he had learned from his experience with cancer, he still wasn't a partic-ularly good friend. There were countless examples of his failing to react when someone needed his help or when his offer of assistance was more in line with what he needed or wanted to do rather than what the friend needed from him. Ben was at the top of a pitch, and Jimmy was below, getting ready to ascend.

Ben watched a small eagle riding the updraft about fifty meters off the rock. It was just having fun, enjoying being alive that day and coasting along the invisible rails of a natural amusement for raptors, not hunting, pure play. It called out in that screechy voice shared by all birds of prey and was soon joined by another young bird, per-haps a sibling. One after another, they whooshed past Ben, curiously inspecting what this strange human—tethered to another below who was sipping sweet-smelling coffee from a shiny aluminum bottle—was doing, looking so comfortable in their exclusive avian domain.

Banking violently to the left, the birds abruptly vanished, and Ben's thoughts returned to his failings as a friend.

"Hey! You ready up there?" came the voice of Jimmy Jason, Ben's climbing partner. Jason was the perfect climbing partner for Ben. Almost 2 meters tall but weighing less than 80 kg, Jimmy could virtually slither up a wall like a snake, with an ability to read cryptic sequences on technical rock faces. On particularly long, difficult pitches with distantly spaced hand and footholds, Ben would encourage Jimmy to lead. Jimmy relished the dangerously exposed sections of rock, elegantly moving upward until he reached an anchor, then tie off and bring Ben up with steady calm.

"Yeah, sorry. I was just watching those eagles," Ben apologized.

"What eagles? Nothing has been flying around here for the past couple of hours except us."

This had happened to Ben before when he was rock climbing. He saw eagles. Jimmy never saw them, nor did any of his other climbing partners. He reached up as high as he could and clipped into the next eyebolt, jammed his right fist into a crack, leaned back, and stepped up to a tiny ledge in the cliff with the toe of his climbing shoes. He slid the heel of his hand up another 20 cm of the crack and then, with his free hand, found another ridge the size and shape of a clothes hanger that allowed him to wrap the fingers around up to his second knuckles. Shifting his weight to his foot, he brought his other knee up to his chest, found a nubbin of rock and confidently stepped up. In this manner—left hand, right foot, right hand, left foot—he moved steadily up to each successive eyebolt over a 40-meter pitch, clipping in and proceeding to the next until he felt a tug on the rope.

Ben finished the pitch, pulled up to a small ledge, set up his anchor, and clipped in his harness with a sling and a locking carabiner. After settling in against the rock wall as comfortably as possible, he shouted down, "Belay on, come on up," he called to Jimmy, receiving the reply, "Climbing!"

The pink and green 10.5-mm rope passed swiftly through his belay device until Jimmy's shiny orange helmet came into view. He could smell Jimmy's sweat in the clear, otherwise scentless air as he caught his breath at their perch at nearly 4,000 meters. Jimmy rested his head against the light gray granite of El Muerto, pressing his cheek into the cool rock. There was no sound, save for their breathing. Not even a hint of wind. They both hung limply from their webbed nylon harnesses.

Ben and Jimmy loved climbing together. It was their chance to get away from all irrelevant conversation. It was as if in the simple fact of entrusting their lives to each other and the relatively low-tech equipment they used, the world was distilled into the sounds of movement and words were conserved, their only discourse related to their physical actions. It was the experience that was shared. The experience was so sublime, so brutally real, their concentration on leverage with the risk of falling weighed in a fraction of a second before each reach and step, that chatting would be so superfluous as to be annoying.

The communication of shared action. This was both highly evolved as well as intrinsically basic. Ben wondered if the fact that their relationship was primarily limited to a common love of a recreational activity rendered the status of their friendship superficial. But how could that be? They had technically saved each other's lives innumerable times. They had known each other since childhood. Had experienced the deaths of friends and family and endured serious illness suffered by each other. Didn't that put things on a higher plane?

Again, his concentration drifted. He thought back to a lesson in communication he had learned from a short-lived love. For reasons about which he still wasn't clear, he had broken up with an amazing girl and done it in an abominable way. She had her facts wrong; he wasn't seeing someone else that he was leaving her for, and she would never understand the conflicts he was facing in his life at that particular moment in time, but nevertheless, she had scored a direct hit to his heart when she sent him a note that read,

> *I need you to put your phone away and give me the courtesy of time and the respect that I deserve.*
> *I need you to listen without interruptions to my confusion and my questions.*
> *I need you to hear my hurt and to see my pain.*

I need you to help me overcome the distress you have caused me and that I wholeheartedly allowed you to cause.

I am telling you this so that maybe you will never be so selfish in the future. People are not toys to be played with!

I hate what you have done to me. I hate that I let you get this close.

I hate who you are or maybe who you have become. I cannot decide!

I hate myself for trusting you; you are someone who truly deserves no trust from anyone.

You are right. You need to work on you.

Please take responsibility for your behavior in what I am sure will be the first time in your life.

I am a fool and hate feeling stupid; I allowed you to make me feel stupid.

I feel like you left me that night Barbara came over to be with her despite your telling me this is not true.

I feel like you wanted to maximize my hurt to make it easier for you to walk out.

I cannot begin to even tackle the lies of what you said we had and where you wanted our relationship to go.

It's too painful!

Your ego is much bigger than it deserves to be.

I used to love your confidence and ego; today I realize it covers your many insecurities.

I know that I am still very much in love with you, and that makes me want to vomit. In fact, I will vomit you out of my mind and out of my life because you make me sick!

The rawness and truth of those words had stung. More than stung. Stinging is a temporary discomfort. He felt tattooed with shame. It was like everything that he'd learned about friendship had been forgotten, like the cancer experience had never occurred, and he had not grown, but rather diminished as a person somehow. Looking up, he noticed that one of the eagles had departed. He wondered if he would ever change as he watched the remaining eagle above him, riding the updrafts, gliding down, and swooping up like a surfer on an endless curl.

CHAPTER 17

Rachel

Present, Mississippi

RACHEL WAS BREATHING heavily from sprinting down the tree-lined lane that led to her property. She reached the mailbox and spun around and jogged back to the rickety wood and wire bridge that spanned Milton Creek. Carefully crossing the ancient structure, she picked up her pace beneath the ancient oaks and continued along the narrow, winding county road that led to town. A blaring horn and screeching tires startled her out of her Zen-like focus. She had unwittingly drifted off the shoulder of the road and was running several feet onto the pavement where the shadows made it difficult for a motorist to see her. The driver shouted some unintelligible obscenity at her and flipped her the bird as he disappeared around the next bend. Sufficiently startled back into reality, she once again turned and, this time, ran all the way to her front door. Without taking the time to shower and change, she headed straight for her laptop to put the beginnings of her plan into action.

It was actually quite easy for Rachel to find Ben's coordinates. As a writer, he was registered with several writers' associations including the Writers Guild of America, East. He had a well-developed Facebook page for his readers, as well as a LinkedIn profile. Although not specifically providing any address, it was clear that he currently lived in Istanbul. She wondered what had taken him so far away from the States. Without any feelings of guilt whatsoever, she started digitally stalking Ben, learning about his friends and rereading his books, his interviews, and the short essays he occasionally published in a wide range of magazines and newspapers. She paid particular attention to his Facebook timeline, noting the dates and places he had visited and trying to tie them to which of his friends he had no doubt seen.

Rachel was sitting in her small office just to the right of the foyer of her large antebellum home, illuminated by the soft early-morning light coming through the translucent threadbare curtains. She furiously attacked the keyboard, searching for anything and anyone tied to Ben Jacobson.

Several names continuously appeared: Johan Niedermann, Kateryna and Vladyslav Buglakova, Bamkiz Safavi, Howman "the Blitz" Steinblitz, Donald Malgerry, Ipek Elmayiyen, Lale and Kaan Güzeli, and Jimmy K. Jason. She was able to define the parameters of some of their relationships with Ben by the posted photographs: Johan with sportfishing, Donald with flying and sailing, Jimmy with mountaineering. Kaan, Lale's son, it seemed was a good friend and ski buddy for Ben and Donald. She couldn't fathom his friendship with Ipek. She seemed to come from a different world and certainly was young enough to be his child. Bamkiz had disappeared from her personal radar screen since graduation from Duke. What role, if any, did this descendant of Persian royalty now play in Ben's life? Based on the Facebook timeline, they saw each other infrequently and always in remote places where there was local political and social unrest, but great food and beautiful women aplenty. Rather strange places to go out for dinner or cruising for booty, or so it seemed to a girl from Colliersville, Mississippi.

It wasn't like she was looking for a needle in a haystack in poring over all of Ben's Facebook friends. Rather, it was an effort at using social media as a means of making an approach to Ben without embarrassing herself. She had already left a cryptic recommendation for one of his books on Amazon. She had started reading a few of the others, only to put them down because they were too shallow and middlebrow for her tastes. She noticed that he had recently posted some links and comments regarding the current struggle between two factions in Turkish politics. That wasn't like the Ben she knew from their university days, when the most political he got was to run an unsuccessful campaign for president of the student government. She remembered that his issue was to save the Duke Forest from development for faculty housing while all the other candidates were clamoring for more budget control of the student council. He used to mock them for that. The council's total annual budget was less than he would make in a single night with one of the rock concerts he produced. Not surprisingly, he lost. Student politics was even more arcane and unpredictable than national politics, often focusing on the wrong issues entirely.

The more she dug, the more the pieces started to fall into place. Ben had, thus far, led an interesting life. A fair degree of success in the private sector and then, in his forties, a distinguished career in the foreign service. Interesting also because usually it was the other way around. People usually began in government service and then reaped the rewards of this experience in private life. Ben had gone forward by going backward in his typically unique manner. He brought his private-sector experience to the government, working as an official on the front lines of diplomacy, not as some inexperienced but socially connected political appointee. And now he was living in Istanbul, of all places. Funny that she had recently been thinking of taking a trip there.

Rachel next delved into the backgrounds of some of his close friends. Of all of them, Donald Malgerry proved the most fascinating to her. He had made his enormous wealth solving problems he encountered in his medical practice by engaging the country's top young biomedical engineers to invent devices that did what human hands could not. Renowned as one of the foremost reconstructive surgeons in the country, Donald detested sending a patient away with less than perfect surgical results. Not surprisingly, his first creations were employed in his own procedures: implants of optic nerves and facial muscles, jaw hinges, microcapillary filters, and tiny blood pumps. These he installed in the face and other delicate parts of the body to nourish transplanted tissue and muscle with fresh blood and targeted antirejection drugs. They were designed to be removed after the patient fully recovered and the danger of rejection or necropathy had passed. Donald's biggest contribution, both to medical science as well as to his net worth, was inventing a means of transplanting major organs from a donor to a recipient of different blood types without fear of rejection. The drugs he patented also enabled large-scale blood transfusions without regard to blood groups, a crucial life-saving factor during global disasters. This complex system was patented and sold by Donald to a major pharma company for the astronomical sum of $13,800,000,000.

Rachel learned that with this money, Donald had endowed several humanitarian organizations, including a worldwide flight-for-life fleet of planes, helicopters, and pilots; a series of medical colleges in sub-Saharan Africa; and a traveling museum of surrealist art. He was now retired, if you could call a peripatetic existence flying among his medical schools and researching venues for his art museum, buying and selling aircraft, and angel investing in biomedical start-ups *retirement*.

Lale was all over the web. Innumerable photographs both at society events and professional symposiums, impeccably dressed according to the occasion. Sometimes Lale was accompanied by her son, Kaan, other times with interesting-looking men, but often with other beautiful women who looked like they spent their lives shopping in Bergdorf Goodman, Harvey Nichols, Neiman Marcus, or wherever it was that glamorous Turkish women buy their wardrobes. Author of a dozen books on international business law and countless legal articles in scholarly journals and a part-time professor at the Koç University College of Law in Istanbul, Lale seemed to have endless energy and a bottomless pocketbook. Rachel knew that she was no match for this woman.

Rachel found a fair amount of press on the man known colloquially as the Blitz. A middle linebacker at the University of Maryland in his younger days, Howman now ran a successful advertising agency. She could see that he was fiercely loyal to his friends and unrelenting to those who had wronged him. From a recent photo she found on Google Images, the Blitz strangely resembled a gray-haired version of Lenny Kravitz. Strange because she remembered that Ben had once mentioned seeing a young Black singer/guitarist who went by the name Romeo Blue in a small New York club in the West Village. He had an infectious smile, tough, street-smart attitude, steely blue eyes, and an amazing voice. Ben had correctly predicted that this performer would eventually become a huge star. It was funny how Ben always noticed things like that in people. Although not a super-star like Lenny Kravitz, the Blitz was obviously someone you could always depend on, she learned from the many testimonials and comments written on his LinkedIn and Facebook pages.

Rachel rose from her desk and climbed the stairs to the bedroom she had occupied on and off for over fifty years. She stripped off her sweaty sports bra, socks, and shorts and appraised herself critically in the mirror. She rarely missed an opportunity to check herself out in this manner. She thought that she looked virtually the same as she did when she was in her thirties. She wrapped her hair in a towel, changed her mind, threw the towel on the floor, turned on the faucet, climbed over the tub rail, and stood under the cool spray of water from the gracefully curved showerhead.

Rachel had a prodigious collection of shampoo and conditioner. She chose a mandarin orange-scented shampoo and a wild berry conditioner. Her hair was, for want of a better word, lustrous. She could have been a model for one of the big hair-care brands with TV ads of women flinging their tresses about in wild abandon. She liberally applied the gel-like shampoo and worked it into her scalp, bending backward into a yoga pose and letting the water run across her chest and stomach like a warm caress. Then the conditioner, Rachel enjoying the berry scent like a child with a strawberry ice-cream cone. She lost herself in the sensuality of scent and the strong hot water cascading from the oversized showerhead she had recently purchased from a Swedish fixture company online.

Her ears were filled with shampoo, and the powerful cascade of water drowned out the ringing of her cell phone. Although she subscribed to a caller ID service, the screen merely indicated Wireless Caller. Whoever had dialed Rachel subscribed to an app that defeated the caller ID. Not that it mattered. Rachel was too busy with herself to have answered the phone anyway.

CHAPTER 18

Ben

Present, Istanbul

BEN ROSE AND paced the room. He had been lost in meditation over his sister and how he had met and briefly dated a girl named Sara who appeared as her doppelganger. Maybe it was the anxiety that something bad would happen to Sara, leaving him alone again, that caused him to run away from her so abruptly. Intellectually he knew that there was a vast difference between Sara and his sister, Laura. Age, the nature of the relationship, and his own maturation all defined their separate places in his life. He walked over to the credenza that ran along the wall at a right angle to his desk and tenderly lifted the silver-framed photograph of Laura and him at the beach standing with an enormous German shepherd. The dog's name was Kaiser. He was a majestic animal, intelligent and protective of the twins and remarkably adept at keeping them from fighting during their occasional sibling battles.

Kaiser had died barely two months after Laura had succumbed to her cancer, and his parents had separated and left their home shortly thereafter. His mother first, and then early one morning a week later, his father went to work and never returned, leaving the boys alone with their grandparents. Here he was, so many years later, still haunted by the memories of those experiences. No chance for reversal or redemption. Not with his sister, his parents, or Sara. Ben had become a victim of himself and his dread of abandonment and the sorrow of losing someone he loved. Deep inside, he knew that this was keeping him from sustaining any one-on-one relationship with a woman, much less having a family of his own.

He gingerly returned the photograph of him and Laura to its place within the small, informal shrine he had assembled in her honor. He had work to do on the biography of Lale's family. Ben reluctantly returned to his desk and stared at the computer screen, trying to remember where he had left off.

He leaned back pensively in his cracked leather desk chair. The wheeled tripod base was unstable at best, probably even dangerous, inviting an embarrassing crash to the floor in front of someone, sometime. But that was Ben, always living on the edge of disaster. He had some illogical belief that its very instability was like a Pilates exercise in developing core balance and abdominal strength. However, he positioned himself in it, he was forced to constrict his muscles to keep it vertically and horizontally aligned so that his weight remained evenly distributed. Two of the legs already had visible cracks that looked like any excess pressure on them would cause them to break. Despite the wobbly legs, it was obvious that the now-cracked upholstery had once been supple and expensive Italian leather. The chair originally belonged to a famous Turkish lawyer who, despite his rigid rule against fraternization with junior associates, broke his own taboo and had an affair with a twenty-three-year-old working in the firm. This led to the temporary banishment of the associate to an office outside of Turkey, then an unplanned pregnancy, and then an absurdly expensive divorce, all of which activities distracted him from his responsibilities as managing partner of the firm and his being ridiculed in the Istanbul legal community. Shortly after the embarrassing and highly publicized divorce, his law firm began to disintegrate, the clients following their attorneys to their new firms. The once-powerful lawyer retired to his yacht in the south, now spending his days as a lonely, bitter man afloat on a sea of regret. Ben loved the fact that he had bought the chair of this former heavyweight hypocrite for a mere twenty dollars.

Ben allowed his eyes to close for a moment, his mind a slide-show of his own loves won and lost. He knew that he shouldn't be so harsh on himself. He also acknowledged that the attorney in whose chair he now sat was luxuriating on an eighty-two-foot yacht some-where in the Aegean while he, Ben, sat with writer's block in his small office.

So he forgot about that final disastrous trip to the Bahamas with Sara and thought about all the good things he had going for him in Istanbul. A large mug of now cooling *elma chai* (apple tea) rested precariously on his thigh. Brewed with a heavy dose of honey and a couple of heaping tablespoons of Splenda, it was sweet enough to make most people gag. But that's the way he liked it. That was how he wanted life to be—extraordinarily sweetened with both the natural and artificial.

He stood up and opened the door to the small balcony, gazing toward the German consulate across the street. They let him park his car in one of their diplomatic spaces unless a major function required its use for a visitor. He appreciated this favor because he loved that car, a 1997 Porsche Turbo, the last of the air-cooled Carreras. He figured they tolerated him and his vehicle because it was a classic German car. There were even guards who kept an eye on it as long as it was there, but he didn't recognize the tall man standing near the Porsche. He wasn't dressed like the other guards. He wore a cap and elegant wool coat that had been in fashion twenty years ago. Then Ben watched as one of the regular guards came out of his lit-tle booth and addressed the man. After a few minutes of chitchat, the man walked away. A car enthusiast, probably, Ben thought. A tourist. Maybe one of those Russians that had been hanging round lately. Certainly, all the locals had become accustomed to the per-fectly maintained dark blue vintage Porsche. He watched the man walk down the street to the next block and cross the street just after a metro bus passed, narrowly avoiding being run over by a swerving taxi blaring its horn in protest. The man then made his way back up Inönü Caddesi until he was by the door to the Chinese restaurant directly below Ben's office.

The man stood there for at least fifteen minutes, occasionally talking on his cell phone and smoking a cigarette, but never looking up in Ben's direction. If their roles and positions had been reversed, Ben thought he would definitely have felt the fellow's eyes on him. The window was partly open, and Ben could smell the distinctive odor of Chinese food mixed with the cigarette and the diesel fumes of the buses that continuously passed through the Gümüşsuyu neighborhood. He heard with the familiarity of a local denizen the building crescendo of afternoon rush-hour traffic. And he thought that this man somehow looked out of place, even under the most benign circumstances—vaguely European, but not a typical Italian, French, or German. Ben could discern from his position overhead that he wasn't speaking English. Something that sounded Slavic. He decided that it was time to leave his office, anyway, and perhaps he would chat up the fellow before crossing to his car.

Dumping his laptop in the old worn Prada briefcase (it was a fortieth birthday gift from his father in a rare moment of acknowledging paternity), he grabbed his jacket and glided down the curving staircase. Again, he was assaulted by the smells of kung pao chicken, oyster sauce, and fried scallions. He pushed the button to release the automatic lock and stepped outside toward the curb. He didn't see the man with the cap and coat, so after waiting for a break in the traffic, he darted across Inönü Street and unlocked his car while casually waving at the guard. But the man in the cap and coat saw Ben. He had simply stepped into the Chinese restaurant, waiting in the shadow of the door.

Ben just sat in his car, absentmindedly listening to the melodic strains of the sunset Maghreb call to prayer. The Arabic words rang out from no fewer than five mosques within walking distance from where he now sat, performed with a wide variety of talent by their respective muezzins. Ben loved the way that they were all a second or two out of sync with one another. It provided an asymmetrical effect that reminded him of how an echo bounced around the walls of Maple Canyon in Utah, one of the best places for bouldering and rock climbing that he and Jimmy had ever found. The irony of sitting in a vintage Porsche, on a street in Istanbul with turn-of-the-century

European architecture, thinking about a 5.12 climb in a canyon in Utah, while listening to a melodic cacophony of Arabic words in a Turkish city wasn't lost on him.

Allahu Akbar (God is great), *Allahu Akbar, Allahu Akbar, Allahu Akbar.*

Ashhadu an la ilaha illa Allah (I bear witness that there is no god except the One God), *Ashhadu an la ilaha illa Allah.*

Ashadu anna Muhammadan Rasool Allah (I bear witness that Muhammad is the messenger of God), *Ashadu anna Muhammadan Rasool Allah*

Hayya 'ala-s-Salah (Hurry to the prayer/Rise up for prayer), *Hayya 'ala-s-Salah.*

Hayya 'ala-l-Falah (Hurry to success/Rise up for salvation).

Ben thought about the fact that most of the citizens of Istanbul hadn't a clue what these Arabic words meant, and he wondered why the call wasn't performed in Turkish. He thought that it was a brilliant move of the Catholic church in the mid-sixties to forgo the Latin Mass in favor of Mass in the local language. Why not the same for the *ezan*? He turned the key, the old air-cooled, turbo-charged engine roared to life, and he shot away from the curb, squeezing between two taxis, the smell of burning oil in his nostrils.

The man in the coat and hat remained in the doorway, talking quietly on his cell phone.

CHAPTER 19

Rachel

Present, Mississippi

RACHEL WENT ONLINE the next morning, and after visiting the *Huffington Post* site and looking for her favorite columnist Samantha Revelstoke's latest piece on feminism, she clicked over to the *Daily Beast* and saw the following from James Brower:

> In the wake of revelations the NSA spied on foreign officials, Vicky Harley, the State Department's top official for Europe, has been caught on tape planning a deal to end the Washington-Ukraine-Trump-Biden crisis and she had a message for her European counterparts: "Fuck the EU." Adding insult to her self-inflicted career-ending injury, she added, "And fuck the corrupt Dems and those sexist Republican bastards."

A YouTube video uploaded by an anonymous user has publicly revealed a private conversation between Vicky Harley, Assistant Secretary of State for European Affairs, and Peter Welch, a staunch Republican and US Ambassador to Ukraine. In the tape, the two officials discuss a plan to broker a deal between the Ukrainian government and certain unnamed officials of a local energy firm to declare Hunter Biden *persona non grata* in exchange for another large tranche of foreign aid from the US which they probably would have received anyway.

The origin of the recording is unclear. It was uploaded by a user named Maidan Puppet, a reference to the Maidan Square in Kiev where protesters had fought the government and the Russian accusation that the protesters were puppets of the United States and the West. The video was first reported in the *Kyiv Post*.

Harley told Welch she had discussed the plan with UN Undersecretary for Political Affairs Eugene Pressman, a former senior US State Department official, and that he would appoint a UN representative to help move it forward. Former Vice President, now Democratic presidential candidate, Joe Biden would also be brought into the plan at the right time, according to Harley.

"That would be great to help glue this thing and to have the UN help glue it," she said. "And you know, fuck the EU and fuck the corrupt Dems and those sexist Republican bastards."

"I think we're in play," Welch tells Harley about a plan to join the corrupt energy company and the Bidens into one profoundly guilty unit, apparently being attempted by the White House behind the scenes.

"It's just not going to work," she said.

"Maybe, maybe not. We've got to do something to make this thing stick together because if it does start to gain altitude, the Russians will try to do something behind the scenes to claim that this was all a corrupt American kabuki dance," responded Welch.

If the Russians did want to turn the idea to their advantage, taping and leaking Harley's private conversation would be a great way to do it, experts said. Roby Penfield, the former White House senior director for Russia, defended Harley, saying that she was just recognizing that the EU was becoming an obstacle for dealmaking in Ukraine. He diplomatically forgot to make mention of her comments on the American political parties involved.

From her web searches, Rachel had seen that Ben was often standing alongside Penfield and others from the bureau that was concerned with Russia and its neighbors. She had also found photographs of Ben and Penfield fishing together, presumably off the coast of south Florida. Numerous articles and essays had been written by someone who sounded suspiciously like Ben although his name was never associated with the writings. Furthermore, the purported authors of those articles, harshly critical of Russia and its activities in Crimea and along the eastern border of Ukraine, didn't seem to actually exist. At least, she had been unable to find any other articles or references to them on the web.

Rachel had heard through the grapevine that Ben has several close friends in Ukraine and often spent time in Kiev with a woman and her young son. She had no idea what he was doing there, if it was government-related or merely social. She became anxious while she thought of Ben's predilection for places in turmoil: his years in Tajikistan during their civil war, Eritrea during the last years of its long war with Ethiopia, Bosnia-Herzegovina at the close of its war with neighbors Serbia and Croatia, Peshawar and the Northwest Territories of Pakistan immediately prior to the invasion of Afghanistan by US troops, and others which she probably didn't even know about. Over the past few days, she had done a lot of research on Ben and managed to get the e-mail addresses and telephone numbers of many of his closest friends, even connecting with some of them on Facebook.

She commenced a casual campaign of contact with Ipek, Jimmy, Kaan, Johan, and Bamkiz. She tried calling Kateryna, with no success. Her efforts occupied the better part of twenty-four hours due to the extreme difference in time zones between Mississippi, Denver, Istanbul, Accra, Kiev, and Sydney, the last known address of Bamkiz. But her first call was to Donald. She had learned that he had a fleet of planes used for medical evacuations, including a jet that could easily handle a transoceanic flight.

"Is this Donald?" she inquired timidly when his line was answered by a man with a slightly elongated New York accent. The man answered affirmatively.

Without hesitating for even a fraction of a second since it had taken two shots of Southern Comfort followed with a lemonade chaser, Rachel launched into her story about surprising Ben. Donald never interrupted. It wasn't even possible. He was mesmerized by the tone and sweetness of Rachel's Deep South accent. He did, however, Google her as they were chatting and looked at photos of her from the images tab. Suitably impressed with both her academic credentials as well as her straightforward beauty, he listened carefully. When she finished with a request that he fly with her and some of Ben's friends to Istanbul or wherever it led them, he put her on hold, called his PA, had him assign all his surgeries to his partner, put everything requiring his presence in regard to his biomedical R & D company in suspension for two weeks, and sent a text message to his long-distance copilot to put him on notice that they would be leaving on the Gulfstream in the morning for a ten-hour flight.

Returning to Rachel, he said, "I don't know what antebellum fantasy you crawled out from, but I'm intrigued. I'm also always ready to help Ben. His father virtually raised me from a young boy after my father died, and I'm forever in his debt. I was also getting a little bored, to tell you the truth, and I think that ten hours with a beautiful model of Southern gentility is just what I need. And I'll bring along one parachute in case either of us becomes so miserable we want to bail out."

"Oh, I doubt that would ever happen," she said with confidence. She too had done her research on Donald. It hadn't failed to impress her that he had founded a successful biomedical firm that developed and patented prosthetic jaws; eyes with lenses that interfaced with the optic nerve, artificial cheek and eyebrow muscles that allowed traumatically injured patients to wink, smile, and frown; and breast replacements that had become the rage of every woman that had undergone a radical mastectomy in LA or New York. Although he always enjoyed challenging surgeries the most of all his professional activities, over 90 percent of his substantial income was derived from his biomed business. Donald had also pioneered the concept of time-sharing and later fractional ownership of aircraft. In addition to their use for medical evacuations, every one of his seven planes was fully subscribed with corporate as well as individual users, most of them friends or former patients. Both Rachel's mother and aunt had died of breast cancer, and she believed that she carried the gene as well. Maybe someday, she would screw up the courage to have genetic testing and, if the marker was found, follow the example of Angelina Jolie and, depending on her personal impressions of Donald, perhaps let him do the work.

Meanwhile, she had sworn everyone to secrecy about the reunion, a promise she would ultimately regret.

CHAPTER 20

Ben

Present, Istanbul

THE TELEPHONE AWOKE Ben from such a realistic and action-packed dream that it seemed to be incorporated within the unconsciously generated scenario. Five times it rang before Ben was able to discern the difference between dream and reality. "Yes?" he inquired groggily, rolling over and propping himself up on one elbow.

"Wake up, Ben. It's me," Kateryna said in a tight voice. "I think we've got a problem."

"What? Is Vlady okay?"

"I heard a noise, like a squeak, and it woke me up. I went into Vlady's room to check on him. The big window was open and he was sitting upright, very stiff. His eyes were wide-open in big fear. He said a huge man who smelled bad had woken him up and said that his friend Ben was in serious trouble if he didn't come to Kiev immediately. I called the police, but they haven't arrived yet. It's been over an hour. I'm sorry to have woken you, but I'm shaking."

Ben could hear it in her quavering voice.

By now Ben was fully awake. "Okay, Kateryna. Can the police do anything, you think?"

"I'm not anyone influential here. I'm not rich. I can't pay them extra money to prioritize an investigation or a search. They will just take a report and tell me to go back to bed." She was getting shrill with fear and frustration.

"Okay, okay. I'll be there on the morning flight, and we'll figure out what this is all about. Get as much rest as you can. I know that you won't sleep, but you won't be any help if you are physically exhausted too. Wait for the cops and get their names for me. Call your IT guy at the firm to put a tap on your phone and a bot or a worm or whatever they call it in your e-mail address in case anyone tries to call you or e-mail you. Don't leave the house. They may be watching you. Hell, they may even be listening to us as we speak. I don't want to say anything more on the phone."

Ben switched on the light, went downstairs, and started bringing up his clothes and his black Rimowa carry-on. Then he made two calls to old friends in the intelligence community with experience in the CIS countries. He knew that the chances of Kateryna having had any dealings with someone with a personal agenda against him or her were slim to none. Her rather short-lived boyfriends had all been meek, intellectual lawyers more concerned over the elegance of their suits than caring for a single mom. However, a lot of unpleasant characters knew of their close friendship and still bore more than what could be called a grudge against him. He had certainly left a trail of destruction in several of the former Soviet satellites, including Tajikistan and Kyrgyzstan. Corrupt remnants of the Soviet puppet governments had been neutralized and their assets seized by new government officials.

Together, Kateryna and Ben had also identified, located, and even managed to help disassemble a violent gang of former convicts who were acting as the unofficial henchmen of Viktor Fedorovych Yanukovych, the Ukrainian president who had been deposed years ago. That had led a joint task force of agents from the governments of Ukraine and the US to another group of Moscow-supported separatists wreaking havoc in the eastern part of the country. Although many of these men had been arrested or killed by Ukrainian intelligence operatives and military forces, no doubt some had escaped across the border to Russia. There was no shortage of men who would gladly harm a child as retribution for something Ben had done to them in the past, and it was no secret that Ben was the loving godfather of Vlady. Terrorists needed little excuse to act in circumstances that promoted their interests, in other words to identify the soft target and strike where they had a weakness. Nothing had actually happened to harm the boy. But the message had been delivered clearly and concisely to great effect. Kateryna and Vlady were two of the five people Ben deeply cared about.

From his former colleagues, he got two lists of names. One list was very short. It contained names of four trusted men and women who would provide round-the-clock protection for Kateryna and Vlady. The second was longer. It contained a list of places he could go to obtain information for cash, weapons he couldn't carry on a plane, aircraft and pilots for hire without having to file an accurate flight plan, an SUV under a false name, and people with safe houses in Tajikistan, Russia, Georgia, Kazakhstan, Uzbekistan, and Belarus. These were all countries where men lived who would joyfully rain on Ben's parade, men who would, without hesitation, put a woman's or a child's life at risk for an ulterior motive like evening out an old score with someone like Ben. He would give copies of both lists to Lale.

Suddenly, all thoughts of previous girlfriends and amorous adventures evaporated from Ben's mind. Unfortunately, they were replaced by an overwhelming sense of guilt and apprehension. In particular, it was the guilt that started to eat into him. He noticed this as he was filling the little black leather bag in which he kept his shaving supplies, medications, and other essential personal things. He couldn't decide whether to bring Tylenol or Apranax. He kept thinking about how many extra razor blades he might need. Which toothbrush? Which hairbrush? Stupid things he shouldn't have had to think about. Innocuous decisions that became crucial to…what? This was why he always kept a go bag in his office at State. So not to have to worry about such decisions. On one level of his consciousness, he knew what was happening to him while at the more basic level of converting thought to action, he was becoming helpless. He needed a cold shower to clear his mind and effectively return to the task at hand.

After his brain had been shocked back to reality, within minutes, the little bag was packed. He would carry his Dopp kit, iPad, laptop, external modem, and chargers in a small leather Tumi backpack and appear like a typically casual but affluent American tourist.

Ben knew that the first flight out of Ataturk airport to Kiev Boryspil Airport was TK 8816 departing at 5:55 a.m. That gave him over two and a half hours to make the flight. No traffic at this early hour. His Miles & Smiles platinum card gave him business-class service at economy prices. He arrived at Ataturk at 4:30 a.m. and still had time for a very quick breakfast at one of the little kiosks serving early-morning travelers.

CHAPTER 21

Rachel

Present, Mississippi

IT WAS 11:00 p.m. in Colliersville and 3:00 p.m. in Sydney. She caught Bamkiz on Skype just as he was about to leave his office for a massage. His back had been acting up recently and he didn't hesitate to tell Rachel about it in exhaustive detail. The fact that Bamkiz had averaged an extra pound per year since he had graduated from Duke apparently had significantly contributed to his back problem.

"I'm so sorry to hear that, Bammy, but maybe if you had taken a little better care of yourself, perhaps fed your mind instead of your stomach these past oh so many years, you could be spending your money on theater tickets instead of with chiropractors and masseuses. So with all due respect and consideration for your personal, vertebral issues, can I cut to the chase here, darlin'?"

"That's one of the things I always loved about you, Rachel," Bamkiz said, "your sweet Southern politeness, adorned with a scorpion's sting to the most sensitive part of my fragile ego. That and your legs. I assume that you've still got those as well."

"My legs are fine, as is my acerbic wit and *shugah*-coated vitriol, if that's how you prefer to categorize it, no doubt born of the parsimony that results from a meager salary. Meanwhile," she continued before he had a chance to riposte, "I wanted to organize a

119

reunion of sorts. For Ben. Kinda like a *destination reunion* of sorts. In Istanbul. That's where I tracked him down. With you, me, Jimmy, the Blitz, and some of his other friends we don't really know. A guy from Ghana, a woman from Kiev—"

"A woman from Kiev? Why only one?"

"Stifle your imagination, Bamkiz. You may have been the reputed descendant of Alexander the Great once upon a time as far as freshman girls were concerned, but now you're just an overweight refugee from a dead ayatollah, with a back problem and probably a bad prostate from a dearth of sex."

"Which is precisely why I need several women from Kiev."

Rachel smiled broadly. She couldn't fail to appreciate the innumerable superficial differences between Bamkiz and her—she tall, quick, and lithe and he bulky but powerful, slow, and hairy. She was the real deal, born, bred, educated, and working in the South. He was always a fish out of water, a Persian of royal blood who could trace his ancestry back for a thousand years who had to flee his homeland as a child when his father was assassinated, only to return for a few years and then have to leave again when his relative Shah Reza Pahlavi was removed from office in a 1979 revolution. Rachel had her aristocratic Southern drawl, Bamkiz his exclusive private school-acquired Oxfordian English accent. Her undernourished libido was in a fight to the death with an irrepressible romantic streak. His corpulent body was infused with testosterone, yet in a state of perpetual sexual frustration. Not to mention that they had lived for the past twenty-five years more than halfway around the world from each other. Yet they managed to pick up where they had left off so many years ago. Essentially, they were cut from the same cloth, hence their shared affection for Ben.

"What made you think of Ben after all these years?"

She explained about her resolve to do something to change her life, which basically hadn't changed all that much since they last saw each other. She touched on the disastrous relationship with her last boyfriend, Ross. "You threatened to shoot him with your grandfather's gun?" Bamkiz exclaimed incredulously.

"And his ego along with it, I'm afraid."

"So you found a box of old photographs and now you want to arrange a cheery reunion of Dukies and an introduction of assorted others? And what do you hope to accomplish with this folly? Do you think Ben will forgive you for cheating on him with that scrawny, unwashed hippie? Really, old girl. Why would—"

Rachel interrupted his negativity, "Because it will be fun and completely different, and no one gives a damn about what absurd mistakes we made so long ago. That's why. I've been checking on Ben. He has his family, friends, and a damn interesting life compared to me. His world has expanded way beyond the confines of Durham, as has yours, I might add. You have changed lives and lifestyles many times. From a life of privilege in Iran and England to that of a bohemian student space oddity at a university in a small city in North Carolina to an evolving political and socioeconomic firestorm in Tehran and now a quiet existence living under the radar in Sydney."

"Go on. Proceed with the monologue. I do love to hear the dulcet, lilting tones of your antebellum voice."

"I'm sure that everyone has changed, Bamkiz—except me, that is. And I do so want to change. And I want Ben to know, as ridiculous as this may sound, that I have regretted that night every waking hour for the past forty-three years."

"Yes, that sounds suitably absurd. Why would he care?"

"He probably won't. And that's my point exactly. New beginnings for old friends. Get it? But please don't breathe a word of it to Ben. Okay?"

"Okay, Rachel, my dear. You put it together and send me the details. I wouldn't miss it for the world. I'm certain that Ben will be there and suitably surprised. I spoke to him just a few days ago, and he was complaining that he was working on something that would keep him in his office for the foreseeable future. Anyway, I haven't been to Istanbul since, uh…Who was that chap? Bülent Ecevit was calling the shots. I always admired his mustache."

Next, she called Jimmy. The Fred Astaire of big wall rock climbing. The master of 5.15 on the YDS grading system. Not that Rachel had any idea what that meant. She just knew that he was always hanging upside down from something, somewhere. She had connected with him on Skype earlier that week. She found him sitting on the back porch of his cabin in the Sangre de Cristo range in Southwestern Colorado. "Jimmy, meet Ben and me in Istanbul. On Wednesday. We will surprise him."

"You and Ben? What am I missing here? It's kinda been a long time for you guys, ya know."

"That's exactly the point. Better late than never. And all that clichéd stuff. Spontaneity. Isn't that what you always said you lived by?"

"Yeah, but not when it comes to, what, like a ten-hour plane flight?" Jimmy hated long flights with the claustrophobic conditions of an economy-class seat, breathing other people's farts, jet lag, bad food, waiting in lines, packing, unpacking, repacking. If he couldn't drive there and carry everything on his back, he wasn't going.

"Actually, from where you are, it's more like a four-hour flight and then an eleven-hour flight, but so what? You can just sleep the whole way if you want. I'll even think about paying for your flight."

"Really?"

"Really. But you must keep this a secret from Ben."

After she finished with Jimmy, she called Donald again. Actually, she should have called him first. He had planes deployed all over the world and offered to fly everyone to Istanbul for free so long as they didn't mind the occasional stopover to pick up or drop off one of his executives or flight crew. She called Bamkiz and Jimmy back, got them lined out, and returned to her list.

Jimmy would begin the tour in Denver for the flight to Reagan National, and then Howman would join them to be picked up in DC by Donald with the same plane as it made its way eastward. Johan was actually fishing the Great Barrier Reef with some Aussie friends, so he would join Bamkiz on a plane due to depart in thirty-six hours from Sydney. There wasn't much of a bite, anyway. The grander black marlins and other big pelagics had left the reef a week earlier, and he was tired of catching grouper and yellowfin tuna. He could stay at home in Ghana and do that fifteen minutes from his dock.

Rachel couldn't obtain a phone number for Kateryna, so she left her a message on Facebook inviting her to come to Istanbul. Then she gathered her courage and placed the call to Lale, who certainly would know the whereabouts of their mutual friend.

CHAPTER 22

Ben

Present, Ukraine

BEN'S FLIGHT ARRIVED on schedule at 8:00 a.m. to a city under siege. Several months ago, Ben had refocused on the turmoil in Ukraine when he read an article in the *Times* that reported, "Ukraine's decision to freeze its signing of a mutual defense and trade agreement with NATO and the European Union in favor of a closer relationship with Russia constitutes a stunning triumph for Russian President Vladimir Putin, a major geopolitical defeat for the West, a jaw-dropping course reversal to the EU, and a tragedy for the long-suffering Ukrainian people, a majority of whom see their country's destiny as part of Europe."

In an internationally disturbing case of *déjà vu*, anti-government Euromaidan demonstrations began in Ukraine on October 21, 2019. They were triggered by President Nikolai Nemchenko's confounding decision to abandon closer ties with the European Union in favor of the country's eastern neighbor, Russia. The turnabout was the result of a secret meeting between Nemchenko and Putin in December during which the Russian president offered Ukraine a $30 billion bailout and a steep percent discount on imported natural gas. The demonstrations turned deadly in late December when at least five protesters were killed by gunshots during a police assault on the crowd. The standoff was still firmly established at Maidan (Independence) Square, site of violent demonstrations in November 2013 against former President Viktor Yanukovych, when Ben landed.

A few days before, an estimated one hundred thousand people had gathered to protest in central Kiev, clogging all the approaches to the city and polluting the sky with thick clouds of black smoke from burning tires and debris. This was the tenth consecutive Sunday that mass demonstrations had been held to protest the government's decisions and policies. Behind a wall of concrete, wood, and tires, a huge stage had been erected by the people.

"We repeat our demands so the world can hear. WE DO NOT WANT TO BE RUSSIANS! Putin cannot buy us with his black money and dirty gas! We demand early presidential elections," the leader of the resurrected Strike (Udar) opposition party, Lina Poroskova, roared from the stage. For the benefit of the foreign press covering her speech, Poroskova reminded everyone that the opposition wanted a forward-thinking westernized Ukraine, not to go backward toward Russification, as was still happening in the east. "Come to Independence Square, Nikolai, and debate with the people, debate with Lina," Poroskova told the cheering demonstrators.

But now most of the hordes of protestors had returned to their homes and jobs, their anger at the government unabated but put on hold for another workweek. Ben waited in the early-morning cold in front of Boryspil International Airport, looking for his usual driver. Neither the driver nor his blue Mercedes C-Class was anywhere to be seen. A few taxis came and went; other drivers approached him and offered cut-rate fares. There wasn't much activity at the airport at this hour. He felt cold. Despite his fleece and warm jacket, he wasn't dressed for standing still in −5° centigrade temperatures. He called Kateryna to ask about the driver as sometimes he was late because of another customer. "Hey. I've been standing outside the airport for twenty minutes looking for Viktor. Are you sure he knew to pick me up?"

"Yes. I called him at six this morning. And hello to you too, Ben. Welcome to smoky Kiev."

"Sorry. Didn't mean to be rude, Kat. Good morning. I'm tired and cranky, I guess. And fucking cold."

"What is cranky?" she asked.

"Like the way Vlady gets when he doesn't want to wake up in the morning and get dressed."

"Yes. Cranky you must be. It was such an early flight. I am so sorry that the driver isn't there. I shall not use him anymore. Can you just take a regular taxi? I will tell the driver the address and how to come with these traffic problems we have now."

Ben began walking toward the area where one could usually find a licensed taxi when Viktor the driver and another large man waved him down from the blue Mercedes that had just pulled to the curb. "You Mister Ben? You come with us."

Ben didn't like the fact that he would be sharing the ride with a stranger. He considered calling Kateryna and asking her to talk to Viktor about what was going on. But he was too cold and cranky. Exhausted from lack of sleep, his Gavin de Becker "gift of fear" intuition was dulled. Then again, he never had the gift of fear. He had what was more of an instinct that trouble was near. That "something is wrong with this picture" kind of feeling. Unfortunately, it was in hibernation mode at this particular moment in the morning cold of Kiev.

The big man got out from the passenger seat, took Ben's bag, and put it in the trunk. He politely asked for Ben's coat and folded it neatly, placing it in the rear seat. Motioning Ben into the front passenger seat, he said, "My name Yura."

As they pulled away from the curb and left the airport, Ben called Kateryna to tell her that he was in the car with Viktor and a big guy named Yura. Ben told her sotto voce that the guy smelled like he had never taken a bath in his entire life and that he would see her and Vlady soon.

"You are coming to Maidan to be with protest?" Yura announced.

"No. Whatever gave you that idea?" Ben responded.

"We know this. We know you. American-government man. We know."

"I think that you have been misinformed." Ben was trying to be polite despite his being *cranky.*

Yura looked at Ben quizzically. Apparently, his English was limited to saying small groups of words in a deep growl that was intended to be frightening. Ben would have to dumb it down and speak to him in much the same way he had communicated with Vlady when he first started English preschool.

Yura: "You will speak to him."
Ben: "Who?"
Yura: "My boss."
Ben: "No. Viktor here is taking me to my friend's house."
Yura: "Maybe later. Not now. Now you go to Boss."

Ben looked over at Viktor, whose tears were making it difficult for him to drive. The car pulled from the forested side of the highway into the lane that led to town. He looked back at Yura and only then saw the muzzle of a Grad AR bullpup sweeping back and forth between the seat backs. He felt even colder now. With a strong feeling of self-loathing, he recognized how he had stupidly missed all the obvious danger signals. Viktor had been purposefully late, hoping that Ben would get disgusted and take a cab. Unlike every prior occasion when he had always jumped out to greet Ben with a hug and two kisses, Viktor had remained in the car while Yura had engineered Ben into the front seat, placing his Rimowa carry-on in the trunk just in case Ben had some type of weapon inside. The Grad had been under Yura's big coat the entire time, held in place with a black strip of Velcro, which is one reason why he looked so extraordinarily bulky.

Ben had also missed the sour smell of fear emanating from Viktor's armpits. He was quite familiar with that smell from others he had been with in stressful situations in the past. And Ben had a sharp sense of smell. But perhaps it had been dulled by the cold. At least this was how he intellectualized it during the seconds of analysis he underwent formulating an escape plan. What he failed to take into account was that Yura was a professional. He saw Ben starting to reach for his seat belt, anticipating that he would grab the steering wheel from Viktor to cause an accident. He knew that Ben planned to jump out of the car in the ensuing pandemonium; probably he and Viktor would be injured as they would not have the benefit of safety belts.

As Ben's right hand went back and down, then across his waist, clicking the belt into place, Yura quickly unwrapped a roll of silver duct tape and wound it around Ben's head and the head restraint of the passenger seat. When Ben's hands automatically rose to his face, Yura continued wrapping to firmly affix his hands to his head and the seat back. Ben was effectively blinded, gagged, immobilized, and in an extremely awkward, uncomfortable position. Yura then took Ben's nicely folded coat and draped it over his well-wrapped body. "Drive, *dolbyeb*" (dickhead), Yura ordered Viktor, and the car lurched back into traffic, steadily gaining speed as Yura pressed the muzzle of the Grad deeply into Viktor's seat.

To his credit, Viktor never gave up trying to attract attention, and it was only when he had unsuccessfully attempted to drift into the high-speed lane and be hit by a fast-approaching BMW 3 series that Yura ordered him to pull over and open his door. "*Nu vse! Tebe pizda*" (That's it! You're fucking dead). Yura casually put one bullet into Viktor's brain and let the body fall out of the car. He quickly dragged it into the forest, returned to the car, wiped off the blood splatter that had hit the driver's side door and window, and got behind the wheel. "Nice try, Viktor," he muttered in Russian. He hit Ben against the side of his head with the butt of the weapon and reminded him that if he had any thoughts of escape, he would end up like Viktor. Then he reached into Ben's pocket and removed his cell phone, tossing it in the general direction of Viktor's body. After he heard it land in a soft pile of leaves and pine needles, he thought that he should have taken out the battery. It was unprofessional to forget such a thing. But Yura was slightly lazy and rationalized that he would be far away before the Ukrainian police could locate the cell phone by its GPS or whatever technology they employed for such things.

The bigger mistake Yura made was not noticing Viktor's iPhone still connected to the charger inside the glove box. Ben had realized this about the same time that he felt his phone being removed from his pants pocket and heard it being thrown outside the car. While his was an old iPhone 8, he had brought the expensive unlocked iPhone 11 for Viktor from the States the last time he came to visit Kateryna and Vlady, together with an iPad mini for the boy. He prayed that Kateryna wouldn't call Viktor's phone until after they had arrived at their destination, and no one was in the car to hear the distinctive ring. He had downloaded "Lara's Theme" from the movie *Doctor Zhivago* for the old guy, hoping the man appreciated the irony. Ben doubted Yura would feel the same way.

Meanwhile, he was getting angry. He hated to have his head restrained in any way. It reminded him of one rainy morning in Washington when he had been rear-ended hard while he was waiting at a red light. The old guy who hit him had been looking for a building number and failed to see either the traffic light or Ben's light gray SUV. Due to the severity of the crash and Ben's painful injuries, an ambulance had been called. The medics had quickly ascertained the trauma to Ben's neck and gingerly eased him from his car and strapped him safely to a stretcher, securing his head with Velcro straps to avoid further damage in the event he had sustained serious vertebral injury. After an eternity of weaving in and out of the heavy, weather-related traffic, Ben had an anxiety attack about not being able to lift his head. This was the same feeling, but without the reassuring words of a kindly ambulance attendant and the ability to, at least, see the underside of the roof of the emergency vehicle and the equipment that adorned its walls.

Ben used all his skills to estimate the length of time and distance they drove. Yura no longer talked to him; only occasionally speaking in a low voice into his cell phone, alternating between a strangely accented Ukrainian and poor Russian, presumably to give updates to his "boss." Ben had always suffered mildly from allergies, hence was quite anxious only being able to breathe through his nose. The other problem was it forced him to continuously inhale the rancid odor from Yura, a distasteful proposition even if he had been able to breathe through his mouth. To add insult to injury, Yura had turned on the radio, pushing buttons until he arrived at a Ukrainian pop music station that seemed to be limited to heavy metal music. Thankfully, and as it was soon to prove, fortuitously, he kept his window open and had the volume turned up so high that the windshield wipers were vibrating against the glass and a loose door panel resonated from the bass of the subwoofer in the trunk. The gentle strains of "Lara's Theme" didn't have a chance against such cacophony.

But Ben heard it. Or at least he thought that he heard it. He moved his right leg forward until it was pressed against the underside of the dash, under the glove box. The next time Viktor's phone received a call, Ben felt it rather than heard it. Yura, meanwhile, didn't hear anything except Blood of Kingu while happily imitating the death growls of lead singer Roman Saenko. Ben, always a slave to irony, felt his lips strain against the duct tape while he inadvertently smiled at the fact that this would probably be the only time he would prefer the raucous screams of an unintelligible metal band over the melodious tones of Maurice Jarre's timeless composition.

After stopping twice to refuel and after Ben had felt the vibrations of the phone at least twenty times, the car began to slow. Ben estimated that they had been driving over ten hours based on the pain from his bladder. With the radio still blaring, he felt the tires transition from macadam to concrete and the air become close, as if they were in a shed or garage. Thankfully, the phone had stopped ringing awhile ago. The tape was torn from his head and unwound from around his body. The engine was turned off, and Ben was unceremoniously pulled from the car and roughly pushed a few steps up into a room. Abruptly, a metal chair was pushed hard behind his legs, causing him to sit involuntarily. He could smell Yura moving behind him and then felt his wrists being tightly bound to the arms of the chair with plastic zip straps. He was allowed to pee in a can placed in front of him.

Hours passed so slowly that it was as if time had distorted to accommodate a melting clock painted by Salvador Dali. He had been sitting for so long that he was beyond uncomfortable, with excruciating cramps in his legs, back, and neck. After a while, he came to embrace the pain, as if it was a solipsistic concept, confirming his very existence. His mind was active, thoughts flitting about, wondering whether Kateryna had contacted the police, the US embassy, Lale, or any of his friends in Kiev. Had she thought to have Viktor's cell phone GPS traced? Had Yura found that phone? What of his cell phone's GPS? He was desperately thirsty. The building was empty of noise-dampening materials. It was cold, yet not as cold as the outside air. With the tape still over his eyes, the world remained black.

Sound echoed. Feet scraping against a stone or cement floor. He felt a searing pain as the duct tape was ripped from his mouth, replaced by a leather gloved hand that encircled his head. "My name is Colonel Stanislav Nevski and I can easily break your neck," said a disembodied voice with a Moscow accent.

At the moment, Ben was more concerned that his lips had remained affixed to the tape than about having his neck broken. If they had wanted him dead, he knew that he wouldn't be sitting there wondering if he would ever be able to kiss a beautiful woman again. "Why would you want to do that?" he asked. "Then you would never find out the answer."

"I already know the answer," the Russian said. "But you don't know the question."

"Actually, you have many questions," Ben responded. "But I will only answer one, so choose wisely."

The gloved hand was removed from his head, only to return behind a punch to Ben's left ear that sent daggers of pain through his face and neck. Involuntarily, he moaned; the pain was so intense. The last time he had been hit like that was in eleventh grade when he was fighting a pseudo hippie on the back lawn of his high school. He thought about that. The memory cut through the pain and made him very angry. He had destroyed that kid, but of course, his arms hadn't been bound to a chair. Returning to the present, he realized two things. Since Colonel Nevski had remained behind him, it meant that he was probably left-handed. It also meant that the man knew how to inflict pain without causing loss of consciousness. The first was good for Ben. He could block well with his right and counter-punch with his left. That information was not particularly useful at the moment as he was immobilized. The second was not good. Ben wasn't very good with enduring physical pain.

"Are you finished being clever?" the Russian asked.

"I've been called many things," Ben said. "But clever was never one of them."

"*Nu ti dajosh!*" (You've got balls!) Nevski laughed.

"*Potselui menya* u *zhopu*" (kiss my ass), Ben replied.

"*Zatknis! Ty menya dostal! Yobni yivo*" (Shut up! I've had enough of you! Beat him), the Russian said to Yura and left the room, wondering where Ben had learned his street Russian.

CHAPTER 23

Rachel

Present, Mississippi

RACHEL GENTLY RETURNED the wireless phone to its base. She'd had a brief conversation with Lale, who'd at first been somewhat suspicious of her identity and connection with Ben. But after confirming a few very intimate details regarding Ben, Rachel had firmly established her bona fides. It was only when she felt comfortable discussing her concerns with Rachel did Lale reveal the disquieting news that Ben had lost contact with her after taking an early morning flight to Kiev. "It's probably nothing to worry about," Lale had told her. "Ben is not so good keeping in touch sometimes. But he was supposed to call me to tell me what was going on there with the little boy, Vlady."

After finishing the call with Lale, she went online and booked a flight to Washington's Reagan National Airport. She sat at her desk and looked at a small religious icon of the Madonna and Holy Child that her mother had bought in Sofia, Bulgaria. She felt great sorrow that she would never hold a baby of her own like that but also relieved that she would never experience the sorrow of losing that child to an early death. Although Rachel wasn't a particularly religious person, her mother had been devout and collected religious objects from all her travels. Next to the icon of Mary and Jesus was another larger one of the crucifixion. She had never liked that image. It was too graphic for her tastes. She could almost feel the suffering of Jesus on the cross. She had recently finished a book by Boris Groys titled *Art Power*, where he wrote about digital imaging and the concept of what constitutes an original and if, in fact, an original of a digital image even holds any validity as an original. Alternatively, perhaps every reproduction of a digital image, being so perfectly exact, was an original in and of itself.

This led her to reflect on God and whether it was appropriate or even possible to create an image, digital, in ink, paint, or sculpture, of that which was divine. She had heard the word *God* expressed in many ways: the Invisible, Hashem, Yahweh, Allah, Elohim. She felt that it was more an amalgamation of countless images and stories. Rachel personally liked the term *the Invisible* because that was how she perceived God. Something that was, indeed, invisible but everywhere, more in the form of an *energy* than an old man with a white beard or even a beautiful young woman as some of her feminist friends ascribed to. The Invisible with its energy was everywhere, appearing in both static and dynamic form. A magnificent mountain like the Matterhorn and a roaring cascade like Victoria Falls. A symphony with seemingly divine inspiration and a painting as immortal as the *Mona Lisa*. Wonders and miracles, both mundane and fantastic. As Groys wrote, "The Invisible remains invisible precisely by the multiplication of its visualizations." In Rachel's opinion, that about said it all.

Rachel liked to pray despite believing that prayers were never individually heard. Nevertheless, she felt that prayers made the one praying feel better, and at the very least, they were doing *something* during a stressful time. Rachel then dropped to her knees in her bedroom, arose, and, with outstretched arms, walked slowly walked and prayed to the energy of the Invisible. She prayed that Ben was safe and that this was just some technical problem with his cell phone or the result of some misunderstanding with the local police or that he had gotten food poisoning on the plane and had been taken to a local hospital. Some plausible, although improbable, explanation for his disappearance. She refused to let herself get all stressed about it. Annie always said, "Don't get to worryin' 'til there's something to actually worry about."

Her favorite place to pray was in the bathroom, sitting on the small, tufted stool at her mother's vanity table. As she prayed, she looked at herself. She never prayed with her eyes closed. She thought that was dishonest or, at best, might be dishonest. She wasn't sure which. Just that closing one's eyes when confronting one's deepest needs and wants wasn't correct. If you couldn't look yourself in the eye when praying, wishing, seeking something that was to ascend to the level of the metaphysical would be akin to getting completely soused on gin and tonics and then taking a lie detector test. She also liked to look into her lovers' eyes while having sex. Not that she had been doing much of that lately. And she also didn't stay with a man very long if he wouldn't or couldn't look into her eyes, at her face, at her body while making love. She learned so much from looking into a man's eyes during sex. If he was an honest man, that was when he was *most* honest.

She lost her focus, though, and started to look at her neck. She didn't like the way it had changed as she aged. She had often heard that a woman can disguise the age on her face with Botox, filler, and makeup, but nothing short of cosmetic surgery could fix a neck. Clothing could hide the problem, but it was too damned hot and humid in Mississippi to wear silk scarves around her throat. She had been saving a few hundred dollars a month over the past three years for such a surgical procedure and probably had more than enough, with some left over for those tiny crow's feet at the corners of her eyes. Hell, just because she was a Southern intellectual didn't mean she couldn't be a little vain. But perhaps that money would be better spent on an extended trip overseas. Perhaps she could entice Donald into giving her a deal on some cosmetic surgery. Suddenly, she felt guilty, worrying about such superficialities while responsible for the logistics of such a complicated and speculative reunion. People were depending on her. She understood something relatively annoying about herself. As often happened when she wasn't as entirely committed to a radical idea as she wanted to be, her deep thoughts had devolved into the realm of the superficial.

She returned to her computer, completed the purchase of her ticket to Washington, and then purchased some tickets for Bamkiz to fly from Sydney to Istanbul with Johan. *There*, she thought. *It's done*. Her long-saved, hard-earned money flying through the ether on tickets for people she hadn't seen in ages. But the definite action was a catalyst for her to get moving, get organized, and prepare the house for a lengthy absence.

Rachel contacted Doyle, an old family friend who agreed to house-sit so long as he could bring his bluetick hounds, Rory and Mert. She put all the utilities on auto pay to her credit card and arranged for a $500 per month credit at the Colliersville General Store for anything Doyle might need to care for the house, garden, or himself. She made sure that Doyle's mother, Maggs, who ran the store, knew that the credit didn't include alcohol but could be used for night crawlers should Doyle have a need to wet a line in lieu of wetting his whistle.

She drove to Hattiesburg and purchased an iPad with 64 gigs of memory from a discount electronics store and downloaded two seasons of *The Good Wife*, *Catherine the Great* HBO miniseries, three seasons of *Killing Eve*, and the first and only season of *Mrs. Fletcher*. Although generally detesting reading books in electronic format, she downloaded *Cutting for Stone* by Abraham Verghese and Neil Gaiman's novel *The Ocean at End of the Lane*. She downloaded about 150 of her photos from iCloud where, in an unusual fit of technical ingenuity (at least for her, a middle-aged nontechnically oriented woman from a small Southern town), she had uploaded and stored them. They included scanned pictures of her family going back to the mid-1800s, their slaves, the main house and outbuildings, and livestock. Also in the mix were scans of letters her aunt had received from a noted Southern writer, including one written shortly before he died that repeated his famous words: "Don't grieve for me. I've had a wonderful time."

While at work, setting up the new iPad with all this content, she reread that letter. It reminded her of something Ben once said to her during a particularly somber conversation. "When I die, if I do ever have a tombstone, since I think I'd rather be cremated than buried, ya know, all I want my tombstone to say is, 'Here lies Ben. He had a good time.' That's it. No Ben Jacobson with years of birth and death and survived by so and so. Just those eight simple words."

She shivered at the thought of a tombstone for Ben, banished the image from her mind, and instead concentrated on choosing some music to add to the iPad—Emmylou, Pure Prairie League, Dave Alvin, Gangstagrass, Jesse Dayton, and Brennen Leigh, and in a moment of overly saccharine nostalgia, "Stand By Your Man," sung by Beverly Staunton.

CHAPTER 24

Lale and Ipek

Present, Istanbul

LALE SAT AT a table outside the House Café in Nişantaşı by the Teşvikiye mosque. She felt entitled to a cigarette, something she had given up for the fifth time in twenty-five years, then restarted today to assuage her stress. She hadn't heard from Ben in a disturbingly long time and was beginning to worry. Maybe it was time to call Kateryna and ask if she had heard anything from Ben. Who knew where he could be by now? Over twenty-four hours and neither a call nor a message, something uncharacteristic of her good friend. All these people about to descend upon her whom she didn't know and Ben, the guest of honor at his own reunion, nowhere to be found. What kind of surprise party is that? A surprise for all the guests, she supposed.

She was vaguely aware of the parade of people strolling along Teşvikiye Caddesi, some pausing at the shop windows of Calzedonia to gaze at the lingerie or at the dresses displayed in the window of Max Mara facing the café. It was a gray, chilly day, and the electric heater overhead did little to warm her as she sipped her double espresso and smoked her Vogue. A woman at the next table offered her another cigarette as hers burned down to a stub in the silver ashtray beside her. She politely refused and concentrated on her contacts in the cell phone. She called Ipek.

"*Canım*—it's Lale. *Nasılsın? Iyimsin?* (My dear. How are you? Are you well?) "Have you heard from Ben lately?"

"*Iyim, Lale Hanım, sen nasılsınız?* (I'm good Lale, and you?) No, I haven't spoken to him for the past three days. Is everything all right? You sound—tense."

"I am more than tense, Ipekcim. I'm very worried. He took a flight to Kiev yesterday morning, and I haven't heard a word, and Kateryna called and said he never arrived to her home. This isn't like Ben, you know. He's very good at checking in with me and my brother on a daily basis, updating us on the book he's writing and where he's going on the phone and on WhatsApp. The first thing he always does is send me a new photo of Vlady…but…but…nothing. I'm frightened. Kat is in panic. I got a call from an old college girlfriend of his, and she's coming tomorrow with a group of his friends to surprise Ben with some kind of reunion. Just what I need. What I am supposed to do with them? I've got clients to meet with and deals to finish, so much work in my office. I don't know where they will stay, what they will do. Ben should be here to meet them. I'm sitting here like a moron who doesn't know what day it is. What am I supposed to be doing? Should I call Chuck at the American consulate? Maybe he knows someone in the embassy in Kiev or one of Ben's old State Department friends who can find him. I'm…I'm…"

"Slow down, Lale Hanım," Ipek said softly. "*Rahatla* (relax). Stay where you are. I'm just up the street at Cities Mall. I will walk down to you."

Five minutes later, the two women were sitting together with a pack of Ipek's Winstons between them. Lale took one of Ipek's cigarettes and nervously twirled it with her fingers. She didn't want to smoke it; just to hold it was comforting on some subliminal level. The two had never been that close despite their common connection with Ben. Lale was among those who never quite understood his relationship with the much younger woman. Ipek was too old to be his daughter, too young to be his wife, but as attractive as she was, just perfect for the role of a girlfriend for a guy going through a midlife crisis. Maybe he was sleeping with her. But that didn't make sense either for two reasons. One was that Ben never considered himself middle-aged. He had managed to arrest his development somewhere between twenty-five and thirty-five years of age. The second was that Ipek had always had male friends like Ben; he had been friendly with most of them. She wasn't sure about Ipek's boyfriend status, though. It seemed from Ben's comments that Ipek had trouble initiating and sustaining romantic relationships with men. But while she knew her concerns about Ipek were probably unfounded, she remained vigilant. At least until now. Ipek's immediate response to her cry for help and her shared concern elevated her to a new level in Lale's estimation.

"*Dinle* (listen), Lale. Don't worry about Ben's friends coming. I will handle all that. I will call his friend Aydin Hazeri and put them all in his little hotel in Arnavütköy. It's called Villa Deniz and has only six rooms, which should accommodate all of them quite nicely. He really loves Ben, and I'm sure that he will provide them with a couple of cars too. After all, he has about twenty. They're kind of old, but I think they all run."

"*Iyi fikir* (good idea), Ipek. He is as hospitable as he is sweet. You do that please. It's nervousing me all these strange people coming that I don't know what to do with. Do you think they can be helpful? Or are they coming just for a holiday?"

"Well, I don't know them either, but I'm sure Ben has told me stories about them. I think that his old stories are funny. Not just because they usually *are* funny but because Ben always thinks that he's so young, yet for someone who has so many stories and experiences, it's as if he's one hundred years old."

"I know, I know," Lale agreed, chuckling. "And sometimes he takes so long to tell the story and get to the point that you start thinking that you will be one hundred years old before he is finished and reaches the punching line."

Ipek, whose English wasn't much better than Lale's, wondered about that last phrase. *Punching line?* Desperate for conversation with an intelligent, glamorous, and worldly older woman, Ipek briefly told Lale about how she had just broken up with her fiancé, Bekir. She decided that she wasn't attracted to him anymore, and she was never satisfied by him sexually. So *boşver*. Forget it.

"What goes on in the bedroom is very important," Lale acknowledged although she had personally never been all that interested in the actual sex act with the men in her personal life. She felt it was just something that men always expected out of her, so she usually just went along with it if she generally liked the guy. Love was more of a spiritual thing for her, and she wondered about Ipek's priorities when it came to relationships.

The two women returned to the matter at hand. Ipek told Lale that she would check with Aydin on the car situation when she called him about the hotel rooms, something she knew she better do before it was too late. She kissed Lale on both cheeks and started walking back up the street, slightly embarrassed that she had let her lips get so close to the other woman's. That was definitely not an air-kiss. Glancing backward over her shoulder, she saw that Lale was lost in her own thoughts.

Lale was thinking about how it was so much more interesting to enter a person's life when they were somewhere between the ages of forty and sixty, so much more to talk about, so many more stories to tell and relate. One's reach was greater. Both in terms of the education gained from simply living a life rich in friends and experiences and in learning from books, classes, business, and social encounters. Some of it was found in the typical events of living; she had been married twice, divorced twice, and then had a few lovers. She'd raised children and then seen them fly out of the nest. She'd founded a law firm with three partners she had known since childhood that had grown to thirty-seven attorneys since its inception. They were currently having discussions with a large New York firm that wanted to merge. She'd lost friends along the way, saved friends, become disillusioned by friends, and felt abandoned and hurt when betrayed. In addition to her many years in Istanbul, she had lived in Geneva, London, Paris, Venice, Marakesh, and Papa'ete in French Polynesia and was always surrounded by crowd of acolytes.

Her academic career could be characterized as eclectic. She'd studied mechanical engineering at her father's insistence only to switch her major to eighteenth-century French literature after one year and then abruptly started over in the faculty of law at Galatasaray University as a compromise to appease her father. She'd managed to seduce nearly every brilliant professor she studied under while playing academic assassination with those who she reviled as idiots. To her, it was more of an intellectual game than any atavistic, physical, or chemical attraction or compulsion. She acknowledged her intense but unfocused sexuality, but in fact, she understood that she was never really attracted to or turned on by any of them. It was as if while they were entering the intimate areas of her body, she was penetrating their minds. Interestingly, Lale was only vulnerable to things of great beauty, whether it was a dress, a painting, an animal, or a poem. Human beauty she appreciated but heavily discounted as a minor, superficial attribute. She'd learned as a young girl that there was often an inverse correlation between good looks and good friends. Not always, but enough to make her wary of beautiful people.

But this girl Ipek was different. Although not beautiful in a glamorous, fashion magazine kind of way, she had a strong, edgy sexuality and a totally natural attractiveness about her. Smart and serious, funny and irreverent, Lale could clearly understand why Ben liked her so much. Ipek was definitely what the Americans called a tomboy, but a very feminine one for sure. Lale resolved to get to know her better and incorporate her into her life in some useful way. Ipek may be young, but she was interesting and clearly had an old soul.

For Lale, Ben didn't fall into any particular category with regard to his appearance. To her, he was beautiful, but she always referred to him as ugly. This was a typically Turkish concession to the superstition of the *nazar*, the evil eye that brings misfortune to those whose fortune has been too good. Therefore, babies were never fussed over as being too beautiful for fear of attracting the evil eye. A friend of hers who had recently married a famous lawyer in Istanbul had fallen out of her fourth-story window, breaking her arm, leg, and several ribs. Virtually everyone who heard the story responded with one word: *nazar*. The more she thought about it, the more she began to think that Ben's disappearance might likewise be related to the *nazar*. For someone so intelligent, sophisticated, and well educated, this superstition might seem counterintuitive, yet there it was: the Turkish explanation for all things unfortunate.

Lale was a control freak. Among her law partners, close friends, and family, this was a source of both jokes and irritation. She exercised no self-restraint when it came to telling drivers how to drive, doctors how to diagnose and treat, chefs how to cook, her kids how to act. And Ben, well, she always tried to tell him how to do everything, including how to write the book about her family. He generally ignored her in a good-natured sort of way, occasionally indulged her with barely disguised reluctance, and often rose to the bait and had a heated argument over something he forgot within minutes. Lale, on the other hand, never forgot an argument or act of disobedience. These transgressions were compiled like an unabridged history of the world. If she had known how irrelevant they were to Ben, she'd probably have a heart attack.

Her reaction to his being incommunicado vacillated between extreme annoyance and sheer panic. She blamed him for upsetting her despite knowing that was irrational and narcissistic. She also feared life without him as her *American friend from Washington* and didn't know how she could cope on her own with the myriad of situations he was so adept at handling. She needed the comfort of being on his arm at certain social engagements, as well as his thoughtful support of her during her many crises. Lale resolved to turn her fear and annoyance into thinking about positive action if that's what was required. She was good with telephone calls, so she called Kateryna.

CHAPTER 25

Ben

Present, Eastern Ukraine

ANOTHER DAY HAD passed. Yura had hit him in the face with a telephone book, mumbling something about how he'd seen this in an American movie and how it would hurt but not scar. Then he allowed Ben to stand up, unzip his fly, and take out his penis and told him to pee in the can he placed in front of him. Yura expressed an inordinate amount of interest in the fact that Ben was circumcised and asked if it felt different when fucking a woman.

"How would I know, you dumb shit? It's not like I had a lot of sexual experience when I was less than eight days old," Ben replied and then turned away from the can and pissed on Yura's boot.

Yura hit him in the face again with the book. Ben fell backward, and his urine sprayed about the room, wetting Yura's clothes in the process. Yura kicked him hard in the ribs and left the room, saying, "*Zhri govno i zdohni!*" (Go fuck your mother!)

Although at this point thoroughly confused about why he was being held captive, who precisely was holding him, and where he was in relation to Kiev, Ben was remarkably quite calm, all things considered. However, after about three hours, he became concerned being left alone with Yura, who understandably was not going to be too keen on coming to feed him or provide him with water, much less allow him to relieve himself.

"*Preevyet, Yura!*" (Hello, Yura!) he called out. "*Prasteete. Eezveeneete.*" (I'm sorry. Excuse me.)

"*Poshyel k chertu!*" (Go to hell) Yura's voice came back from another room.

"Come on, brotha. I've gotta move my legs, take a dump, get some water," Ben pleaded. "Gimme a break." An elaborate deception was beginning to take form in his head. If he could get free, even for a moment, he might be able to incapacitate Yura and escape. He could quickly grab Viktor's cell phone from the taxi, if it was still there, and if not, there must be a road nearby where he could flag down a passing motorist and make his way to a phone to call for help. At this point, he knew that nothing good could come out of remaining in captivity for much longer. Although at the moment he was more concerned with self-preservation than the need to address the anxieties of Kateryna or Lale, he had thought about them while tied to the chair. They must be worried sick about what had happened to him by now. He dropped his head to his chest in frustration and allowed himself a brief nap.

The last time his blindfold had been removed, he had noticed a small coffee table and wooden chair in the corner of the garage, along with a large metal toolbox against the wall. When Yura finally came into the room and released him to take a bathroom break, he positioned himself far enough behind Ben to avoid being the human equivalent of a fire hydrant. Ben pretended to become dizzy when he stood up and took a few steps, fell hard against the little table, and broke off a leg from it while he was on the floor. When Yura bent over him to pull him up, Ben rammed the pointed end into Yura's groin and rolled away as the big man collapsed. While Yura writhed in pain, Ben clambered over to the toolbox and found a large monkey wrench to use as a more definitive weapon. Smashing the back of Yura's head, Ben then used it to break the padlock and open the door.

It was the middle of the night. Without his jacket, the February evening's chill quickly penetrated Ben's thin frame through to his bones. He debated going back inside to look for a coat but then noticed an old parka hanging inside a truck parked outside. The heavy wrench easily shattered the vehicle's window, and he reached inside and grabbed what turned out to be the perfect garment for his escape—a deep green pleated hunting coat with waterproof fabric and a detachable hood. Its owner, judging from its size and relatively clean smell, definitely not Yura, had courteously left gloves in the pockets and a foldable locking knife with a six-inch blade nearby on the seat. Ben quickly searched through the compartment under the dashboard, half expecting to find a map and compass the way his luck was currently going, but he was disappointed to find nothing more than a sales receipt and disposable lighter. He scuttled over to the vehicle that had once been Viktor's taxi, and finding the door wide-open for some reason, he retrieved the driver's cell phone from the glove box. The battery had long since died, but Ben believed that the chances were good that he could find a charger once he could make it to a town. Quietly and remaining low to the ground, he slipped back into the shadows. He was fortunate that the cab's interior light had burned out.

He moved into the darkness of the surrounding woods, just in case the building had video monitors, and circled approximately 120 degrees around it and walked forward for perhaps 300 meters. He moved with the utmost stealth, employing all the skills his father had taught him as a boy on their first hunting trip in the Adirondack woods. The evening dew left a layer of moisture on the ground cover, and his soft shoes helped him avoid the crunching sounds usually made when walking on leaves. Several large birds were having a heated discussion overhead, and Ben tried to time each step with each noisy outburst. Putting the outside of each foot down and slowly rolling the sole inward, he timed his deep breaths to coincide with each step. He varied his pace: one step, four steps, two steps, three steps. He listened carefully at each pause. There was no sound other than those birds, which, oddly enough, seemed to remain exactly overhead regardless of how far he traveled. Then he stopped, sat down on a log, and quietly listened for the sound of cars or other evidence of civilization. He thought about those birds, still overhead, continuously cawing to one another.

A searing pain shot through his head and the breath squeezed from his chest as his chair was suddenly kicked backward, and Yura stood over him, unzipping his pants. Ben realized that he had been dreaming and had never left the building, much less incapacitated Yura. Gasping for breath, Ben immediately understood what Yura had in mind by way of retribution. He quickly forced himself to close his mouth and turned his face to the side. At least the bag had been removed from his head so he could resume his visual reconnaissance of the interior of the building.

The tool chest was still where he had seen it earlier, as was the door and its shiny new padlock. The floor smelled like damp concrete, and Yura still smelled like a swamp with rotting weeds. He could see up to some of the clerestory windows and appreciate that it was night. He risked a glance toward his captor and saw that he was about to be urinated on. "Can I tell you a joke?" he asked the big Ukrainian.

"What joke?" Yura replied. "You about to get pissed on and you will tell me joke?"

"Why not? Here it goes. An Italian is drinking in a New York bar when he gets a call on his cell phone. He hangs up, grinning from ear to ear, and orders a round of drinks for everybody in the bar, announcing his wife had produced a typical Italian baby boy weighing twenty pounds. That's about nine kilos. Nobody can believe that any new baby can weigh in at twenty pounds, but the Italian guy just shrugs, 'Dat'sa 'bout average backa home. Like I said, atsa my boy, a typical Italian bambino.' Congratulations showered him from all around, and many exclamations of 'Wow!' 'Bravisimo!' 'Unfuckingbelievable!' Two weeks later, he returns to the bar. The bartender says, 'Hey, you're the father of that typical Italian baby that weighed twenty pounds at birth, aren't you? Everybody's been making bets about how big he'd be in two weeks. So how much does he weigh now?' The proud father answers, 'He's a fifteen pound.' The bartender is puzzled, concerned, and a little suspicious. 'What happened? He already weighed twenty pounds the day he was born!' The Italian father takes a long swig of Sambuca, wipes his lips on his

147

shirt sleeve, leans into the bartender, and proudly says, 'My wife, his mama, she Jewish. We had him circumcised!' Ya know what, Yura?"

"What, *zasranec* (asshole)?"

"You obviously aren't a typical Italian bambino."

"Fuck no! I am a Ukrainian man."

"You obviously don't get it. But that's okay. Did you say your name was Yura or *Balvan* (moron)? Ya know, I'm not very good with remembering foreign names. I forget."

Yura brought his boot back to deliver a viscous kick to Ben's head when a familiar authoritative Russian voice barked, "*Balvan!* What do you think you are doing? With your dick hanging out and your foot on his chest? How can you get a *minet* (blow job) if he can't breathe?" The Russian pushed Yura away, glanced at his crotch, said, "*U tebia ochen malenki hui, skolka, pat centimetra?*" (You have a very small dick, what, five centimeters?) and pulled Ben back to a proper sitting position.

"*Spasiba*," Ben thanked him.

"Let's dispense with your crude attempts at speaking my elegant language. English will do fine from here on." He opened the door and five men dressed like partisan fighters entered. Three stood by the door and two approached Ben and the Russian. "Now we have some questions for you, and I don't want any games. I will do the translating. They don't speak English."

"Okay," Ben acknowledged. "But who are these guys?"

"These guys," Colonel Nevski mimicked, "are some brave local fighters whom I am advising on behalf of my government. We believe that you are still quite involved with the joint efforts of your government and the new false Ukrainian government to force the truly Russian people of the eastern provinces to remain Ukrainian against their will."

"You're a day late and a dollar short, my friend. I left all that behind over a year ago. And do forgive me for that colloquialism."

"I assume that means we missed our opportunity with you, Mr. Jacobson. But we have seen our patriots occupy the city halls of Luhansk and Donetsk and are monitoring the radio and telephone traffic between American advisors and Ukrainian commanders."

"How are local guys who claim to just be farmers able to do that? Russia maintains that you aren't here to support them. But you are here, aren't you?"

"Never mind how they are able to do that. Over seven hundred Ukrainian soldiers were captured by those *farmers* today, and the Ukrainian government is in hysterics over what they call a full-scale invasion by Russian troops. Ha! That certainly won't be necessary." Nevski walked behind Ben and dug his thumbs into twin pressure points on either side of his neck.

Ben winced from the pain. "As I said, I'm out of the intelligence business. I'm a simple biographer working in Istanbul for a wealthy family that couldn't care less about Ukrainian-Russian affairs."

Colonel Nevski spoke over the top of Ben's head to the partisans. He told them that Ben was claiming to be out of touch with his former employers. That they should work on Ben a while to determine if he was being truthful. Then come get him from the truck to have a final interview with Ben. Ben knew just enough Russian to know that this wasn't going to be good.

"Before you go, Colonel," Ben interrupted, "if these fellows don't speak English, how are they going to know if I'm telling the truth? Perhaps you need to stick around for the fun. That is unless you are uncomfortable with torture."

The otherwise taciturn Nevski looked nonplussed for a second. Regaining his composure, he said, "Good point, Mr. Jacobson. Are all American intelligence officers as clever as you?"

"Only when we are facing an imminent abuse of our human rights," Ben replied.

CHAPTER 26

Rachel, Howman (the Blitz), and Donald

Present, Donald's G650ER jet

REMARKABLY, THE LOGISTICS of the confluence of friends had been accomplished without even a hiccup. Currently, Rachel, Jimmy, and Howman were relaxing in the cabin of the Gulfstream with Donald taking his turn in the cockpit while the pilot had a nap. Jimmy and the Blitz were wondering why they were making this extremely long journey without having heard anything from either Lale or Ben.

While Rachel pretended to be asleep but was actually listening to their quiet conversation, she heard them acknowledge to one another that this entire escapade was ridiculous. For that's what it clearly was—a ridiculous escapade. How had they allowed this strange Southern woman from Ben's distant past to talk them into such an arduous journey for her thinly disguised motive to reunite with a memory? After all, he was *their* friend. She was merely a college fling who had broken his heart. What were they getting themselves into? Maybe they should have waited until there was some concrete information that would provide at least a plausible guaranty that they could enjoy an actual reunion of best friends. Each had their individual theory on what may have befallen Ben and the possible reasons behind his being incommunicado.

Howman thought that it was the US government that was behind everything as he lived in Washington. Even now, so many years later, the Blitz was still trying to digest the revelations by Edward Snowden about the extent of NSA surveillance. He postulated that it must be the Ukrainian intelligence agency thinking that Ben was somehow connected with the Russians' expansionist dreams. And Jimmy, ever the contrarian, rebutted him by positing that this was all about the Russians thinking that Ben was a Ukrainian agent along with Kateryna.

"We will land in less than four hours, folks, so let's put the speculating on hold and try to sleep. We need to be sharp when we arrive in Istanbul. Lale said that she will meet us in a big Mercedes van with a friend named Ipek. So that's one less thing to worry about," Donald announced from the cockpit. "And one more thing. You remember the corrupt former president of Ukraine, Yanukovych, who disappeared from Kiev years ago? Maybe he's with Ben."

"Are you serious?" Rachel exclaimed.

"C'mon, Rachel. That's Donald being funny. He likes to laugh in the face of adversity," Howman corrected her.

"Remind me of that the next time I run out of fuel at fifty thousand feet," said Donald, doing a little tail wiggle with the rudder of his plane. "And by the way, that former Ukrainian president never surfaced anywhere in Ukraine, as far as I know."

"Not funny, Donald," Rachel admonished. "Some of us are not fearless flyers, so kindly mind your business and get us there in one piece." She had lost her concentration due to fatigue and the ceaseless chatter of the others. Everyone soon settled down and pulled the black suede cloth eyeshades on and poked the little gummy plugs Donald had provided into their ears.

Rachel adjusted her seat back to a forty-five-degree angle and closed her eyes. While her body relaxed, her mind raced. What was she bringing them into? She hadn't been able to confirm anything with Lale or even Ben, for that matter. Maybe Ben was just traveling outside of Turkey and they'd arrive like fools with no one to see and nowhere to go. But wouldn't Lale have called her if that was the case? She had mentioned that Ben had to depart on a quick trip to Kiev and should be back in a day or two. But now a week had passed with no word from Ben and Lale had seemed quite concerned. Rachel resigned herself to following Lale's lead and not panicking until there was something to panic about. In reality, this was none of their business, and if something bad had indeed happened to Ben in Ukraine, how could a group of middle-aged folk from Persia, Turkey, South Africa, and the States possibly do anything more than muddy the waters and further exacerbate the situation?

She took a long slow breath inward through her nose. The chemically treated, recirculated air felt so unnatural, causing her to grimace mid-inhalation. Was she the leader of this group? Her rag-tag army of Ben's old good-time buddies? She knew that Ben would appreciate their efforts, but he certainly never would expect anyone to put themselves at risk for him. She wondered if and how Ben had evolved from the emotionally skittish guy she knew in college. She doubted he could have changed all that much despite what he had written about his survival of cancer. Yet how much could anyone be expected to really change despite experiencing a personally earth-shattering catharsis or trauma?

She thought about what she did know about his life during the intervening years since they had last been together. She had felt supremely guilty about cheating on him. It was like an ever-present weight she carried around with her. Not oppressively heavy but nonetheless there, it was like a little stone in her psychic handbag. When she analyzed it (and to prolong the metaphor), she hadn't given much weight to Ben's value as a person at the time of her unfaithfulness. He was a nice-looking, bright, fun guy from a background far different than hers. His being so familiar with New York, his world travels at such a relatively young age, his Corvette, and his easygoing self-confidence were what made him so attractive to her, a sheltered Southern belle who had rarely been outside rural Mississippi. She knew that other than the big bruise to his ego and a momentary sense of betrayal, there were no other discernible injuries he could have suffered. Hell, he had even admitted to having a brief affair with an older woman in Manhattan that same summer. Some lady who had sold him a brass bed, she remembered. But he had been so passionate in his guilt and plea for forgiveness that she had immediately caved to his tenderness. So when it was her turn to stray, she hadn't attached much significance to it because, in context, it really hadn't meant anything to her.

Years later, after a string of disappointing lovers and relationships, she was surprised to catch herself thinking about how life could have been with Ben. But maybe this was all fantasy, a form of cognitive recreation and self-indulgence mixed with intellectual masochism that had no basis in reality. They were essentially children at the time, students without responsibilities or financial concerns, no stress other than turning papers in on time and waking up in the morning and getting to a lecture. How would it have ended up over the course of thirty years and the tribulations of adult life? Births and deaths, jobs hired for and fired from, career changes and health problems, other lovers, perhaps, or the numerous temptations one faces very every day one is out in the world.

She knew the reality about him, at least the reality during the time of their relationship. Ben was a man who treated his friends better than his girlfriends. He always used to say, "Friends are for life. A lover's for one night." Where had she fit in? Where would she fit in now? Obviously not as a lover. He probably had several women in his life now. She had read that Istanbul was full of great beauty, both architectural and female. No, she didn't think that she wanted him as a husband or even as a lover.

Reclining in that luxurious cream-colored leather seat, she came to understand that she wanted not only what he represented back in the seventies—fun, insouciance, and self-confidence—but to try to correct him. To save him. To teach him to understand that for a permanent and successful relationship between a man and a woman, you needed to be not just friends as well as lovers but vulnerable and consistently present in each other's lives as well. This was what made a complete, lasting bond between two people. Apparently, Ben had never known that kind of partnership. She knew about his twin sister's death and his parents' breakup. Without doubt, she would have major scars to excise. More than anything else, these three characteristics were what all the other men in her life had lacked.

CHAPTER 27

Bamkiz and Johan

Present, flying to Istanbul

"What's your last name again?" Johan asked Bamkiz.

"Afrastani-Ehteshami-ed-Dowleh-Abbas-Mirza Safavi," Bamkiz replied, writing out his name after seeing the reaction on Johan's face.

"That's quite a mouthful, Bamkiz. And you apparently still haven't lost your virginity."

"What? My dear man, I'll have you know that I lost my virginity when I was a mere lad of nine years old."

"Could have fooled me, mate. You've still got your hyphens intact."

"If I had a dollar for every time some fool made that stupid pun, I'd be a rich man." Bamkiz rolled his eyes at the weak joke. "If it pleases you and is easier on your limited South African intellect, you can call me Peter English."

"Where did that come from? I can say your full name as well as anyone. Wait a minute, let me think for a second. Bamkiz Afrastanihyphenenteshamihyphenvoodooswamihyphenmizeria," Johan blurted out.

"Let's stick with Bamkiz or Peter English," Bamkiz smiled. "And I'll tell you where that moniker came from. Back at Duke, I had an English professor, Dr. James Kingham Burnside, during my freshman year. He liked to call the roll at the start of each class and assigned us seats. Rather a rigid fellow, but with the most mellifluous Southern aristocratic accent." Bamkiz closed his eyes for a moment in silent reflection, hearing Professor Burnside's voice in his head. "At the first class, he had the list of students in his hand and commenced reading and noting presence or absence of each of us. Yet after an Abramowitz and an Adams, he came to me. He just stared at my name. 'What is this?' he said in consternation. 'Is this some kind of a joke?' I stood up with as much regal bearing as I could muster with the eyes of about sixty other students upon me and said, 'My dear man, my name is pronounced Afrastani-Ehteshami-ed-Dowleh-Abbas-Mirza. I'm a direct descendent of the Qajar Dynasty which can trace its history back over five hundred years.' 'So you say, young man!' he snapped at me. 'But I'll be damned if I have to repeat that painful sesquipedalian moniker three times a week for an entire semester. So if your royal eminence will so indulge me, I will call you by a name that's easier on the tongue. I have a wonderful nephew named Peter. I've always been partial to that name. And since you have that lovely English boarding-school accent, your last name will be simply English. Peter English. A fine Anglo-Saxon name.' And ever since then, I was known on campus as Peter English. I got quite used to it, in fact. The women who knew me and liked me sometimes called me Bammy in that typically American affectionate way. My good mates called me Bam. Sounded macho, I suppose. My rugby sevens certainly embraced that. Put it on my jersey, in fact, rather than trying to fit the entire name."

"That's a nice story, Bamkiz. So despite your currently decrepit appearance and being a wee bit overweight, you're telling me that you're a tough fellow. Rugby. The game of those with a yen for brain damage, broken collarbones, and dislocated shoulders. Played a bit in secondary school myself. Before discovering the joy of catching really big fish with really light tackle. Do you know if Duke still has a team?"

"Indeed it does, Johan. And yes, I broke my collarbone and dislocated my shoulder, not to mention tore the cartilage in my right knee so badly that I am still limping around thirty years later. So I think you were smarter than me. Fishing seems like a much safer pastime."

"Safer so long as you don't get pulled overboard and eaten by a great white. We had quite a few of those off South Africa." (He pronounced his home country as one word, *Soufrika*.)

"We have a few around Sydney's beaches as well, which is why you won't catch me bathing in those waters. That and my reluctance to scare off the ladies by being mistaken for a walrus. I've heard tales that men such as me are built for comfort, not for speed. But I must admit, I do yearn for the crunch of an opponent's bone in a maul and the stink of sweat in the scrum. What a game! I'll never understand why the cheerleaders and sorority girls at the university always preferred the American football players to us sevens. Bunch of poofs if you ask me. What with all that padding and helmets and whatnot."

"Maybe because the American footballers always took showers after the games, mate," Johan chided.

As they flew northward, the two men chatted about their lives: Johan so committed to the growth of Ghana, dynamic, driven by financial success, and the heady feeling of influence on a national scale; Bamkiz, quite the opposite, content to live out his days in relative peace and tranquility after experiencing the terrors of the Iranian Revolution in late 1979 and most of 1980 before he was able to make his way to safety in Switzerland, England, and, later, Australia.

Bamkiz shifted uncomfortably in his seat. Finished with the ahi tuna salad that had been graciously served by the flight attendant, he loosened his belt and stretched out his legs into the aisle. "I was like a bearded puppy dog, following this energetic blond from Darwin all around the less inhabited parts of the country." He glanced over toward Johan to ensure that his audience was still conscious.

"I'm listening, just very relaxed," Johan said, catching the glance.

"I suppose I was the same as Ben," Bamkiz acknowledged. "Just not accustomed to commitment, especially when the woman requires work to keep her satisfied. Not sexually, of course. I mean physical exertion with life's little duties." He finally abandoned her on a walkabout near Alice Springs as the temperature reached 120° Fahrenheit and made his way to the coast, settling in a suburb of

Sydney. There he met another blond, this one a local girl, married, and settled down to a more or less quiet life. "Oh, Nanni, what a dear love of mine," he reminisced. "She found a lump in her breast and was gone within a year. Only thirty-two years old. Diagnostics weren't what they are now back then. She fought the good fight, and Ben flew all the way from Colorado to help us with everything. He was like a combination chauffer, housekeeper, telephone-answering service, home health-care provider. Anything we needed. He stayed until the bitter end and then helped me bury her. Finally, after a couple of months of tending to a very worthless me, he scooped me up and took me to London to drown my troubles in piss-warm beer and lukewarm mates who kept trying to fix me up with inappropriate women. I did manage to consistently beat them bloody in backgammon, which also helped support our lackadaisical lifestyle."

"How long did you fellows stay in London?" This was a story involving Ben that Johan had never heard.

"Ahhhh, I don't precisely recall," Bamkiz answered. "Perhaps two or three months. Then one morning Ben announced that he had to leave and serve his government. All quite cryptic, you understand. And off he went to God knows where, and I returned to Australia to fly solo."

He continued the recitation of his life story to Johan. In response to stepping in dog shit on numerous occasions while walking his Rottweiler around a nearby park, Bamkiz reacted by inventing a simple plastic mitt that could be used as a glove to pick up doggie droppings, turned inside out, and closed with a Ziploc system. After patenting his "A turd in the hand is worth two in the bush" glove, Bamkiz then lobbied the local government, successfully convincing them to pass an ordinance requiring people to clean up after their dogs or face stiff fines. News of this new law spread throughout Australia and was so well received that within a few years, all municipalities had passed similar laws. Holding the sole patent on his simple and inexpensive disposable glove, he earned a substantial income and virtually retired at the age of thirty-five. That lasted for about five years until, suffering from terminal boredom, Bamkiz reentered the economy with a vengeance, again as an inventor, devising online gaming software for young executives who lacked the formal management skills to control companies employing scores of undisciplined yet highly creative young people.

Bamkiz removed a small lightweight laptop from his satchel. "Observe," he commanded Johan. "In the process of designing software for your typical undisciplined yet well-educated and intelligent youngster, I came to understand organizational behavior at a uniquely high level as it applied to these kids. Control is not a weapon to be wielded by a superior."

Johan interjected, "Pardon me. So how does one get their subordinates to do their bidding?"

"Ahhhh, my antiquated friend. Herein lies the trick. Control should be applied in a more rewarding fashion, à la Pavlov. In fact, control must be exercised more like *out of control.* This is something that I am uniquely qualified to demonstrate, having lived out of control for nearly my entire life." He smiled broadly and spread his arms wide. Looking out the window at the clouds rushing by below, he told Johan how he had written a new management software program he called Herding Cats and sold it to tech start-ups, as well as the better known mid-to-large-sized companies with a strong youth culture. It was in a game format, with the winners qualifying for everything from Apple iTunes credits and Uniqlo gift cards to vacations in Ibiza and Iceland. "You know," said Bamkiz, "as far as I'm concerned, I've never worked a day in my life. And for that matter, I don't think that Ben has either."

Johan readily agreed, saying essentially the same thing. The two men silently appraised each other, appreciating the common life philosophy with their mutual friend, Ben Jacobson. The Persian was always fishing for ideas, though, while the South African just fished for grander blue marlins. Yet neither really knew what Ben was fishing for at the moment.

CHAPTER 28

Ben

Present, Eastern Ukraine

BEN STOICALLY ENDURED the beating by the partisans from the Donetsk and Luhansk People's Republics and the endless questions from Colonel Nevski. Finally convinced beyond a doubt that Ben didn't know anything current about US-Ukrainian military intentions for Eastern Ukraine, Nevski threw up his hands in disgust, admonished the partisans for wasting his time, and departed with the suggestion that they keep Ben and attempt to collect a ransom for him. "This American must have some rich friends. Perhaps you should contact that wealthy Turkish lady he's writing the book for. If she wants her book finished, she'll need the writer back."

While the partisans tried unsuccessfully to contact Lale, Ben sat, immobilized, strapped uncomfortably to the chair. The partisans had begun to threaten his friends, Kateryna and little Vlady, as they were unable to identify or reach any of Ben's other friends with money for ransom. Obviously, they knew how to find Kateryna and her son as they had already accomplished that the night before Ben was abducted.

Ben overheard, but couldn't understand, a heated conversation over a sat phone in Ukrainian with a woman he hoped was Kateryna. He gathered from his elementary knowledge of Ukrainian, different

159

from but essentially the same as Russian, that they had managed to get her attention. For the first time since he had been taken at the airport, he felt hopeful. Kat would certainly know who to contact and how to handle this situation with sensitivity and finesse. Just as long as she didn't think that she could handle this alone, he would be all right. Surely the embassy would come to his aid and negotiate his release.

Then he remembered with a chill that the US official policy is to never negotiate with terrorists. He and Kateryna had managed to have many of the separatists officially classified as terrorists by both the American and Ukrainian governments. This had certainly come back to bite him in the ass. So where did this leave him, other than somewhere between Luhansk and Donetsk?

Two hours later, the rusty metal door burst open, allowing a frigid but welcome blast of air into the large gray space. A vaguely familiar, tall, and elegantly attired officer strode authoritatively inside. In relatively unaccented English he said, "Mr. Jacobson, my name is Colonel Aleks Volosovik. I am here to take over from Colonel Nevski." He looked toward the group of partisans and barked an order at them. They grudgingly made their way to the door and stood outside like agitated guard dogs.

The feeling of hope evaporated. Thinking that he had finally managed to convince his captors that he was of no value as either a hostage or a source of information, he was back to where he started with a new inquisitor. The colonel found another chair and pulled it up to sit across from Ben. "Please call me Aleks," he began.

Unnecessarily, Ben explained to Aleks about how he had merely befriended a Ukrainian single mother and her son in Kiev, and somehow that had evolved into a geopolitical conspiracy theory with him at its center. Aleks nodded calmly, stood, and left the building without another word, leaving Ben stupefied, wondering what he had said or done to so immediately alienate this colonel. After spending several hours refining his explanation of the misunderstanding, he decided on the direct approach with this more sophisticated Russian officer.

At the next opportunity, as Aleks sat down across from him and offered him an unwanted cigarette, Ben began a monologue of his points of argument against the presumed theory while Aleks noted that Ben had apparently stopped smoking. The Russian placed the cigarette between his own lips, lit up, and slowly, pensively exhaled the smoke toward the ceiling. What else had he missed in his observations of Ben in Istanbul? He removed his elegant gray wool coat and draped it over the back of his chair, not wanting to accidentally drop any ashes on the fine garment.

"Colonel Volosovik, Aleks, my friend, I believe that we are sitting here due to a truly global misunderstanding."

"How so, *comrade?*" the Russian inquired with a sarcastic emphasis upon the archaic Soviet word.

"If you will permit me to outline my explanation until its conclusion, I will afford you the virtually unlimited opportunity to pose follow-up questions when I'm finished."

"Proceed," Aleks affirmed.

"True, I often worked in concert with certain US intelligence agencies, as I believe you and Nevski either did, or currently do know, with either FSB or the Foreign Intelligence Service, your SVR. True. I first came to Turkey while working at the State Department, but not as an intelligence officer. Merely as an international real estate manager looking for land to buy for a new US consulate in Istanbul and subsequently for land for a new embassy in Ankara. True. I have had close relations with a succession of American diplomats in Istanbul, Ankara, and Kiev. True, I have had some contact over the years with members of the Turkish Parliament. True, I also performed the same functions and duties in Kiev and have met and remained friends with many private Ukrainian citizens as well as some government officials in that city. True, I often socialize with diplomats resident in Istanbul from many other countries, such as Spain, England, France, Belgium, and the Netherlands. But if you look at my diplomatic résumé, you will note that I also served extensively throughout Africa and South America, the Balkans, Scandinavia, and Western Europe. But that was my job then, not now—to establish new embassies and consulates and improve the physical security conditions of existing embassies and consulates.

"I was not a spy. I was a real estate guy. And now? I'm still not a spy. I'm just an ordinary American expat living in Istanbul, writing articles, columns, and a family biography, commissioned by a beautiful Turkish lawyer who happens to be an honorary consul—the operative word being *honorary*. I stay out of politics and keep my opinions to myself. I do not attempt to become involved in the internal politics or external concerns of any nation, America included. I have a best friend who is a single mother living in Kiev. I help out with her young son. He's a great kid and doesn't have a father. So to prevent your further wasting your time trying to figure out just exactly what I'm doing here and why I'm doing it, I have a proposal. Come with me to Kiev, and I'll introduce you to them, and you will see that I speak the truth. I'm not a spy or any kind of foreign agent with some agenda for or against Ukraine, Turkey, or Russia."

As soon as those last words left his mouth, Ben regretted uttering them. He shifted uncomfortably in the chair and gazed out of the small dirty window to his left. The bare lightbulb over his head cast a sickly yellow brushstroke over their faces. Damn! The last thing he needed was to get Kateryna and Vlady involved in this. On the other hand, they must already know about them. Otherwise, how had they been so successful in luring him to Kiev? Who had paid the nocturnal visit to Vlady's bedroom?

"I know all that, Mr. Jacobson. *We* know all that," Aleks corrected himself. "Of course, I will report this conversation to my superiors, and we will see if they are swayed by your candid explanation and will see things in a different light." He leaned forward with his hands on his thighs. "But you have to admit that you certainly have a unique profile—the perfect cover for an intelligence agent. However, in this case, for ironic and totally unrelated reasons, I tend to believe you. The problem for you is that not only must I convince my superiors but also their counterparts in Turkey and Ukraine. We will speak again tomorrow." Aleks rose and athletically put his arms through the sleeves of his tailored overcoat and started to leave. At the doorway, he turned and once more offered Ben a cigarette. "I will ask these men to unbind you and see that you are properly fed and have the opportunity to clean yourself. My apologies for not being able to offer more luxurious accommodations." He left without looking back toward Ben.

There! That was it. The first confirmation that there was a triumvirate of intelligence agencies looking into the innocent yet seemingly clandestine activities of one Ben Jacobson—US citizen, resident of Turkey, godfather of a Ukrainian boy. Unfortunately, Ben was not buoyed by this news. Rather, it depressed him more than ever. His story was too full of coincidences to be believed, just as he wouldn't believe it himself if he was sitting on the other side of the table. Likewise, the facile acquiescence of Aleks didn't seem to ring true. It was almost as if it was easier for Aleks to let Ben believe that his scenario was accurate in order to camouflage another motive entirely. Ben may have been naive, but he wasn't stupid.

CHAPTER 29

Rachel

Present, Istanbul

Customs and passport control proceeded perfunctorily due to their arrival in the private aircraft at the executive airfield. As she rolled her big wheelie into the bright Istanbul sunshine outside Istanbul's Hezarfen Airfield, Rachel instantly understood who was waiting for her. Replete in Chanel, the thin, black-haired, fortyish woman behind the big Persol sunglasses standing by the Mercedes van talking on her cell phone had to be Lale. Hezarfen was Istanbul's only airport exclusively for private jets, located a little south of the main Ataturk airport that also catered to an international clientele.

To avoid the possibility of being ambushed by the paparazzi that hung around the general aviation terminal at Ataturk airport in the hopes of catching some celebrity or member of the social elite with someone not his or her wife or husband returning from a romantic getaway, Lale had instructed Donald to choose this lesser-known airstrip. Lale had wisely decided that a quiet entrance into Istanbul would be best for Rachel and her eclectic entourage.

Lale raised a finger to Rachel in a *bir dakika* (just a minute) gesture, which, in any event, was unnecessary because Rachel was waiting for the rest of the group to come out of the building. Lale had arranged for a second vehicle driven by Ipek for the travelers, and a very tall, well-dressed man who introduced himself as Nusret began to load the valises into an old Range Rover parked just to the rear of the van. Rachel had heard about Lale's incessant cell phone usage but came to understand that it was because she was the consummate organizer. So long as this call was on their behalf, she could hardly complain.

Rachel was fully inculcated with southern hospitality and was curious about the similar level of gentility she had heard was characteristic of the Turks. As the volume of Lale's voice rose to an extraordinary level (she was to soon learn that this was typical of Turkish women and cell phone conversations), she began to wonder if she had been misinformed. This woman was seriously upset with someone.

A small Lear screamed overhead on its ascent, momentarily drowning out Lale's histrionics, and Rachel turned to see Donald, Jimmy, and Howman emerging from the small terminal building and directed them toward Nusret and the Range Rover where Ipek was organizing the loading and translating for the travelers. Lale finished her call and rushed over to engage Rachel in an embrace that was overwhelming both in terms of its physical strength and the familiar scent of an intriguing mix of almond and white magnolia, with just a hint of orange blossom and vanilla. Rachel decided it would be politic if the first words spoken to Lale were complimentary. "I love your perfume! What is it?"

"Elie Saab's L'Eau Couture," Lale replied, clandestinely sniffing Rachel to see if she was wearing anything. Whatever had been so upsetting to her five minutes ago apparently had been forgotten.

Not to be taken for a foolish American, Rachel quickly acknowledged the smell test and said apologetically, "Honey, I've been traveling for seventeen hours, I know I need a shower, and my Yohji Yamamoto Love Story has long since worn off. And I'd be damned to waste any more Yohji on these pitiful excuses for men."

The two women laughed conspiratorially, newly bonded by their femininity and an appreciation of these expensive scents. "I love that Yamamoto bottle. I saw it in Beymen the other day. So sweet, the purple."

Rachel wondered who or what Beymen were, assuming that some men of a certain bey class or something were selling perfumes. She was to learn later that it was an upscale department store in Istanbul that could hold its own with Saks Fifth Avenue or any other major purveyor of quality fashion. She was also surprised that Lale could be blithely talking about perfume when Ben had been missing for more than a week and her guests were here on a rescue mission, not for a party. It was only much later that she was able to understand that this was Lale's coping mechanism. Shopping, thinking about fashion, talking of superficial things as her means of self-medicating. If a trial or contract negotiation wasn't going her way, Lale would inspect the shoes or earrings or business suit worn by the other party's attorney. This was her trick for refocusing.

Rachel, on the other hand, was feeling completely out of her element and fighting the urge to slip into hysteria. Fortunately, jet lag was having a calming, almost soporific effect. The familiar trappings of her everyday Southern lifestyle were far behind her. Turkish was such a strange-sounding language with all the words ending in *cam* (pronounced "jam"), *caz* (pronounced "jazz"), *cak* (pronounced "jack"), *tamam* (okay), *yok* (pronounced "yolk," meaning "not"), *evet* (yes), *hayır* (pronounced "higher," meaning "no"), *tabı tabı* (pronounced "tubby tubby," meaning "of course"), and all the people's names ending in sounds like *oğlu* (pronounced "oh lew," meaning "son of"). Not to mention all the *canım* (pronounced "ja num," meaning "my dear") and *aşkım* (pronounced "ahsh kum," meaning "my love") and the men calling each other *abi* (pronounced "ah bee," meaning "older brother" even if the person wasn't necessarily older, more like the Turkish version of the American slang *bro*.) As a professor of literature, she had taken note of the fact that this was a language spoken and written in the passive voice, with the verb always at the end of the sentence, as in "the ball red the boy kicked."

Rachel had been prepared to see throngs of headscarf-clad women, but these were nowhere to be seen at the private jet terminal. It looked pretty much the same as the terminal in the States from which she had departed with Donald and the friends. Once she entered the city proper, she assumed this would change. As they drove into Istanbul, navigating through the insane traffic congestion, she reflected on the fact that within any single part of the city containing merely three acres, more people could be found than in all of Colliersville's three square miles. She thought of all the human personal histories. The tragedies, the success stories, the drama, the characters, and both the everyday life as well as the extraordinary events that these people would experience—riots, protests, funerals, weddings, births, betrayals, relationships, suffering, and joy. The stuff that life was made of. Were these lives the same or far different from their counterparts in rural Mississippi? This was her professor of literature's mind at work—looking for the poetry in every moment and the story playing out in front of every backdrop.

When they drove past the ancient aqueduct connecting the watershed of the northern forests to the heart of Istanbul, Rachel was overwhelmed by a sense of human history and wished that they would have more time to be tourists and do some sightseeing to all the places she had read about. The Grand Bazaar, the Cistern, Topkapı Palace, the Ayasofya (also known as the Hagia Sophia), and the Blue Mosque were all places on her bucket list. Would she see them on this visit? Probably not, and she immediately felt guilty for even thinking like that. In any event, their route did not take them anywhere near such places as all were located in the Sultanahmet historic district, and they were weaving through traffic on the Trans-European Motorway from Büyükçekmece to the Levent business district and then down on local streets to the little neighborhood of Arnavütköy.

Rachel kept one part of her brain focused on the discussion among Lale and her colleagues as they argued about how best to proceed with respect to the hunt for Ben. Although she was the one who had put this somewhat aimless, disorganized mission in motion, she was so distracted by the sheer size of Istanbul that she found it hard to participate in the conversation. She watched passively as the highway diminished to boulevards, and then boulevards shrank to narrow, twisting streets barely wide enough for the van to pass between the haphazardly parked cars lining both sides of the road. Rachel gradually felt her focus return, as if the narrowing lanes had compressed her mind rather than just the streetscape. The men were questioning Lale about Ben's last known whereabouts, her phone calls with Kateryna, whether the US embassy in Ankara had been contacted (it had), and what Interpol had to say (nothing). As they pulled up in front of the charming little Villa Deniz, disembarked from the Mercedes Vito, and collected their bags from Nusret, it was clear to her that they were looking at a completely different kind of reunion than originally anticipated.

CHAPTER 30

The Friends

Present, Istanbul

RACHEL WAS TAKING stock of their current situation, counting people, counting luggage, and, as three *kargalar* (ravens) landed on a telephone pole across the street, counting crows. The appearance of the crows confused her. Years ago, a student had presented a paper to her about superstitions involving birds. Rachel vaguely remembered that one crow was unlucky, two crows meant something funny was about to happen, and three crows portended death. This disquieting thought was interrupted when an old topless black Jeep Wrangler suddenly screeched to a halt behind her. Jumping back from the curb, she turned her head to see two improbable-looking fellows start shouting their greetings to Howman and Jimmy. Johan and Bamkiz had arrived, completing the team.

Aydin, Ben's Turkish friend who owned the Villa Deniz hotel, came barging through the building's ancient French doors. He gave a big hug and innumerable kisses to Lale and introduced himself to the others. He and Bamkiz understood immediately that they both had their origins in Persia and, also being of a similar body type, had an instant rapport. Johan, having met both Lale and Jimmy on prior occasions, gravitated toward them. Even though she had been the organizer, Rachel felt somewhat isolated and stood apart as greetings and introductions were made. She followed the group into the hotel and climbed the twisting, creaking stairs to her room, exhausted, desperate for a few hours of sleep. The famous and infamous Turkish men in the old black-and-white photographs that lined the hallway seemed to follow her with their eyes. Earlier, when she had begged her companions to allow her to take a longish nap, they had immediately agreed and made a plan to reconvene in the lobby at 8:30 p.m. and walk to a nearby *balıkçı* for a fish dinner overlooking the Bosporus. After confirming that her translation services were no longer needed, Ipek left with Lale to return the Mercedes van to a rental agency.

Fifteen minutes after Rachel's door closed behind her, Aydin, Jimmy, the Blitz, Donald, Johan, and Bamkiz were huddled around an old wrought iron table on a second-floor balcony of the hotel, overlooking the busy street locally known as Birinci Cadessi (First Street) and to everyone else as the shore road. Although barely twenty-five feet above the sidewalk, they could clearly see across the Bosporus to the identical road that ran along the Asian side of the strait. About a dozen men were lined up along the seawall with their long fishing poles jigging for sardines, elderly couples strolled arm in arm in the waning sun of the afternoon, and screeching gulls coasted on the breeze reliably provided by the constantly changing currents of the dark, broiling water. Occasionally, a vendor with a rickety pushcart would call out, advertising the simits, grilled corn, or chestnuts he was selling.

Aydin knew nothing about Ben's prior activities in the intelligence community other than what he had heard and originally dismissed as typical Turkish rumor and gossip. He now listened intently to the conversation among the other men, some of whom had known Ben for virtually all his life.

"So you guys know about Ben's friends in Kiev. This woman named Kateryna and her son, Vlady," Jimmy said.

"Never heard of them," Johan replied, as Bamkiz nodded.

Aydin elected to join the discussion. "I've met them both. Ben had them come to Istanbul twice during the past year, and they stayed here in the Villa Deniz. Intelligent, pretty woman, little rascal of a boy, *ama çok tatlı* (but very sweet). I observed that she and Ben had an interesting relationship. Clearly, they loved each other, and he doted over the boy, but it was obvious that Vlady wasn't Ben's son. He was way too smart and handsome."

The others chuckled at that while digesting this information. "So what was their deal?" Johan asked.

"Now that's the million-dollar question," Jimmy responded. "I used to give Ben a boatload of shit about Vlady really being his son, but he really slapped me down about that, reminding me that he had probably been sterilized from the chemo and radiation when he had cancer years before Vlady was even born."

"Yeah, I kinda suspected something like that, too, but then I remembered what Ben went through with that and how they had asked him if he wanted to freeze some sperm. So I dropped that idea," the Blitz added.

"Well, did he?" Bamkiz asked.

"What? Freeze his sperm?" Jimmy replied.

"No, he didn't," Donald intoned in a low voice. "There will never be another Ben Jacobson."

"*Allah korusun* (God forbid)! Two Bens," Aydin exclaimed. "The world could not stay on its axis with two Bens."

"Let's get back on track, gentlemen," Jimmy suggested. "We're talking about why in hell Ben was rushing off to Kiev so early in the morning after a phone call from Kateryna and what's happened to him since. I spoke to her on the way here from the airport, and she hadn't heard anything, and the US embassy wasn't being particularly helpful. Fuck! They didn't even acknowledge that Ben had been working with the Ukrainians to nail some bad guys in the eastern part of the country a coupla years back. And he and Kateryna even got some kind of official commendations that were presented by both governments. It was like…uhhh…ya know, public record. Not in the newspapers or anything like that, but I saw the photos from the awards ceremony."

"What are you saying?" the Blitz interrupted. "Ben was back in the game as some kind of double agent or what?"

"No, man. Ben wasn't any double agent. He worked for us, and Kateryna worked for her country. They had been like Mr. and Mrs. Smith for years. You know, the Angelina Jolie, Brad Pitt spy movie, 'cept they never fought with each other. Never even the slightest argument. Always had each other's backs. Ben never gave me any specifics, but it didn't take a rocket scientist to figure out they were up to some scary shit."

Bamkiz leaned forward. "Do you know anything more specific, Jimmy? Like what was the last thing that they worked on together? Give us some kind of a starting point."

Jimmy leaned back as a waiter brought them a round of Efes beers. The glasses, frosted and coated with a patina of ice, were labeled with the blue, gold, and white oval logo of the largest local beer company. As soon as he left, Jimmy looked around the table. "I'm not sure what I'm allowed to say here. We've got a South African-Ghanaian, a Turk, an Iranian—"

"Persian!" Bamkiz loudly interjected.

"Okay, *Purrrrrsian*," Jimmy acquiesced sarcastically. "But since I don't think that this is currently a matter of American national security and I'm not under any duty to maintain confidentiality or anything, I'll tell you what I think. And as I tell you, keep in mind that I'm sort of thinking out loud." And Jimmy proceeded to relate what he knew—and thought he knew—about Ben and Kateryna and their fight against the Ukrainian separatist movement.

CHAPTER 31

Kateryna

Present, Kiev, Ukraine

THE ROOM WAS dimly lit by an antique Russian desk lamp, the walls a somber gray, matching the sky outside. Drawings and watercolors produced by Vlady during various stages of his young life competed for space with framed photographs of Cappadocia rock formations, ski holidays in Mürren, Austria, and Mediterranean beaches with Ben and Vlady in silly poses. The vanilla scent of a small votive candle permeated her office. Kateryna was feeling frustrated, frightened, and nervous. She had exhausted all her contacts in the government ministries, the police, and the US embassy with respect to obtaining either their cooperation or any information about Ben's whereabouts and the identity of who had taken him. She had enlisted their mutual friends in Kiev to follow up every bit of information they could find that might remotely provide a clue as to Ben's fate.

Vlady was still traumatized about the night visitor to his room and what had befallen his godfather. He was becoming a thorn in her side as since the night the mysterious visitor had come to his room, he had attached himself to her hip (she felt that those two English expressions she had picked up from Ben were quite apt in this case) and was making it extremely difficult to attend many of the meetings she had scheduled with officials who might be of assistance. She sat at her desk in the office, silently crying as a light staccato of raindrops began to patter against her office window.

Kateryna did not consider herself to be a strong woman. Following the precepts of Sun Tzu, she felt it best to be conservative with her self-assessment. She recognized her strengths but resented that they were purely intellectual and emotional rather than practical and physical. Her emotions were always getting in her way, clouding whatever cognitive abilities she possessed and in the present case, impeding her analysis. She slapped her hand down on the desk, feeling the sharp sting of pain. Focus!

At virtually the same moment that her hand made contact with the wood veneer, the storm loudly announced its arrival with a robust thunderclap, the wind riding hard on its heels. The trees outside her window shed their remaining leaves; some adhered to the pedestrians below as they scurried for cover from the rapidly intensifying rain. All color left the sky except for an ominous charcoal gray—really more of a tone than a color—and the smell of ozone infused the air mere seconds before lightning struck the golden dome of Saint Michael's just uphill from her building. Suddenly, she felt profoundly empowered.

While obviously she knew that the slap of her hand had not brought on the powerful storm, at some subliminal level the power and fury of the cloudburst infused her with positive energy and an irresistible motivation to travel to the east of the country. She strongly intuited that Ben was in that direction. It had to have something to do with the work that she and Ben had done on behalf of their respective governments in identifying and locating the leaders of the separatist movement. She would pack her car with supplies and head in the direction of Luhansk, where she believed their greatest enemies could be found. Although she was not 100 percent comfortable with the idea of undertaking such a journey without the companionship and protection of someone like Ben, she knew that she would be better off alone than with any of her local male friends or former colleagues from the Ukrainian intelligence community, most of whom were well-intentioned, but not particularly effective if things became violent. Like her, they were all analysts, not soldiers. And as a woman traveling alone, she could dress down, keep quiet, and fly under the radar.

Kateryna began working the phones with a vengeance, only getting up from her desk to remove the thick green cable-knit sweater Ben had bought her for her birthday. She incessantly brushed her hair back behind her ears, a habit she indulged whenever she was anxious. In the midst of arranging for her mother to come into the city and take care of Vlady for a few days, she remembered something so obvious that it made her shake for a moment. With today's generation of cell phone technology, virtually everyone was connected to everyone else, if not actively by voice, then passively by GPS and proximity to cell towers. Kateryna decided to begin her search by contacting an old boyfriend who was a tech manager at Kyivstar, the largest Ukrainian telecommunications company.

Andriy was several years younger than her. He worshipped her, a fact that ultimately led to the failure of their relationship. He was more of a sycophant than a boyfriend and ridiculously insecure. She didn't like that in a man. They had ended it peacefully, and she had kept in touch, if for no other reason other than allowing him to be immeasurably helpful on tech-related issues, such as the one at hand. She called him at his office.

"Are you warm and dry, Andriy? I hope that you weren't caught in the storm." She correctly intuited that it would be best to express some concern for his well-being before hitting him with a request for a difficult favor that was to benefit another man.

"Oh yes, Kateryna dearest. And you? Are you fine? Where have you been? What have you been doing? I have tickets to a Dynamo Kyiv match tonight. Would you like to come with me?"

Kateryna rolled her eyes at his old-fashioned way of speaking and suggestion she accompany him to a football match, a sport she found to lack in both scoring and personal relevance. "Well, actually, Andriy, I must ask you for a small favor. Can you help me track the location of a cell phone if I give you the number, using GPS perhaps?"

"No problem. Give me the number, darling."

The term *darling* made her cringe, but she quickly gave him the cell numbers of Ben and her driver, Viktor. Then she remembered that Ben would call that a twofer.

CHAPTER 32

Ben

Present, Eastern Ukraine

IT HIT HIM like a thunderbolt from the storm that had just arrived from the west. Not only was the Russian the fellow he had shared a smoke with in Dushanbe, he was also the same man with the cap and coat who had been eyeballing Ben and his car from the doorway of the Chinese restaurant near his office not long ago. Now he was thoroughly confused. He had been under the impression that his predicament was due to some confusion about his professional status and the reasons for his travels and his relationships in Istanbul and Kiev. But perhaps this wasn't the case. Somehow the same man had been hovering around him in three completely different locales without ever coming out and defining his interest or intentions.

Obviously, they didn't want him dead. The Russian had attempted to interrogate him, both directly and passive-aggressively. Such efforts had been futile, partially because Ben was completely ignorant of the purpose and certainly without any hidden agenda. So why go to all the trouble of having a thug like Yura kidnap him, kill Viktor the driver, beat him and hold him hostage in this dark, dank place for so many days, and then, when fear didn't produce any answers, reverse course 180° and have the Russian come with his transparent attempts to play good cop?

The Russian, Aleks, had allowed him to walk around a bit, albeit always with Yura and his bullpup submachine gun. They had released him from the uncomfortable confines of the metal chair and thrown an old mattress and wool blanket on the floor to let him sleep horizontally. He had never been so appreciative of this simple pleasure, the musty stench of old bedding a small price to pay to eliminate the painful neck cramps that came from sleeping in a sitting position with his head lolling from side to side.

At the moment, Ben was pacing back and forth across the twenty-meter length of the garage. He was frustrated, bored, angry, and sad. Outside it was raining hard, and the rapid fire sound of the drops on the metal roof was deafening. The noise only served to further annoy Ben. He felt that he had literally entered purgatory. Ben knew from his university studies in comparative religion that purgatory was considered a state or condition, not a place. Therefore, although he was essentially a nonbeliever in any religion, he didn't think that he was technically in *the* purgatory but rather that this entire bizarre experience was some kind of a test of his soul. Could he endure the beatings from Yura and the quiet insistence of Aleks, not to mention the separation from his friends in Istanbul and lack of communication with Kateryna and the rest of the world?

He remembered an old episode of the television series *Game of Thrones* in which the dwarf, Tyrian Lannister, was being held captive and was given the opportunity to make a confession. His captors expected him to confess the attempted murder of the boy, Bran Stark. Instead, he surprised them by delivering a history of personal transgressions, which was highlighted by his detailed explanation of how he had ejaculated in the turtle soup being served to the House of Lannister. This memory, in turn, led Ben to a brief reminiscence of a porno movie made by a college friend who had, together with several other men, ejaculated onto a large salad bowl to provide a very special organic dressing as a prelude to the film's requisite bacchanalian orgy. Eventually, it was the feeling of disgust at this rather unsavory memory that returned his mind to the present.

Ben knew that he was terminally bored and also realized that this was an extremely hazardous condition to be suffering from given his present circumstances. The challenge was to keep his brain active and immune from depression and other nonproductive states of mind. Back to the concept of purgatory. Yes, he was physically alone and a prisoner, but nothing was preventing him from experiencing complete freedom and companionship if he unbound his mental constraints. He knew from reading about people kept in isolation for extended periods of time that the mind tended to reorient itself into an artificial reality that accommodated the captivity of the body. This had both positive and negative effects. If guided toward the light, it kept one from being hopelessly lost in despair. Ben tried to remember everything he had learned while reading a primer about Kabbalah that Lale's brother, Mustafa, had given him many years ago. At the time, he hadn't taken it very seriously, and certainly he hadn't become a student of Kabbalah, partially because he distrusted anything that came into vogue due to the publicity generated by celebrities like Madonna, Gwyneth Paltrow, and Demi Moore, all sporting their little red string bracelets. He had even worn one himself although more for the cocktail chatter value than any real belief that it would protect him. Unconsciously, he glanced down at his wrist. No red string, just the irritated skin from his ties.

Ben had read in the little book that Kabbalah was an ancient amalgam of teachings that purported to reveal how the universe and life are inextricably coordinated. The word *Kabbalah* means "to receive"; thus, it's the study of how to receive fulfillment in life. Ben had attempted to explain the teachings of Kabbalah to his friend Jimmy Jason while they were taking a break halfway up the Riffelhorn near Zermatt. He asked Jimmy if he had ever been overcome with the feeling that he wasn't as fulfilled as he had the potential for—the feeling that the harder he tried to achieve such fulfillment, the more it eluded him.

While perched on a narrow rock ledge three quarters of the way up the crag, Jimmy and Ben spent the next twenty minutes enjoying the brilliant sunshine and talking about the concept of personal fulfillment, not just being temporarily happy or having a fleeting sense of peace and well-being. Ben was trying to explain to Jimmy the importance of making an actual connection to the Energy, his concept of God, and maintaining that connection so as to obtain a permanence of fulfillment. "My understanding of Kabbalah, and keep in my mind that I'm below neophyte level, is that it's like a recipe for living. It teaches that all the branches of our lives—health, relationships, professional career—are derived from the roots and trunk of the same tree." This was what Ben considered the Tree of Knowledge that every kid learned about in Sunday school, the central library of life that contained the technical, metaphysical, and spiritual tomes that explain how the universe works at its most basic level.

Ben told Jimmy, "The Kabbalah teaches universal principles that apply to all peoples of all faiths and all religions regardless of ethnicity or where you come from. The beauty of studying Kabbalah is that you can't be forced to think in a particular way. There can be no coercion in spirituality." The men looked across a great valley toward a facing peak and were silent for a few minutes. Acknowledging the philosophic oxymoron of his explanation, Ben explained to Jimmy, "I like Kabbalah in its most simplistic form because it apparently applies to anyone of any faith, even someone like me. And you know how I feel about organized religion." Jimmy looked at his friend, nodded with a smile, and went back to staring across at the dirty brown glacier below. "It's all about connecting to the Light, and not about following strict religious precepts, superstitions, or mandates from long-dead prophets and their acolytes."

Jimmy nodded, muttered with dramatic sarcasm, "Whatever, dude. The beauty of nature releases your inner profundity," and then more loudly announced, "On belay," and prodded Ben with the toe of his climbing shoe to get him going back up the cold brown rock wall.

Ben's mind returned once again to the present. It was difficult to connect to the Light in such dim surroundings and under such opaque circumstances. He decided to conduct an inventory of everyone he had wronged who could even remotely be considered as responsible for his capture and detention. Unlike Rachel, he was not one to make lists. This required a mental discipline that did not come naturally to Ben's normally haphazard style of analysis.

Although Ben was generally amicable, he had a short fuse when it came to certain kinds of people. He hated bullies as he himself had been bullied several times as a boy. Ben reminisced about the time he was confronted by Bruno Signatelli, an older kid on the playground when he was in fourth grade. He came home from school frightened to death and told his father that he was going to get badly beaten someday soon. Unfortunately for Bruno, Ben's father immediately went out and bought a punching bag for the basement gym and gave him a short course in fist fighting for success. His father kept it simple. "The guy who lands the first punch to the other guy's nose wins the fight. Period. I don't subscribe to that old maxim of letting the other guy throw the first punch because if he knows what he's doing, you'll be flat on your back in a second. Hit 'em in the nose as hard as you can with your entire body behind it. When he goes down, if he tries to get up, give him a shot to the ear and tell him that the next one will send him to the dentist for a new set of teeth." This was typical of the highly pragmatic advice always provided by Ben's father.

This made complete sense to a nine-year-old boy, who practiced for hours without gloves on that little punching bag. A right to the nose and a roundhouse left to the ear. The next day, when Bruno strutted up to him with his entourage trailing behind, a nasty smirk on his face, saying, "I'm gonna put your face in the dirt, Jacobson," Ben followed his father's instructions to the letter.

Bruno had a good twenty pounds on Ben and didn't go down the way Ben's father had promised. Instead, he only dropped to one knee, blood streaming from his nose. He screamed, "I'll fucking kill you, Jew boy!" Fortunately, he had his eyes closed in pain. Then Ben remembered to throw the second punch, a wide, looping slam to Bruno's right ear that had the desired effect of stunning him and sending him to the ground. The entourage of older kids scattered when Ben turned around to confront them with a feral gleam on his face. It was then he learned the power of optics. In other words, what you see isn't necessarily what you get. If they had seen him in a true light, they would have torn him apart. Instead, they saw a violent little maniac, not a bad street rep to have when you weighed less than one hundred pounds and stood well under five feet tall.

Ben also learned the power of politics and the fickle nature of cliques. As is usually the case, no one particularly liked a bully such as Bruno; his friendships were based more on fear than fun. When the teachers came to investigate the fight, there was unanimity in the students' reports, even from Bruno's former entourage. Bruno had been picking on everyone and had thrown the first punch at Ben.

The second encounter with a bully was a mere two years later when Ben was in sixth grade. A mean little kid named Bobby Aronofsky suspected that his *girlfriend* liked Ben better than him. Notwithstanding the fact that Barbara Laine barely acknowledged Bobby's existence and could hardly be categorized as a girlfriend, he ambushed Ben as he was walking down a crowded hallway with his arms wrapped around a stack of books. This time, it was Ben who caught the punch in the nose. He dropped his books and could barely avoid vomiting from the pain. "Stay away from Barbara" was all that Bobby had said.

Ben was mortified that a physically inferior kid had gotten the better of him through planning and stealth. He decided that he could play the same game, likewise in the open and in full public view. Bobby had a biology class immediately after Ben's class with the same teacher. There was a vertical window in the middle of the classroom door which afforded a view of whoever was about to enter from about ten steps back. Ben stood just out of view at an angle from the door, waiting for his adversary to approach. The door opened outward, and as Bobby was reaching out to grab the knob, Ben came running at the door with his weight behind it. The door hit Bobby square in the face and sent him reeling backward into a group of eighth graders who didn't appreciate a sixth grader crashing into them and spilling their Cokes. When they saw who it was, they made short work of Bobby, stuffing his puny form into a nearby locker and latching the door firmly shut.

But Ben's current predicament wasn't some dish of revenge served extraordinarily cold by the likes of Bruno Signatelli or Bobby Aronofsky. He wondered what his father would advise him to do now. Obviously, Ben didn't think that anyone from his past in the US would take the trouble of intercepting him in Dushanbe, Istanbul, or Kiev. No, this was revenge as much as twenty years in the making. It had to be someone from between 1998 and 2000. That was when he made that visit to the Alpha Group interrogation facility after the arrest of Chechen commander Salman Raduyev. Why else would the Russian be involved as a common denominator and also explain the involvement of a Chechen like Yura? Who had he crossed during those two years?

CHAPTER 33

Rachel

Present, Istanbul

SHE WAS AN exceptional cook, courtesy of long hours spent in the kitchen with Aunt Annie. As Annie grew older and more forgetful, it was up to Rachel to always check the ingredients and cooking times of their dinners shared with friends and family. As time went on and Aunt Annie grew weaker and less attentive, Rachel began to experiment with Annie's traditional Southern cooking, adding more exotic herbs and spices and substituting quinoa for rice, salmon for catfish, and truffles for the locally farmed shitake mushrooms. She deconstructed traditional recipes and reconstructed them to her own personal tastes.

Oddly, perhaps it was the deconstruction part that proved most challenging for her. She knew that she couldn't simply replace coriander with cumin and that coriander is the same as cilantro leaf although the taste bears no resemblance to that of its seeds. Each variation of every ingredient had its own unique proportions, and she couldn't assume that two teaspoons of one would equate to two teaspoons of another. Consequently, through trial and error, Rachel became an expert at breaking down a recipe into its most basic elements as a prerequisite for reconstructing it into a more innovative and enticing meal.

While engaged in this process, she often compared herself to a reality checker of sorts. One who understands the fundamental nature of things and thus achieves proficiency in the ability to discern reality regardless of its manifestation. This process was difficult enough when employing the senses of taste and smell, but the reality of the present conundrum was made more complicated by the lack of information and the different cultures and people involved. So again, she went back to the basics.

She needed to deconstruct the present situation. A missing friend. A phone call in the middle of the night from a friend of his in a different country. A mysterious midnight visitor to a child. A plane boarded and disembarked. A missing taxi driver and his vehicle. Kateryna had called Lale not twenty minutes ago and informed her that a friend at one of the local cell phone providers had traced Ben's cell phone to a gravel shoulder along the motorway into Kiev. The police said that they were looking into it but wouldn't share any really helpful information. Typical. Kateryna's friend also advised them that he had seen a call from the taxi driver's phone that registered on a cell tower in a remote location in Luhansk Oblast in easternmost Ukraine. They told the police about this. However, due to the politically unstable and violent conditions there, no local police officers were available to conduct a search.

Sitting at the large table with Ben's friends at the fish restaurant *Mavi Balık*, overlooking the roiling waters of the Bosporus Straits below, she withdrew from the conversation and speculation and began to reassemble what they knew of Ben's situation. Unfortunately, unlike one of Annie's recipes, she had damned little to work with. At least on the surface.

But Rachel knew that here in the former city of Byzantium, things were most probably not as they appeared to be, nor could the vast agricultural lands of Ukraine be compared to the fertile fields of Mississippi. The French cliché was *cherchez la femme*. As a professor of literature, albeit Southern, she had read widely and had remembered the trivia that this phrase probably originated with Alexandre Dumas père in *Les Mohicans de Paris*, written in 1864 and used in the form *cherchons la femme*. In the present case, it wasn't a single femme;

it was at least three who all intersected in one way or another with Ben: Ipek, Lale, and Kateryna—not that she suspected any of them of being directly responsible for Ben's disappearance. However, she did believe that somehow the answer lay hidden with at least one of them. It was a shame that although she had the right idea, she had the wrong women or, to be more precise, woman. Young woman.

CHAPTER 34

Ben

Present, eastern Ukraine

A SUPINE BEN was stretched out, thinking, on his pungent-smelling mattress. The odor was an annoying distraction, obfuscating focus, frustrating mental acuity. His own odor, emanating unrestrained from his clothing, unchanged since the beginning of his ordeal in Eastern Ukraine, was adding to the potpourri. The room was dimly lit by the suffused light of false dawn at 5:30 a.m., not that he had a watch or knew the exact time. He slowly rose and ambled over to the bucket against the wall and took a piss.

When he had exhausted the contents of his bladder, he circumnavigated the room until he came back around to the metal chair and sat down. Ben craved music. He was missing the soundtrack of his life. He imagined himself at the symphony, his favorite place for free association and reminiscence. He conjured up his cognitive jukebox and pushed the button for Johannes Brahms's Concerto No. 2 in B-Flat Major for piano and orchestra, Opus 83: IV Allegretto grazioso. Lively yet not overwhelming. Good "wake up and concentrate" background music, especially since he hadn't heard any music since he unplugged the earbuds from his iPod after landing at Boryspil Airport.

Ben's head began to clear after about ten minutes. It was the concentration required to actually remember the entire movement that had a therapeutic effect. The visual of the little rolodex of songs from a Seeburg Wall-o-Matic table-side extension reappeared in his head and he selected the 2009 hit by Mumford and Sons "Little Lion Man." He thought it particularly apropos of his current circumstances. *"Weep for yourself, my man. I really fucked it up this time. Didn't I?"*

Ben felt like he had definitely fucked something up. He just didn't know what it was. He rarely failed to accept blame if it was his and generally didn't try to avoid the consequences of his actions. He might try to mitigate the damages but never ducked responsibility. This was like the time he was prosecuted for *stealing* a library book from the reserved reading room at Duke. Not only was he completely innocent (for once in his life), but it was also absurd that he would filch a book that he already had purchased from the school bookstore weeks before and was sitting on the shelf in his dorm room, plain as day. The charges were finally dropped, but he never forgot the presentiment of malicious prosecution by the university equivalent of the Star Chamber or the awful feeling of impotence in the face of misguided authority.

His recent inventory of potential enemies made between 1998 and 2000 hadn't yielded any realistic prospects—some interesting memories, to be sure, but nothing of value to his understanding of why he was being held by Alek and the Chechen.

Ben also felt the first pangs of depression creeping over him. Why hadn't anyone come to rescue him? Yesterday, he had overheard several men being positioned around the building; he assumed they had been recruited as additional security. This was confirmed when he had tried to follow Yura out the door last night and was abruptly pushed backward by an armed man he hadn't seen before. Yura had just laughed, saying, "The puppy is trying to follow his master." Meanwhile, Ben had no idea of what was going on in his immediate surroundings as he really wasn't sure exactly where he was located. He couldn't believe that Viktor's cell phone hadn't been traced because from the brief glimpses he had from outside, he knew that the taxi was still parked behind the rear of the structure. He didn't know that Yura had found the phone while rummaging through the glove box and tried to call his family back in Chechnya. Then he thought of where Yura had thrown his iPhone after shooting Viktor. Assuming that his phone must have been found by now in close proximity to a corpse, some investigative action had to have been initiated.

This was only the second experience he'd ever had with depression in his life. This time, it wasn't as insidious as with the cancer and chemo. He really felt it beginning to grow quickly. To exploit the phrase, he was wallowing in his abandon. He enjoyed the black humor of imagining a little devil and a tiny angel sitting on his shoulders, the one on the left saying, "Nobody cares about you" and the one on his right whispering, "Don't worry, everybody loves you and help is on the way. Hang in there."

As often happens with depression, Ben wanted to sleep, so he returned to the mattress and lay down. Curling into a fetal position, he pulled the threadbare blanket up to his shoulders and closed his eyes. As hard as he tried, he couldn't consciously conjure up the Seeburg again and listen to music from its little carousel of flip charts. He dozed, listening to the sounds of morning instead.

CHAPTER 35

Friends and Investigators

Present, Kiev, Ukraine

THE UPSHOT OF the dinner meeting the night before was that as unofficial leader of the group, Rachel elected herself to travel immediately to Kiev and join forces with Kateryna while the others remained behind in Istanbul to provide support to Lale and logistics as needed. Lale had put up quite an argument against staying at home, but the friends convinced her that her connections in Turkey far outweighed her value in Ukraine. Jimmy Jason insisted on coming along since he and Ben had literally held each other's lives by the proverbial thread so many times as to grant him the status of being the most physically trustworthy with the best understanding of Ben's behavior under stress. His having won bronze and silver medals in back-to-back Winter Olympics and being a certified trainer in long-gun medallion shooting certainly qualified him in the event firearms were required.

The fact that Rachel had known Jimmy for almost as long as she had known Ben provided her great comfort with respect to having a traveling companion to yet another place where she wouldn't be hearing the kind of Southern drawl to which she was accustomed. The Blitz was well acquainted with firearms and would also be a team member. There was no argument about Donald accompanying them as he was providing the transportation and pilot. Should they need to travel elsewhere in Ukraine, his ability to allow them to set their own schedule was invaluable.

Kateryna and Vlady met Donald, Jimmy, Howman, and Rachel at Boryspil Airport in Kiev at eleven in the morning. Kateryna was waiting behind a line of taxis in a borrowed Range Rover, with Vlady watching a video on an iPad Mini in the back seat. Kateryna had already set her GPS for 15 Holosiivska Street. After quick introductions and a constant stream of questions in perfect English by Vlady along the way, they arrived at the Central Police Department of the Holosiivskyi District. It was an extraordinarily nondescript five-story building constructed of large gray faux stone concrete with frameless windows and faceless guards flanking the door. All the ancient linden and oak trees had been cut down years ago as a result of a government *security assessment* that had determined that terrorists and criminals could hide behind the tree trunks and shoot at police officers. For some bizarre reason, whoever had prepared the report had failed to take into account that the trees were located so near the building that if a criminal had gotten that close to police headquarters, he was probably already in handcuffs or about to detonate a suicide vest. They were met by the US embassy's regional security officer, Karen Lassiter, and an obviously Western-educated police detective who introduced himself simply as Colonel Zakharchuk.

As is typical of most children, Vlady was somewhat intimidated by the austere nature of the police building and the number of serious-looking adults, many of whom were in uniforms and carrying sidearms. RSO Lassiter, herself a mother of a nine-year-old son, recognized Vlady's distress and sought to reduce the tension a notch with some chatter directed at Kateryna regarding the school that both boys attended. At hearing the name Pechersk, he immediately relaxed and focused on her. Vlady, who was immeasurably more comfortable now that he had recognized another schoolmate's mother, began participating in the conversation with the adults. Zakharchuk, himself almost as skilled an interrogator as RSO Lassiter, sat back quietly in appreciation as the woman gently extracted all the facts and observations as were possible to obtain from an eight-year-old boy. Adding to the challenge was the fact that Vlady had been awakened from a sound sleep and had only an understandably foggy recollection of those nocturnal events.

Thirty minutes later, the door opened and Kateryna's friend Andriy from the cell phone company entered. He didn't have anything new to provide in terms of information, except that the battery of Viktor's phone had apparently died as they were no longer able to detect a signal. Zakharchuk began making excuses for the police being unable to send a team to the last known whereabouts of the phone when RSO Lassiter politely but firmly interrupted.

"We have arranged for Beauregard Corp, a private American security firm, to accompany me to the last coordinates received from Kyivstar."

"I will fly you and any other security personnel there at no cost, but Rachel, Jimmy, Blitz, and I must come along," Donald insisted. "We can leave early this afternoon."

"That will not be possible," Lassiter responded.

"Why not?" Kateryna and Rachel asked simultaneously.

"Because the US government cannot be using private aircraft and intentionally putting US citizens and their personal property in harm's way," Lassiter answered.

"Bullshit!" Jimmy growled as Vlady's eyes opened wide at the expletive. It always surprised him when grown-ups spoke like that.

"I wanna go too!" the boy demanded. "Ben is *my* friend. I have a Star Wars light saber too."

"He's the friend of all of us," Kateryna soothed him. "But I will go with Rachel, Howman, Donald, and Jimmy, and you will stay with Ms. Karen's son because you both have school," she rationalized for him. "I will need to help translate for them, which I know that you can do just as well if not better than me, but school comes first. That's our rule."

"No school, no rules, make fools," Vlady intoned mechanically, something Kateryna had drilled into his head when he returned from the first day of school upset that strangers were telling him what to do. This was how he reminded himself that adults were still in charge of him when it came to safety and learning.

Karen Lassiter envied the way that Kateryna had effortlessly taken control of the argument. She wished that she could garner this much respect from her own child. She reconsidered for a moment and made the executive decision that the convenience of the private jet and the government savings on transport justified the risk and breach of protocol. She only hoped that she didn't lose her job and pension over taking what amounted to uncharacteristic initiative for a bureaucrat. The alternative was drafting a classified cable from Post to the Assistant Secretary of Diplomatic Security and the Assistant Secretary for European Affairs at the DOS, waiting for several other bureaus to digest it and provide their opinions, and getting a reply cable to be drafted and transmitted to her. That could take days and might even result in the wrong answer. Part of the problem was that this was a private American citizen, not a State Department official. And even if it had been, Washington wasn't always sufficiently aggressive with their efforts to protect their own. Yes, better to take a risk. It was only her career that was at stake. Failure to take action was not an option. Lassiter stood up and slowly circumnavigated the table, speaking as she walked. "Kateryna, please stay here. My Russian is fluent, so we will not require your translation assistance. The Beauregard security team is already in Luhansk, waiting at the general aviation terminal at the airport for my instructions. I'd much rather be physically present than try to direct this operation from my office in the embassy. Will you be joining us, Colonel Zakharchuk?" She looked down as she said this, knowing that his answer would be negative.

"No," the Ukrainian officer replied curtly. "I have instructed a friend, the Luhansk captain from the Ministry of Internal Affairs, to meet your team at the airport and to provide whatever additional security and logistics assistance you may require. But don't expect much. He's somewhat preoccupied at the moment solving *Ukrainian* problems."

It was all that Rachel could do to refrain from slapping the officious son of a bitch in the face for that last comment. If this wasn't a Ukrainian problem, what in God's name was? An American national kidnapped within its borders in the middle of what essentially amounted to a separatist revolution? Lassiter made eye contact with her, communicating her empathy while warning her to stifle her emotions. Kateryna, on the other hand, ignored Zakharchuk's remark. She was accustomed to such dodges by Ukrainian officials, especially police officers who, if not being offered a sizable bribe, preferred to look the other way when private trouble erupted. Vlady stewed in silence. He was still upset that he would not be going along to rescue his friend.

CHAPTER 36

Ben

Present, Eastern Ukraine

BEN DREAMED INCOHERENTLY, a series of random images and brief actions. Both friends and relatives, as well as many unknown faces, appeared to him in a visual cacophony of overlapping, unconnected events from his past. Random and indecipherable symbols punctuated these *dreamlets*, each more confusing than the last. A rapid-fire somnambulistic slideshow of a young man with piercing blue eyes and enormous hair eating a Fluffernutter sandwich, with a pale blond Scandinavian woman with equally blue eyes; two boys with windbreakers, the older in yellow, the younger in blue, holding a Spanish mackerel and a kingfish; a man standing on a high mountaintop, ice axe raised above his head triumphantly; polo players racing side by side down a field after a white ball; men in suits seated around a dark wooden table at a signing ceremony of sorts; a teenager standing in front of a light blue Jaguar XKE circa 1970; a dark-haired man and his young son at the helm of a sailboat; and a pretty light-brown-haired woman in cap and gown at her college graduation, diploma proudly in hand. A soundtrack came and went, songs from the Byrds' album *Sweetheart of the Rodeo*, strangely interspersed with music from Prince's *1999*.

Then strangely, there came a continuation of the dream about a nurse and a Morgan roadster he'd had the night before his cancer surgery. The nurse once again handed Ben the keys but, this time, climbed into the passenger seat next to him. In slightly Turkish-accented English, she introduced herself as Arzu. Turning on the radio to Power FM, a Turkish pop station, they listened to a medley of 1950s to 1960s era car-related songs beginning with "Little Deuce Coupe" by the Beach Boys:

Well, I'm not braggin' babe so don't put me down.
But I've got the fastest set of wheels in town.

Then a few stanzas of "Little Old Lady from Pasadena" by Jan and Dean and back to the Beach Boys singing,

Well she got her daddy's car.
And she cruised through the hamburger stand now.

Next, Commander Cody and the Lost Planet Airmen with "Hot Rod Lincoln":

My pappy said, "Son, you're gonna drive me to drinkin'
If you don't stop drivin' that Hot Rod Lincoln."

And War's song "Low Rider":

All my friends know the low rider.
Take a little trip, take a little trip.
Take a little trip and see.

And finally, "Maybellene" by Chuck Berry:

As I was motivatin' over the hill
I saw Maybellene in a Coup de Ville.

On and on, a trip through time with the best car songs ever performed: "Little G.T.O." by Ronny and the Daytonas, "409" by the Beach Boys, "Pink Cadillac" by Bruce Springsteen, and, of course "Mustang Sally" by that wicked Wilson Pickett.

"I never heard these songs before," Arzu told him. "I always before prefer the female vocalist songs, like those of Lana Del Ray. But I like these. So…epic." Ben leaned over and kissed her in approval.

Ben not only dreamed in color, he also could have conversations, feel sensations, and, on occasion, smell. Sometimes, he couldn't distinguish his dream from reality for a few days afterward until they faded from memory. This dream was no different. It was at the level of virtual reality.

Ben and the nurse drove into the surreal sunset until night fell. Winding through the trees of the Duke Forest, she suddenly stripped off her uniform and stood on the seat completely naked, her strawberry blond hair behind in the wind like the tail of a comet. This all seemed so real to Ben, and his dream's alter ego acted as if it had indeed occurred before. His memory was on rewind. Images, music, all streaming in a high-speed video downloaded from Ben's unconscious—no time wasted on buffering, no fee or subscription required, and no recollection of how this event had actually happened, albeit with a different car and a completely different girl.

The dream, or rather series of dreams that connected with each other like episodes of the same dream, seemed to take hours. Ultimately, Ben, the nurse, and the Morgan faded to black and he slept deeply, dreamlessly.

Then voices outside, speaking unintelligibly in Russian, awoke Ben. He mistakenly thought he had just fallen asleep, at most a few hours ago. He was surprised to hear Aleks shouting at him, "Wake up, my friend. It's four o'clock in the afternoon! You will sleep through the whole day? I have someone here that I want you to meet."

Surprised at the passage of so much time since his early dawn perambulations, Ben struggled to his feet and rubbed the sleep from his eyes. Before him stood a teenage girl perhaps fifteen years of age. Modestly dressed in jeans and a blue cable-knit sweater under a baggy gray hoodie with the logo of Lomonosov Moscow State University, eyes downcast, she looked eerily familiar.

Aleks cleared his throat. "Ben, meet your daughter, Irina."

CHAPTER 37

Jimmy

Present, American Embassy, Kiev, Ukraine

WHENEVER THEY CLIMBED or skied together, Jimmy was the logistics man. Although he was naturally the better climber, it was Ben who had introduced him to bouldering and, later, big wall climbing. Jimmy was always into the latest gear, which was a good thing since Ben would have been content to depend on old ropes and harnesses. In fact, Jimmy was such a CEO when it came to strategizing a climb that Ben had become accustomed to letting Jimmy not only be lead climber for all the difficult pitches but also choosing their routes and organizing their trips. It hadn't taken much convincing to get Rachel to delegate the Ukrainian operations side of today's endeavor to Jimmy. RSO Lassiter brought him, Rachel, and the Blitz to the embassy for a preliminary meeting with the other members from her diplomatic security team.

There had been some initial grumbling about a mobilization for a private citizen, but after they were informed that Ben was former DOS and the one responsible in no small part for where they were currently sitting, all cognitive dissonance quickly evaporated. Documents affirming Rachel, Howman's, and Jimmy's agreement to keep all actions and conversations confidential and releasing the embassy and Department of State from liability for any injuries or death were quickly prepared and signed. Although it was unusual for the department to allow civilians into what occasionally amounted to a war zone, much less provide them with some logistical support, it wasn't unheard of, hence the form documents that Lassiter had been able to download from the State Department's Bureau of Legal Affairs.

The room was simple yet perfectly equipped for their needs. The newest in fluorescent lighting, whiteboard on three of the walls for writing, as well as a secure landline, VOIP, and sat phone connectivity. A large video monitor was embedded in the fourth wall with PIP that allowed for real-time viewing of video feeds and a detailed map of the eastern part of the country. The room also had a large-format printer that could produce maps and photographs in full color. The furnishings were a standard OBO/PDCS/DE interior design medium gray color composite top conference table and ten matching gray fabric chairs that no longer tilted back due to the distracting effect of a room full of people nervously rocking back and forth. No involvement of the State Department's Art in Embassies program was in evidence on these bare walls. Jimmy decided the best way to describe the conference room was technically functional, elegantly Spartan.

Following the multiple simultaneous conversations that were occurring around her, Lassiter's assistant was quietly preparing a list of equipment they might need. It mostly involved communications gear, medical supplies, tactical vests, body armor, and light arms. They would also take two or three GoPro video cameras to document the action in the event of casualties or serious damage to private property. Somewhat annoyingly, Jimmy was second-guessing everyone on the matter of equipment.

The embassy's commo officer had been in touch with John Beauregard, the owner and team leader of the private security group, and learned that, at least for the moment, all was quiet at the Luhansk airport. Two Sikorsky S-92 executive jet helicopters had been leased from a private broker for a surprisingly realistic price and would be waiting in Kharkiv in the event an extraction from somewhere other than the Luhansk airport was required. Kharkiv was approximately three hundred kilometers northwest of Luhansk, just under an hour flight for the Sikorskys.

Despite his well-intentioned efforts, Jimmy was clearly out of his depth when it came to preparing the technical logistics for such an operation. Nevertheless, Lassiter continually showed him the politeness of asking his opinion on nearly everything. He didn't understand that this was more a means of bureaucratically covering her ass than seriously thinking that he could make any valuable contribution to the success of their impending mission. No matter, he was enjoying every minute of it and trying to act very serious.

The challenges consisted of their lack of information regarding not only the conditions under which Ben was being held but also Ben's actual physical condition: sick, injured, unconscious. Could he walk, or would a stretcher or wheelchair be required? Suddenly, a shout was heard in the room and a remarkably clear black-and-white image of a Quonset-style building came into view, courtesy of a drone provided by a member of a friendly intelligence service. Jimmy and the Blitz immediately recognized Ben emerging from the building, with his typically poor posture and loping gait. Although the image of the man was tiny, he appeared to be moving well, accompanied by a tall man and a small woman of indeterminate features and age. Together, they slowly walked around the building before returning inside. The tall man was walking with a military bearing, close, observant, but physically apart from the other two. As they came back around to the front, Ben stopped and began performing a series of stretches and calisthenics, as if to show anyone watching that he was alive and quite well.

The commo officer had immediately sent the video clip to Washington for further, more detailed analysis. Who were the man and woman? There were several other men standing around the building at strategic points, but all were obviously security, and there hadn't been any communication between them and the principal three players in this real-time confusing drama.

Even after Ben and the other two had reentered the building, Jimmy's eyes remained riveted on the screen. There was something familiar about the young woman. He just couldn't discern what it was. "Can you please play that again?" he asked.

The entire clip lasted slightly more than five minutes, yet it was long enough for Jimmy. He chose a series of frames that consisted of perhaps twenty seconds of Ben and the woman looking directly at each other while they walked and talked. "There!" Jimmy showed the room. "Right there."

"What do you see?" Lassiter asked. "I must be missing it."

"Look at Ben's way of walking, and then look at the girl," Howman said.

"How do you know it's a girl and not an adult female?

"Because she's walking lightly, not with the measured gait of an adult. Look at her hair. The way she flips it with her head and keeps moving it around with her hand." Jimmy looked over at Lassiter. "You don't do that, but maybe you used to before you grew up into what you are now." Jimmy realized that perhaps that didn't come across the way he meant it when Lassiter immediately scowled at him. "I mean, now you have a senior executive position, you are in control of people. Your kid, these folks, your body language says it all. You are an authority figure. That girl in the video, she's the lowest figure in that totem pole of people. She's even deferential to the security guards. See the wide berth that she gives them, only glancing at them surreptitiously. And she's totally focused on Ben. But also with great respect and some distance."

"Okay," Lassiter said. "Run it again."

"But more importantly than just pointing out the apparent social hierarchy, look at the *way* she walks," Jimmy noted.

"She walks just like Ben," Lassiter said in wonderment to the now silent room.

CHAPTER 38

Ben, Irina, and Aleks

Present, Eastern Ukraine

SHE WAS FIFTEEN years old, spoke excellent English, and acted and looked remarkably like him. It was unsettling, to say the least. Especially considering that he had been casually conducting his sex life under the erroneous belief that he was sterile from the cancer treatments so many years ago. Her way of speaking was a reflection of her mother, a White Russian from Belarus who had immigrated to Moscow with her family just before the collapse of the Soviet Union. Irina had Ben's deep-blue eyes and her mother's sultry smile and pale skin. Understandably shy and far more modest and unassuming than her somewhat aggressive mother, Daria, who spoke incessantly of finding a husband and moving to the States. Their affair had lasted just ten days in Dushanbe, where she had been posted as a political officer in the Russian embassy. Ben had known that she was a spy—she had made that obvious—and he had dutifully reported that back to his superiors in Washington as well as the local intelligence community representative. But for the most part, they were on the same side, at least as far as the Iranians were concerned, and not surprisingly he had been encouraged to be open to her attention. As a single man with an uncomplicated social status, this wasn't a problem for him. It became clear to her that Ben wasn't going to whisk her away to a life of leisure in America when he informed her of his departure for Washington, yet they had ended things amicably. He'd never heard from Daria again despite having given her his contact details. Perhaps due to a passive-aggressive mistake on his part, unfortunately those coordinates had not been completely accurate.

Approximately six months after Ben left Dushanbe, Daria had begun showing. Recalled to Moscow a few weeks later, neither she nor any of her coworkers who knew of her brief relationship with the American had made any attempt to find or contact Ben. That was how she had wanted it. Daria was a proud woman. If Ben didn't want her, she didn't want him.

Irina had known nothing about Ben until after her mother had died in a car accident the previous summer. It fell to her uncle Aleks to assume her guardianship. Initially, Aleks had respected Daria's wishes and not revealed the identity of Irina's father, but now the burden of caring for a teenager had begun to take its toll. Handling a very young girl wouldn't have been a problem, but Irina's turbulent entry to the headstrong teenage years was more than he could handle alone. When he was posted to Eastern Ukraine, it became impossible. Thus, it was Aleks, her mother's closest confidant, who had revealed the truth to Irina.

Aleks had always kept close tabs on Ben, especially his relocation from Washington to Istanbul. When he observed Ben's frequent trips to Kiev from Istanbul and his warm relationship with the boy, Vlady, a plan began to form in his mind. He would drop a few hints about the American responsible for the arrest of some of the original separatists to a Russian officer he knew who covertly ran several paramilitary groups in Eastern Ukraine. He would carefully orchestrate a harmless event that would have a high probability of bringing Ben to Kiev. Once in Kiev, he would redirect Ben to an area where he could safely evaluate Ben's interest in reuniting with a daughter he never knew he had. In retrospect, a stupid and irrational plan, overly complex and dependent on too many unknowns. The biggest mistake Aleks had made was to involve Yura, who had all the diplomatic skills of a T. rex and the sensitivity of a storm trooper. But Yura had been willing and available and had been obsessively loyal to Aleks ever since he had secured his release from a detention facility in Grozny. Why the ignoramus had felt impelled to kill the taxi driver and beat Ben was beyond Aleks's comprehension. And then the surprise intervention by Colonel Nevski completely derailed his plans for a peaceful reuniting of Ben with his daughter. There was an American expression that Aleks had learned during his time studying Americans, *clusterfuck*. Well, if ever there was a word in any language that accurately described what had happened here, that was it.

To make matters worse, Yura had also misinterpreted Aleks's feelings regarding Ben and the affair with Daria. He had thought that Aleks intended to punish the American rather than to merely detain him until he could bring the girl to meet her father. Too bad that Ben had no way of knowing that. He still detested the Chechen and didn't trust Aleks as far as he could throw him.

For the time being, Ben was being friendly but restrained with Irina. Despite all evidence pointing in that direction, he was still unsure if this was really his biological daughter or just a clever social engineering project orchestrated by Aleks and some obscure office in the Russian intelligence apparatus with an abstruse goal that at the moment was unfathomable to him.

Yet Ben wanted to believe she was his daughter. He had never had children and didn't particularly like babies. But his relationship with Vlady, what Lale had called "practicing to be a grandfather," had been a rewarding experience for both of them, and an older kid might be fine too. And the cancer doctors hadn't said he would definitely be sterile from the chemo and radiation. Just that he *might* become sterile. Not wanting children at that time of his life, he had probably just heard what he wanted to hear. No pregnant girlfriends. However, he didn't want his hair-trigger emotions to influence his judgment. Better he proceed *yavaş yavaş*, as they said in Turkey. Slowly, slowly. The question was, what to do next?

Aleks called one of his men and asked for some tea for the three of them. After some sharing of personal history between Irina and Ben, he took advantage of a break in their conversation.

"Ben, I apologize for keeping you, quite literally, in the dark. But as you can understand, it was difficult to bring Irina here under the current political circumstances. I had to be sure that she would be safe—that *we* would be safe. Please believe me that I never intended for Colonel Nevski to insert himself, but understand that once I found him here, I had to devise an exit strategy. I apologize sincerely for all the discomfort you experienced. And Yura, well, Yura turned out to be a stupid, sadistic animal beyond my control."

Ben, still amazed at the level of fluency Aleks demonstrated in English, nodded in understanding although not agreement or forgiveness. He had suffered a lot at the hands of this man, and he still had not been allowed to contact Lale or Kateryna. This concerned him greatly. He turned to face the Russian, his back to the girl. "Please allow me to call my friend Kateryna. She can let everyone know that I'm all right. They've probably called the embassy and God knows who else. This was really a fucked-up plan of yours, Aleks. What were you thinking?" Ben asked quietly.

"The mistake I made was in relying on others to understand and follow my orders. Maybe I should have just looked you up in Istanbul and said, 'Ben, remember Daria? Well, she was my sister, and she recently died, and you have a teenage daughter from her and now you must take care of her.' But I couldn't take a chance that you would turn me over to MIT or the CIA and refuse to even meet Irina. There was simply too much at stake." Aleks walked outside for a few minutes and then returned to sit across from Ben. "I've asked one of the men to drive to a village nearby, call a relative in Donetsk, and have them call your friend in Kiev and explain a little about the situation. And tell her that you are fine, of course."

Ben understood that Aleks was worried about a trace on the cell phone signal, yet for obvious reasons he remained silent about Viktor's phone in the glove box of the taxi. "Ya think that's gonna make everything all right?" he asked with no small amount of sarcasm. "You had that oaf, Yura beat the shit outta me, you kept me tied to a friggin' chair. What was that all about? My friends must be worried to death."

Aleks looked him squarely in the eye and said, "I had to be sure."

"Of what? You did the math. You don't need to be a PhD in biology to figure that one out, Aleks," Ben snarled.

Irina was looking down at the floor, silent, trying to melt into the background. She was mortified by the exchange between her uncle and her father. She had known the truth the moment she entered the room and cast a glance at Ben. For her, it was electric. She was shocked to learn of Ben's treatment at the hands of her uncle and even more distressed that her mother had never told her the truth. Whenever she questioned her on the subject of a father, a distraction arose or an outright lie about the death of a beautiful young man from London or Paris or Stockholm. Anything but the simple truth. What was the big deal anyway? She had several friends with mothers but no fathers or fathers and no mothers. This was fairly typical these days. Nobody cared.

Irina brought her left wrist to her face. She inhaled the remaining light scent of apricots from the cologne she had sprayed on herself to smell nice for the first meeting with her father. She'd hoped that he'd like it, but it seemed that he didn't even notice it. Maybe he was too surprised, and he certainly didn't smell too good. After all, she'd had a few months to digest the fact that Uncle Aleks knew the whereabouts of her father. Ben's awareness of her could be measured in minutes. Okay. So she forgave him on that point. But she wouldn't be so quick to forgive her uncle. "May I say something?" Irina politely interrupted in a low voice.

Both men abruptly turned to face her, making her even more nervous than she already was.

"Mr. Ben. Please excuse my uncle for his rudeness," she glared at Aleks as she said this. "This isn't about either of you, really. It's about me. Have you even thought about what I might want to do? Where I want to live and go to school? What I'm wondering about and how I feel about maybe losing my friends? Losing my mother?" Irina looked over at Ben. "You probably don't even want me in your life. I'm not stupid. I know how it is. You already have a life, a family, friends. How would you explain me?"

"Actually, Irina, I haven't given it much thought at all. I'm still processing the fact of your existence." He smiled as he said this to take the edge of his words, honest as they were. "But other than my brother from another mother, Jimmy, I don't really have a family," he added.

"*Processing?*" Irina said incredulously. "You think I am a thing to be processed, like cheese or something?" She lightly scratched her head. "What does 'brother from another mother' mean? You had the same father?"

"No. It just means a best friend who's as close as a real brother, or even closer, sometimes."

"I see. So, no real Uncle Jimmy."

"You can still call him that if you wish. He would probably like that, in fact."

Aleks had kept quiet during this exchange. Strong sunlight was focused like a laser through the small window across the room from where he sat, momentarily blinding him from seeing their faces. "If you will permit me." He stood and exited the building, leaving Ben and Irina alone.

"What are we to do with you?" Irina said in a sing-song voice accompanied with a smirk. "That's probably what you were going to say, yes? But that might be too big a cliché, even for you."

"How do you know what clichés I have in my repertoire? How do you even know that word?"

Exhibiting uncanny maturity and intelligence, she replied, "It doesn't matter. That's what they always say in the British and American films when presented with something like this situation. I don't think that you need to make any decision right now. So let's talk about what I need, what I want. I've been thinking about this meeting with you for some time. Rehearsing how it would go, actually."

Ben was nonplussed by her directness and pragmatism. "Okay," he acknowledged.

"Okay. I like okay. Simple truth. Short and swift."

"Short and sweet," Ben corrected.

"Oh. Yes. *My bad.*" She winked. "Short and sweet. My uncle must soon leave to work with those who want to coordinate a trade agreement with the new government in Kiev. He was surprised at what happened in Crimea several years ago. He doesn't think that would be good if it were to happen here in the east. A big war with Ukraine. That is never good. War, I mean."

"No. War is never good," Ben agreed.

"I have many friends at school in Moscow. I don't want to lose them by going somewhere far away with you. So I prefer to stay there. And I think that you could move there and find a Russian wife. Isn't that what single American men always want to do? Find a beautiful Russian wife?"

"Not me," Ben responded. "I don't want a wife. *Any kind of wife.* Too complicated." He paused. "And Moscow is way too cold. Move to Moscow? *Not gonna happen.* That's another English expression."

"Thanks for the lesson, *Father.*"

This girl was feisty. Yes, sir. Ben was beginning to really like her attitude. Attitude, he believed, was almost as important as a sense of humor. "Here's what I suggest we do. Let's do what an old friend of mine always used to do when confronted by a complex problem. Let's make a list."

"A list?"

"Yes. A list of all ideas we can think of with regard to what we can do. Then we will make a kind of sub-list of what could go wrong, or right, with each idea. Then we can make a sub-sub-list of the best ideas, being the best ideas because they have the fewest bad things that could happen with them. Then we will sit down with your uncle and make a decision. How does that sound to you?"

"Sounds good."

And they got to work, drinking the strong tea, moving around to make the best use of the natural light from the little window, and sharing the earbuds from the tiny iPod Nano she had brought with her on this trip to a new life. Ben noted how appropriate it was that the first song she played was "It's Time" by Imagine Dragons.

CHAPTER 39

Rachel and the Beauregard Team

Present, Eastern Ukraine

WHILE BEN AND Irina were becoming better acquainted with each other and exploring options for her future, Rachel, Jimmy, the Blitz, and the security team had landed without incident in Luhansk. The sky was slightly overcast with a light gray patina of clouds, and it was a few degrees warmer than it had been in Kiev. Colonel Zakharchuk's friend, the local police captain, made a brief appearance and then abruptly disappeared after making a call on his cell phone. They conducted a last check of their gear before loading it into the assortment of vehicles that had been obtained by Beauregard's group. Due to the exigent circumstances, the firearms would be carried by the team members in their respective vehicles. Virtually, all the commo gear (with the exception of their personal cell phones) was loaded into a battered Toyota pickup that was to be the lead vehicle. In addition to a second well-used Toyota truck, two old Russian sedans had been readied.

All the vehicles' windows were strategically cracked to make it difficult for bystanders to identify the passengers. They were also equipped with new virtually silent mufflers painted the reddish brown of rust to maintain the appearance of age while affording at least a modicum of stealth. Unfortunately, the time pressure had resulted in a few incomplete weld joints so that, at least in the old Lada Vaz to which Rachel had been assigned, a tolerable but nevertheless uncomfortable amount of benzene fumes was allowed to permeate the interior of the car.

Great, Rachel thought. *I will be meeting Ben for the first time in thirty-five years smelling like a gas station attendant.*

Jimmy and the Blitz were carefully picking through a cache of weapons with one of the security men. They wondered what kind of firearms Ben's captors possessed, speculating on everything from AKs to old revolvers and maybe some light shotguns used for shooting birds and rabbits. The Blitz was more concerned about what he could use to stop a bullet rather than shooting one. Jimmy, in addition to his Olympic event, had experience with hunting turkeys in the woods of Maryland, duck and geese on the Eastern Shore, elk in Colorado, and target shooting with semiautomatic pistols at the range. He had opted for a lightweight 9 mm Glock and an older Colt M4A1 assault rifle without full auto capability. The latter he had chosen due to safety concerns for the others. He'd never fired anything on full auto and no telling what might happen if things got hairy, and he became excited and started spraying the area with bullets. The Blitz found a massive Sig Sauer P220 .45 caliber semiautomatic handgun holstered in a worn brown leather shoulder strap with four extra magazines and decided to forgo a long gun. Blitz was a close-in shooter.

Lassiter and John Beauregard, the security firm's team leader, were engaged in a heated argument about the correct route. Beauregard was opting for the most direct approach while Lassiter wanted a more circuitous route to avoid detection and make it more difficult for anyone to follow them without being seen. After compromising on taking the main roads for the first half of the journey and then switching to back roads that wound between farms for the remaining ten kilometers of the drive, they set off. The vehicles remained within view of one another, but at all times a good 150 to 200 meters apart. They had agreed that the three vehicles behind the lead truck, a decrepit blue Toyota Hilux, would alternatively pull off the road, watch for following cars, and then rejoin the convoy at a different place in the queue.

In the last car, Rachel and her fellow passengers sat silently as the rural scenery flashed by. Each was engaged in contemplation of what might be encountered when they reached the location where Ben had been spotted. She prayed to whatever god might exist that when confronted by this group of trained security personnel with their state-of-the-art Kevlar vests, high-tech assault weapons, and sexy black commando outfits, the outgunned rebels would quietly surrender and take to the hills. Not that there were any hills that she had observed from the satellite images. She was crammed into the back seat with two huge men cradling assault weapons, making her extremely nervous. In an effort to assuage her anxiety, she tried to casually chat with them. "That doesn't look like anything my daddy used for ducks," she cooed at the man on her left. He had introduced himself as Isaac Hayes, a strange name, she thought, for a Scandinavian-looking fellow from Duluth, Minnesota.

He told her, "It's a FN SCAR CQC like the Navy SEALS use. The thing under the barrel is a grenade launcher. And inside that cutoff shotgun-looking launcher is a very nasty grenade." With an unsettling grin, he added, "So long as you stay behind me, you'll be safe."

Not wishing to talk about weapons any further, she turned to the man on the right and asked, "Do you have a wife or girlfriend?" The man turned to look at her quizzically. To him, the question seemed unfathomably inappropriate for the current circumstances. He never did understand women.

Isaac Hayes said, "LoMo? Girlfriend? He's gay. Doncha know, honey? If you're lonely, you need to talk to me."

Rachel had no idea whether they were serious, so she didn't respond. But then LoMo put his hand on her thigh and invited her to find out just how gay he was. "Actually, I'm bisexual and I've been fantasizing about a threesome with you and my friend Isaac."

No sooner were those words out of LoMo's mouth than the Toyota truck in the lead seemed to lift a meter off the ground, followed by a loud concussive sound. The truck fell over on its side. The passengers were crawling out of the broken windows, dazed from the explosion, searching for their gear that had been scattered on the ground from the truck's open bed.

Men dressed in irregular combinations of camouflage-patterned clothing were running toward them from the surrounding fields. Rachel's driver put their car into a skidding drift to the left, and the two men pushed her down hard. "Stay below the window. Don't look up," LoMo commanded as he leapt from the car and began to lay down a field of covering fire for the injured men from the lead truck. The man in the passenger seat and Isaac Hayes stood back-to-back and fired grenades at two clusters of armed men on either side of the road that were leveling their weapons in the direction of the second and third vehicles.

Rounds fired by one of the rebels began to hit the back of the wrecked truck, and soon a fireball erupted, further shredding and scattering the supplies that had been on the ground and in the back of the truck. A case containing several satellite phones flew through the air, one of them glancing against the side of Jimmy's head, knocking him to his knees. Lassiter pulled him by the collar behind the door of the second truck and, after assuring herself that he was all right, helped him switch off the safety from his gun and directed his fire into the opposite field.

John Beauregard organized two groups of three of his men to deploy in wide arcs to flank the rebels in order to catch both groups of attackers in a crossfire. When his men were sufficiently hidden in the bushes and high grass along the roadside, Beauregard began firing grenades in high arches around the rebels in an attempt to get them to consolidate into tighter groups. The strategy worked. Within minutes, on either side of the road, the rebels were huddled together and waving pieces of cloth in surrender as the security men emerged with their weapons leveled at them, chest high.

As soon as the shooting stopped, Rachel, Lassiter, and Jimmy ran over to the men who had been thrown from the lead truck. The good news was that none were seriously injured. The Blitz was dazed and had sprained his ankle when he was ejected from the vehicle but was otherwise unharmed. The bad news was that all the radios and other communications equipment was destroyed beyond repair, and they were down one vehicle, unfortunately the largest.

Lassiter and Beauregard cursed their stupidity for not evenly distributing the gear among all three vehicles. John took particular responsibility since he had been engaged in many such actions before. But Lassiter, with her rank of senior regional security officer for the Department of State knew that this would be a serious black mark on her otherwise stellar résumé. *Thank God none of the civilians were injured*, she thought. Despite Jimmy's calm, measured firing into the fields and carefully choosing his targets, now she really didn't want to take him and Rachel into an extraction where it appeared more armed conflict would occur. Pressing her fists into her eye sockets, she thought hard and fast about whether she could send them back to Luhansk. But with the destruction of one of the vehicles, there was no way. She was hoping that Jimmy didn't see the face of the man he had shot squarely in the chest, the same man who had been firing at the truck before it exploded.

"How's your head?" Lassiter asked him while pressing a wad of tissues against the bleeding cut from the pieces of the sat phone that had struck him.

"It's much better now that I shot that sonofabitch who blew up our truck," Jimmy answered with a steely look.

Lassiter looked into his eyes. He had what Vietnam vets often referred to as the "thousand-yard stare" and now was known by the more clinical term: post-traumatic stress disorder. She knew that it would take him many months to accept and understand what had just happened, if he ever could. She had been trained and prepared for what occurred although this was the first time she had ever used her weapon for defensive purposes. In the exchange of fire, she had not hit anyone; she had fired over the rebels' heads, hoping that would keep them away from her. But she knew that she had the resolve to kill if any had come within fifteen meters of their position. This would have been her personal kill zone. For everyone it was different. Jimmy had seen the man who shot at the truck, purposefully aimed, and fired. She would have to work with him over the next several minutes to gently bring him back to reality in the manner most appropriate for him.

"You were very angry that the man shot at the truck to blow it up, weren't you?" she asked him. "He was probably hoping that the explosion would kill us all."

"That's exactly what he was hoping, and that's why I shot the bastard."

"Good. I would have done the same thing if you hadn't. He was a dead man walking."

"Really?" Jimmy looked at her, tilted his head, and looked at her quizzically. He wanted confirmation that he did the right thing, not just acting out of anger or some darker, hitherto unrealized need.

"Precisely," Lassiter responded. "In fact, that fellow who was in the front seat of the car with Rachel was just aiming in that direction when you got off the first shot. Just like hunting turkeys, you know. I've done that too, just like you, with my ex-husband. But he never let me get off a shot because he nailed the tom before I even had a chance. So good for you. You got the turkey, Jimmy."

"Some fuckin' turkey," Jimmy observed, not even wanting to walk anywhere near the dead man. Instead, he went over to Rachel. Sitting down beside her as she applied a field dressing to the side of his head, he immediately indicated to her that he didn't want to talk about what just happened. When she was finished, he helped her clean up three other men who had been lightly injured from the blast and observed Lassiter recording some conversation of the rebels on the voice recorder on one of the GoPros that had survived the explosion for later transmission to the embassy. John Beauregard was taking videos with his phone while the other men snapped photos, presumably not for Instagram.

Jimmy knew that he was slowly coming down from a strange place he had gone over the past twenty minutes after the firefight. It had been like being trapped within a cloud. He could see out, but everything was fuzzy. Noises were heard and human speech was intelligible but muffled, and his mind seemed just a step behind understanding what people were talking about. He was confused that the security guys were acting perfectly normal. They were just going about the business of putting zip ties—plastic fastening wraps—around the rebels' wrists and ankles, removing their socks and shoving them into their mouths, and securing them with silver duct tape so they couldn't spit them out. Then they tied them with lengths of nylon cord to some small trees that sprouted from the bushes behind one of the wheat fields. No one would discover them for hours. Lastly, they took the rebels' cell phones to throw into the weeds several kilometers away to confuse any other separatists trying to locate them by GPS.

Jimmy's remaining emotion was anger. How dare anyone try to kill him? He was just a nice guy who liked to climb mountains and fish with his friends. He liked to help people. Not hurt them. He understood what Lassiter had been trying to do: dehumanize the man he had killed by comparing the experience to turkey hunting. Nice try, but what he hadn't told her was that, like her, he had never managed to shoot a turkey either. Ben had always gotten off the first shot.

Jimmy walked over to Howman and helped him to his feet, wrapping the Blitz's arm over his shoulder. Together, they slowly made their way to the other vehicle, and Jimmy settled the Blitz inside. "Ooofa!" the Blitz groaned as his injured ankle rolled over on the floor board as he shifted across the seat. "I don't know how much use I'm going to be once we get to Ben."

"We'll have you guard the trucks when we go in," Lassiter stated as she slipped up quietly behind Jimmy. "Someone needs to keep an eye on Rachel. I feel much better with you in that role rather than one of these Beauregard cowboys."

Of all the events of that morning, two in particular would always stand out for every member of the team. The first was that neither Lassiter nor Beauregard had thought it odd when the local police captain had abruptly walked away from them and made a cell phone call, then left without a word. Secondly, no one from the group, including the team leaders, had thought to check their cell phone for missed calls or text messages before proceeding ahead with the plan to rescue Ben. Perhaps it was because the last noted signal had only been one bar or because before the IED explosion and ensuing destruction of their commo gear, they had thought that they would only be communicating by secure sat phones. Due to this oversight, both Lassiter and Rachel missed two crucial calls. One from Kateryna about the news she received from Aleks's man and another from the embassy to immediately abort the mission and stand down. The consequences of this failure were dramatic and irreversible.

CHAPTER 40

Kateryna, Lale, Ipek, and the Istanbul Team

Present, Kiev, Ukraine

THE MAN WITH a distinct Russian accent would not give her his name. His message was curt and delivered as if practiced for a considerable amount of time. Breathing noisily into the phone, making it all the more difficult to understand him, he said to Kateryna, "Your friend, Mr. Ben, he's okay. He will be released soon, and he is with a friend. When we know more, you will know more. The friend, who I work for, sends his apologies for any distress he may have caused." He paused. "Oh, and do not send Americans with guns. He will be released to you without problem. Very soon," he added.

"Where is Ben? I want to speak to him now!" Kateryna demanded.

"He is not with me. He is with the friend. That is all I can tell you. Goodbye." The line went dead.

Colors and flashing lights swam before Kateryna's eyes, the onset of a migraine. "Stop!" she commanded her brain. "No time for this now." She immediately called Lassiter, but there was no answer. Next, she tried both Rachel's and Jimmy's phones. Likewise, no answer. In desperation, she called the US embassy, and after an interminable wait and being shuffled from one office to another, she reached Lassiter's assistant RSO. She repeated verbatim what the man had said to her and related her failed attempts to reach the rescue party on their cell phones.

"They must be out of range," he postulated. "Our imagery didn't indicate any cell towers anywhere in the vicinity of the building where we saw Ben. Let me try them on the sat phones, but I don't know if they will be turned on. Usually we leave them closed to avoid the expense of keeping an open line and so as not to deplete the batteries."

Despite the tension over this recent turn of events, Kateryna couldn't help but smile at the incongruity of the world's richest country saving a few dollars on satellite phone usage and some spare batteries while spending billions on bombs in Iraq and Afghanistan. "I'll hold on while you try calling them." She didn't want to repeat the experience of tracking him down again through the embassy's telephone gauntlet.

After several minutes, the assistant RSO came back to report that he too had been unable to establish any contact with the team. Kateryna, always the practical one, gave him what turned out to be a fortuitous idea. After calling the ground crew in Luhansk to learn the makes and models of the vehicles in their little convoy, he would call the chopper crew standing by in Kharkiv. He would instruct them to send one heli to scout the roads leading into the area where Ben was last seen. If they were spotted before reaching the building, the heli would intercept them and put them in touch with the embassy.

Meanwhile, Kateryna called Donald on his cell phone. Again, she wondered why she could manage to make all these expensive calls to American and Turkish numbers, and the US couldn't afford to keep its satellite phones open. He answered before the second ring. "Yes," was all he said.

"Hello, Donald, it is Kateryna. I have good news. But with a strange delivery. A man, maybe Russian, called me with a message from Ben that he was all right and we would have him back soon."

"Why strange? You said a strange delivery."

"Because he wouldn't tell me his name or give me any details. And he breathed heavy like he was in a rush. He said he was just delivering a message from his boss."

"That's all?"

"That's all."

"I feel so impotent sitting around on this plane. I wish there was something useful I could do."

"Did you happen to notice what kind of cars the team was driving?"

"Sure. Two Toyota pickups, blue and white, and two little Russian-looking sedans. Why?"

"Because I'm going to arrange a ride on a helicopter for you, Donald. I hope you brought your bifocular glasses."

"I assume you mean binoculars."

"Oh, yes," Kateryna said. "Binoculars," she corrected herself. "You will have a new job as a spotter. Let me quick call the embassy and tell them to instruct one of the helicopter pilots to pick you up in Luhansk by your plane."

In retrospect, she realized that this wasn't the best idea of the day. Flying the extra distance from Kharkiv to Luhansk, landing for Donald and then flying back to the northeast to toward the building would waste valuable time. She called the embassy again and talked the assistant RSO into deploying both choppers, one for Donald and the other to immediately scour the roads for two trucks and two sedans. It was unfortunate that they had no way of knowing that one of the trucks was no longer in play. Barely twenty minutes after takeoff, the two helicopters passed over the well-spaced but diminished convoy without taking serious notice of the two Ladas and single white Toyota pickup below. Fifteen minutes later, one of them spotted the burned-out truck but couldn't discern its color. Assuming that it was just another derelict vehicle used by the rebels as a roadblock, the pilots failed to make the connection between the previously overflown three vehicles and the abandoned truck.

CHAPTER 41

Rachel and the Beauregard Team

Present, Eastern Ukraine

LASSITER HAD INSTRUCTED the security firm's leader to halt the vehicles approximately five hundred meters north of the building behind a copse of evergreens. The Beauregard men had wrapped and taped all metallic objects to avoid accidental noise. John divided them into three small teams, each with at least one FN SCAR CQC and a bag of grenades. The professionals checked one another to ensure that no reflective surfaces were visible, smeared their faces with black and green grease, and refilled their ammunition clips. Rachel was not offered a weapon and sternly instructed by both Lassiter and Beauregard to remain in her vehicle with the Blitz. Jimmy wouldn't relinquish his Colt M4A1, and Lassiter resolved to keep an eye on him. After all, he had tasted blood and was most probably still under the influence of some remaining adrenaline coursing through his veins.

The sounds of the team were muffled. Talk was kept to a minimum, their deliberate movements masked by the sounds of the forest. The birds watching overhead in the branches, never ceasing their constant chatter, maintained a vigilant eye on the humans below. As the birds kept note of the humans, back in the car, Rachel was thinking about Jimmy. She had been impressed by his calm during

GARY S. LACHMAN

and after the firefight with the separatist rebels. He had followed the lead of the professionals, albeit one carefully placed shot at a time due to the fact that his weapon didn't have fully automatic capability. She might have killed the man who fired upon the truck herself, if given half a chance. That was an evil thing to do and had nearly killed several of them with the burning debris from the wreck. She had overheard the conversation between Jimmy and Lassiter. She understood the passive questioning and mental evaluation that the woman had subjected Jimmy to. It was really quite skillful, and mistakenly, she didn't think Jimmy ever realized that Lassiter was gauging his emotional stamina and readiness for what lay immediately ahead.

Rachel was leaning against the opposite side of the truck from where the Blitz was seated. She casually moved about ten meters away from the battered vehicle. She couldn't abide by the decision to have her remain behind with the injured Howman, who was in an exceedingly grumpy mood because he couldn't go with Jimmy, Lassiter, and the Beauregard team. She noticed that Howman was resting with his back to her. With the .45 cradled in his lap, he was facing away from the wooded area the men had entered, looking out toward the dirt road along which they had recently come. She quietly slipped away into the trees, following the team.

Things were definitely not going the way she had anticipated. Naively, she had imagined that they would drive to the building, the Beauregard men would barge in like some Hollywood SWAT team, emerging after the dust cleared with a shaken but smiling Ben Jacobson. Rachel had even embellished this scenario with Ben's overjoyed reaction to seeing her and rushing into her arms for an emotional embrace. However, after the events of but an hour ago and surrounded by these serious men with even more serious weapons, all thoughts of such a day at the beach had completely evaporated.

Rachel began making a mental list of everything that could go wrong. After evaluating twenty-two possible disaster scenarios, she caught up with LoMo, who had heard her approach before she had even seen him crouched with his weapon leveled at her. Weakly pretending like she had been there all along, she asked if they had an extra Kevlar vest. "Unfortunately, all that extra gear was lost when

222

the truck burned, ma'am," he replied. "As we told you before, just stay behind something solid, and do not, I repeat, do not get in front of one of these SCARs."

"I understand. No repetition required." She looked around, seeking Lassiter. Seeing her kneeling behind a tree, conferring with the team leader and looking at a device with a screen about the size of an iPad Mini, Rachel gingerly approached.

"You don't follow orders very well, Rachel," Lassiter snapped at her. "I am most definitely not happy to see you here. I hope that you're ready for whatever comes next. As you saw on the road, this thing's not going according to any plan I know of. I'd prefer that you remained back here."

"Not a chance," Rachel interrupted.

"Okay then. Stay below the bullets and stay behind the men. Try to keep Jimmy back with you too."

After a short hike of a few hundred meters, they all dropped to the ground and began the long crawl through the brush toward the edge of the field bordering the building. Rachel could smell the loamy earth as small clods of dirt were dislodged by those in front of her. She moved over toward Jimmy and pulled him close. "Please stay with me, and don't be a cowboy."

Jimmy nodded but crawled ahead with alarming speed. She had forgotten what excellent physical condition he had always been in from all the rock climbing, mountaineering, biking, and back-country skiing. Rachel felt like an old woman who had spent her life sitting around in sewing circles and at ladies' afternoon teas. After only fifty meters, she was breathing heavily and sweating profusely. *Great,* she thought. *Smelling like sweat and benzene. My face covered in dirt which, good God, is now also deep under my nails. If I live through this day, the first thing I'm going to do is indulge myself at a spa.* She continued this absurd conversation with herself as a distraction from the discomfort of slithering over rocks, roots, leaves, and branches that lay in their path. She was also profoundly frightened, and thinking about a manicure seemed to calm her nerves.

Despite her discomfort, Rachel kept quiet and concentrated to the extent possible on keeping the soles of Jimmy's boots within sight.

After thirty minutes that felt like thirty days, they came to a halt by the northwest corner of the building. The sun was to their back as it filtered through the evergreen branches in uneven shafts of afternoon light. They could clearly see a tall, aristocratic man speaking in what sounded to her like Russian to several other men who looked like the separatists they had encountered along the road. Beauregard motioned for a group of men to flank around to the southeast. This would give them a clear field of fire for the rear and one side of the structure without the danger of hitting any of their own. He kept the rest of them in place, which afforded them a view of the men standing by the side entry door and larger garage bay doors. Jimmy had gone around with the first group while Rachel remained behind a group composed of LoMo, Lassiter, Isaac Hayes, and John Beauregard. That was when Rachel heard the unmistakable sound of Ben's voice.

He was talking in an excited but seemingly happy tone of voice with a girl. By shifting slightly to her left, she could see their heads through the window—Ben with his thatch of brush-cut gray and a teenaged girl with long, soft, brown hair. They appeared to be having an intimate conversation and the girl was laughing at something that Ben was saying. After a few minutes, Rachel saw them rise and disappear from view, only to reappear at the doorway. The tall Russian man and the others didn't seem to care that their prisoners, if that was what Ben and the girl in fact were, had emerged from the building. There was no longer any doubt in her mind that Ben was not in any danger. She couldn't control herself. Standing so quickly that a grasping hand of Lassiter's was unable to restrain her, Rachel screamed, "Ben!"

Two of the Russian's security guards instantly raised their weapons in her direction and were just as quickly cut down by LoMo and Isaac Hayes. The other guards returned fire, with several rounds catching Beauregard in the legs and LoMo in his left shoulder. Ben had thrown the girl to the ground and was covering her with his body while Jimmy and his group came running around the side of the building firing at the men by the garage doors. The air became thick with the smell of gunpowder, and the noise from twelve automatic weapons firing simultaneously was deafening. A round intended for Isaac Hayes snapped past him and found Rachel, knocking her to the ground at Lassiter's feet. Lassiter instantly dropped to one knee and returned fire. Rachel saw the muzzle flashes and heard the crack of bullets as they whizzed by, breaking the sound barrier. The sound reminded her of someone, a Vietnam vet, once telling her, "You never hear the one that gets ya." She couldn't remember if she heard the one that got her. Then she lost consciousness.

Jimmy screamed when he saw that Rachel was hit and turned his Colt on the heavyset guard who had fired in her direction. His first shot caught the man center chest, and his second dropped him when it shattered his knee. Several automatic rounds from a guard in a black sweatshirt hit the Beauregard man to Jimmy's right high in the chest, sending him staggering backward, moaning but alive. The ballistic vest he wore had saved him. Jimmy turned his weapon on the black sweatshirt and fired three rounds into the image of Eddie Van Halen that adorned the chest. Lassiter, Beauregard, and the others systematically picked off the three guards who had continued to fire in a matter of seconds. The others dropped their weapons and quickly ran down the access road. Although the guards had equaled the Beauregard men in number, their training had been woefully inadequate. They were no match for the professionals employed by Beauregard.

Several seconds of silence followed before Ben slowly raised his head to peer around. He instructed Irina to remain down while he grabbed Jimmy by the arm, and together they raced over to Rachel's prone form. Lassiter was bent over her, pressing a sterile Bolin patch over a sucking chest wound, and John was rummaging through his medical kit for a catheter, plasma, and Hextend that was desperately needed by both LoMo and Rachel.

Ben was speechless. He didn't recognize her at first, older and covered in blood and dirt. Rachel Colliers? Here in East Bejesus, Ukraine? This was entirely beyond his comprehension. Jimmy with an assault weapon? And who were these other guys and the serious-looking woman working on Rachel? He remembered Irina and turned back toward where he had left her. But she was gone. It was her wailing cries that drew his attention toward the other side of the doorframe, where he saw her down on her knees in the dirt, pounding her small fists on Aleks' chest.

"Jimmy!" he called. "Help me here. This guy was a friend. Bring the first aid kit and hurry!" He gently moved Irina aside and surveyed the damage to the Russian's head. He knew that there was no life there. A round had entered Aleks's skull just above his ear and exited above his eye leaving an obscene hole. Ben wrapped his arms around Irina and pulled her away. *Why?* he wondered. *Hadn't they received the message from Aleks's man?*

As Jimmy rushed over to Aleks, he glanced at Ben, who slowly shook his head. Jimmy removed his coat and placed it over the man Ben had said was an ally and helped Ben gently pull Irina away. He knew that he would eventually understand what had happened here and walked back over to Rachel without saying a word. At that moment, he realized he probably cared more for this unusual woman from Mississippi than Ben did despite the fact that Ben was the only reason for putting herself in harm's way. He had no idea who the teenage girl was that Ben seemed so concerned with and, frankly, was quite annoyed at his friend's behavior. Looking down at the man in the black Van Halen sweatshirt who lay bleeding out on the ground, he had a thought. He bent down and searched through his pockets until he found a set of car keys and a cell phone. He brought them to Lassiter, who immediately dispatched one of the Beauregard men to drive toward Luhansk until a more viable signal was available. Jimmy and Lassiter quickly wrote a list of names and phone numbers for the man to call together with instructions to call for the helis. They had no way of knowing that they were already on the way, mere minutes out from this scene of carnage, approaching rapidly from opposite directions.

CHAPTER 42

Ben, Lassiter, Kateryna, Jimmy, Donald, Vlady, and Irina

Present, Kiev

THEY SAT SQUEEZED around the small table in Kateryna's kitchen, drinking strong tea and eating the cookies that Vlady had proudly baked. The pleasant smell of oatmeal, cinnamon, and raisins permeated the air, in stark contrast to the acrid stench of stress that underlay the circumstances. Donald was on his cell phone, arranging a medevac with a private company he partially owned while Kateryna was quietly conversing with the hospital. After several hours of surgery, Rachel was resting in the ICU, still deeply sedated. Now that her condition had been stabilized and her lung repaired, the priority was identifying the best thoracic doctor to follow up and prepare her for transport back to the States. The anesthesiologist, Dr. Chub, was an old friend of Ben's and Kateryna's and had proved invaluable in making arrangements for Rachel's immediate surgical care and subsequent transfer to a more secure private hospital. A visiting American doctor who specialized in trauma surgery, Kurt Ludwig, was fortunately on call and had successfully stopped the bleeding and returned functionality to the damaged lung.

Having just completed a short but joyous phone call with Lale and the others in Istanbul, Ben was pensively looking back and forth between Vlady, who was hanging from his arm like a little monkey, and Irina, who was still in a state of shock from witnessing the death of her uncle. He was trying to eavesdrop on the numerous calls that Lassiter had been making from her secure Blackberry while devoting equal amounts of attention to the kids. Irina exhibited the typical signs of shock and depression; her eyelids drooped, and she uttered monosyllabic replies when a question was directed her way. Vlady acted like he was afraid that he'd lose Ben again to some dark forces over which he had no control. He remained glued to Ben's arm, effectively making it impossible for him to leave his chair. It felt almost as claustrophobic as when he had been physically restrained by the silver duct tape to the car seat in Viktor's taxi. He could only hope that Irina would not blame Aleks's death on him and his friends. That would not be a healthy foundation on which to build a relationship.

After the calls were finished, Lassiter stood and cleared her throat. She'd been wrestling with how to deal with the elephant in the room, namely the bloody fiasco they had left behind at the old garage. "I have no other way to say it, people. But we must pretend that all this didn't happen. At least not in the way it actually went down."

"My uncle was killed," Irina spoke in a flat tone, her eyes downcast.

"I know, honey," Lassiter quietly agreed. "I don't want to judge him or what he did. I understand that his intentions were good. But sometimes signals get crossed, and people think things are one way when actually they are something else entirely. Then people get hurt...like today."

"Is my friend Ben your daddy?" Vlady suddenly asked Irina.

She looked up into the young boy's eyes. Something in the perfectly direct way he had asked the question made her smile for the first time in many hours. She nodded her head. Vlady released Ben's arm and moved over to the girl. "But your uncle died?"

"Yes. I loved him very much."

"I'm sad for you," Vlady said and gave her a hug. "But now you have a daddy."

"That's true," Irina said to him.

"So okay," Vlady summed it up. "And I will be your best friend because I'm your daddy's best friend too."

Lassiter cleared her throat again. She didn't want to interrupt the bonding between Vlady and Irina, but she was pressed for time. She had to return to her office and write her incident report. "Listen, I will take some artistic license with the report I have to prepare, and I want to make sure that we are all on the same page. We can never discuss with anyone else what happened. It would make a diplomatic disaster of colossal proportions."

"A regular international incident," Donald added sarcastically.

"You may consider that the source of some bureaucratic comedy, but with the Russians massing at the border and near constant incursions by military personal, no doubt at the instruction of Mr. Putin, directly or indirectly, any violent intervention involving the death of a Russian military officer in which an agency of the US government was involved might appear as a declaration of war on Russia despite its relatively minor size and consequences. This would definitely be frowned upon by the White House and the Pentagon, not to mention my own superiors in Diplomatic Security." She paused to draw a breath. "Therefore, I am respectfully requesting that you forget everything that occurred, specifically during the past forty-eight hours, with a hope, Mr. Jacobson, that you can forgive and forget your ordeal over the past week." She stared at everyone in the room, with a particular glare in Ben's direction. "Do I make myself clear?"

Ben hated when people used that expression. Obviously, the person making such a statement was making themselves clear, and to beg the question was redundant and a hyperbole of theatrical proportions. He was tempted to say, "No, could you clarify that for those of us who have endured imprisonment, separation, stress, and unimaginable sorrow?" Instead, he rose and simply said, "I'm going to the hospital to see Rachel. Y'all look after Irina." And then he left the apartment.

CHAPTER 43

Rachel and Ben

Present, Kiev, Ukraine

RACHEL HAD REGAINED consciousness and was stable—if not psychologically, at least from a physical point of view. She had a morphine drip that ran directly into the IV that ran into the back of her left hand, which helped to dull the pain (but did not entirely succeed). The hospital bed was set at an uncomfortable angle to prevent any fluids from accumulating in her lungs. Lale had arranged for a large private room with a nice window for her at Istanbul's American Hospital in the Şişli neighborhood. The room had a sofa and matching pale green upholstered armchairs for visitors. (Turks made hospital stays into social occasions.) Ben had been stretched out on the sofa, watching Rachel sleep. When he saw her eyes open, he arose and cautiously went to her bedside.

Surprisingly, she was able to think and speak with reasonable clarity despite the drugs and her pulmonary limitations. She looked up into the dark-blue eyes of her former lover and spoke with great sincerity. "I'm so sorry, Ben. So sorry."

"For what?" he responded.

"For indulging a stupid fantasy and popping back into your life without any care or sensitivity to you or your friends. For my audacity. For my egocentricity. For my narcissism. For my melodrama."

She had to stop for a moment to collect her thoughts and catch her breath while Ben stood silently. "Please sit down. It's difficult to converse with you looming over me like some angel of indeterminate purpose." She managed a small smile at her poetics.

Ben pulled one of the surprisingly heavy chairs closer to the bed. As he sat, he noticed that she still looked damn good, considering the passage of the years. "Tell me why you came," he asked in a soft voice.

Rachel began speaking while simultaneously thinking a hundred thoughts, including being embarrassed for how awful she must look, how badly she must smell, particularly her breath as she was cotton mouthed from the pain meds, and what a mess her hair must be. She was also thinking how good Ben looked despite having been locked up in the same clothes for over a week without a shave or proper bath. Shower, she corrected herself. Ben hated baths unless they were part of having sex, and then he always took a shower after climbing out of the tub.

She told him of her failed marriages, her unfulfilled desire to have children, her teaching, the death of Aunt Annie, the burden of maintaining her ancestral home in Colliersville, and how she had become claustrophobic in that little town. She rambled about a stupid boyfriend who had abused Annie. She talked about fishing for crappie in the pond at dusk and sitting in the cemetery thinking about foreign travel. She explained about the box of photographs in her attic that she was suddenly drawn to and staring at their old pictures from better days at Duke University.

She talked about forty years of regret over how she had been so stupid to get involved with a worthless grad student at the expense of her relationship with him. "Ben…"she paused collecting her thoughts, "basically I had a postmenopausal crisis. I was bored teaching another crop of Southern brats who honestly believe they are entitled by their antediluvian aristocracy even 150 years after the fact. My life was at a standstill. The farthest I've been from Colliersville in the past ten years has been Washington, DC, for a conference on William Faulkner, Oliver La Farge, and Sherwood Anderson and their influence on American literature." She drew an involuntary painful breath and winced.

"Stop talking if it hurts. It makes me feel terrible that I was responsible for your pain."

"My deepest apologies, *Ben*. And in the words of one of my favorite authors, 'Don't grieve for me. I've had a wonderful time.'"

"That's kinda like my line, Rachel. You remember that I always wanted my tombstone to read 'Here lies Ben Jacobson. He had a good time.' But now I want to be cremated. Cemeteries are a waste of good real estate. I guess they could just inscribe the urn with the same words."

"Don't be so morbid, Ben. I'm the one lying here with tubes and stiches and pain drugs and you're sitting there looking like a million bucks. So I can see that you are still avoiding reality."

"How do you mean?"

"You have a fantasy life here in Istanbul of all places with very glamorous, beautiful women and wonderful, solid male friends who care for you a great deal and admire your running back and forth to Kiev to be with an adorable young boy whom some might believe to be your progeny. You hang out with twentysomethings like Ipek, and now it appears you have some kind of relationship with a teenage Russian girl. You haven't grown up. You are the same as when you were at Duke."

"Things are not always what they seem; the first appearance deceives many; the intelligence of a few perceives what has been carefully hidden," Ben quickly responded.

"I see you remember your Plato, *The Phaedrus*, I believe. But again, that's the same Ben, deflecting with a pithy comment or quote. And don't demean me by insinuating that I'm not intelligent. You obviously have been in denial about aging. It was one thing when you were nineteen years old, quite another now. So kindly have the respect for me to tell me what's going on in your life. After all, despite my bad timing and ill-advised disobedience of Lassiter's instructions about staying behind, this is why I came to see you."

"I often hurt myself to avoid hurting others," Ben told her. After those words left his mouth, he fell silent a minute and began thinking about their implications. "But now it seems that whatever I will do, somebody else will be a casualty."

"I am merely a casualty of love abandoned and then regretted," she responded quietly. "It's my own damn fault, and I take full responsibility." This reminded her of a song she had listened to on the plane, "Casualty of Love" by Jessie J, atypical of her usual taste in music but nonetheless apropos.

The drugs made her lose her train of thought, and she began to hum and sing the lyrics she could remember. Ben maintained a respectful silence, observing Rachel in her reverie. He knew the song and knew the words and sang the next refrain with her.

Eventually, they both returned to the present. Ben resumed their conversation. "Let me explain a little about what you've encountered. I will try to make a long story short, which, as you know, is difficult for me."

He settled back into his chair and continued, "A little boy named Vlady is my godson. Kateryna, his mother, one of my best friends in the world, is a single mom whom I worked with in Kiev many years ago while I was in the State Department. We've remained close. About ten days ago—I'm not even sure exactly how many days at this pointin the middle of the night, she called to tell us that a stranger had appeared in Vlady's bedroom to give him a warning for me. This scared the shit outta all of us and resulted in my taking a flight to Kiev the next morning. The regular taxi driver who had always met me at the airport arrived late, accompanied by a large foul-smelling fellow. When it appeared that we weren't going into Kiev, and the driver—poor guy—made a few attempts to get into minor accidents to stop the car and attract attention, the big guy shot him and left his body by the side of the road. He taped me to the seat, one of the many uses of silver duct tape being to immobilize people, and drove many hours to the east into one of the Russian-controlled areas."

"This much I know," Rachel interrupted. "Who were those guys? Who is the girl?"

"Now rewind about fifteen years to when I was with State and working in Dushanbe, Tajikistan. I was unhappy and lonely, recently broken up from a great lady due to my own stupidity. I had a brief affair with a woman who was working in the Russian embassy. It was nothing special and mutually acknowledged to be nothing more than recreation. Little did I know that we could have dropped the *re* out of *recreation.*"

"Meaning?" queried Rachel.

"Meaning that the woman got pregnant, and I never knew about it until a few days ago while I was imprisoned by a Russian officer named Aleks, who was her uncle. Aleks was a member of the Russian intelligence service, the SVR RF. Apparently, he had been keeping tabs on me for several years and learned of my relationship with Vlady and Kateryna. Unbeknownst to me, he followed me around Istanbul to learn my habits. Unbeknownst! Damn! I haven't used that word in at least twenty years!"

"Ben! Get back on track!"

"He engineered my visit to Kiev and had me kidnapped with the idea of *softly*"—he made the little imitation of quotation marks in the air with his fingers—"interrogating me over several days to make sure that I would be suitable to raise his niece. Not a pleasant experience, by the way."

"And?"

"There was a glitch in his plan, to put it mildly. Another Russian officer, a military intelligence guy—one who was actively working with the local separatists for a triple A: to arm, agitate, and assist—appeared and decided that I had value as a captive and must be in possession of valuable intelligence information." Ben abruptly stood, concealing a smile at the oxymoron of his being in possession of valuable intelligence. Walking over to the edge of the bed, he continued, "I felt abandoned and forgotten by everyone. I was so worried about Kateryna and Vlady worrying about me, and my friends in Istanbul, I couldn't understand why no one was coming for me despite my trying to leave clues as to my whereabouts whenever and however possible. I was only thinking about myself and my predicament. So if anything, I, not you, are the narcissist."

"Same old Ben. The Dichotomy Man. Only thinking about himself while worrying about everyone else. You didn't think that

Lale and your other friends were worried sick about what happened to you? That they wouldn't be trying everything possible to find you?"

"I guess not. But under the circumstances—"

"Sometimes you're dumb as a bucket of rocks, Ben."

"Thank you, Rachel. You were always generous with the compliments. But you don't understand. I was alone in a dark garage. For days, I was duct-taped to a metal chair. This big stinkin' bastard was beating on me with a phone book. Some asshole colonel named Nevski was threatening me with worse. And then the only person to act civil to me was this aristocratic Russian who suddenly appeared and seemed to know more about me than I knew myself. He beat me at chess and then he'd beat me at mind games."

Rachel raised her eyes, at least as far as she was able considering the meds. "Well, if that don't put pepper in the gumbo! Someone smarter than you." She tried unsuccessfully to sit up. "Damn! I'm dizzier than a betsy bug. Now I bet you've never heard another Duke grad use that old expression."

"Interesting," Ben observed, propping up the pillows and helping her sit up a little. "When you are under the influence, you revert to bizarre but quaint Southern colloquialisms. I wonder where they come from."

"Whatever. This morphine, I don't know whether to scratch my watch or wind my butt." These were all old expressions employed by friends of Aunt Annie when she was a child. Rachel briefly smiled at the fond memories of her aunt.

"I like that one," Ben said with a grin. "Haven't heard that before. Anyway, I'd been driving myself crazy because as time went on, he began to look more and more familiar to me, but I couldn't remember from where. It was just beyond my consciousness. Then I remembered. It was from my time in Dushanbe. He had been a young officer that I often bummed cigarettes from. And then I realized that I had recently seen him hanging around my office in Istanbul, albeit in civilian clothing that pretty much concealed his features. And then he brings in this teenage girl."

"So the young girl—" Rachel refocused the conversation.

"The young girl—her name is Irina—is apparently my daughter. The fruit of my loins, so to speak, from my days of wine and roses in Dushanbe. The Russian was her uncle."

"Was?" Rachel asked. "And why was he raising her? What happened to her mother?"

"*Was* because one of your guys shot him in the head in front of her. And he was raising her because her mother died in a car accident a few years ago. So I'm all she has left."

"Don't you think it's all just too neat and convenient? Maybe you *are* being played."

"I can certainly have a paternity test performed. But my instincts and the chemistry between us are strong."

"And what does your *instinct* tell you? What do you feel about her? Do go on."

"Are you sure that you're up to this? You keep nodding off."

"I AM NOT FALLING ASLEEP! I was just checking for holes in my eyelids." This time, she sat up fully and glared at him.

"My instincts say she is indeed mine. My heart says that I should take care of her. We spent quite a few hours talking and getting to know each other. She has pluck and great intelligence and my kind of sense of humor. I liked her mother a lot even though we both knew it was heading nowhere, and we were simultaneously flirting and spying on each other. I mean, we weren't literally spying on each other. We were just trying to find out what the other people were doing or going to do in Tajikistan. The Iranians were stirring things up there, and we were both trying to determine how far we could go with trusting each other in order to work together against them." This all came out in a great rush of emotion, and Ben stopped to catch his breath. "And what the fuck are you implying?" he asked angrily.

"Now don't go flying off the handle, dear one. I'm just trying to get the facts as convoluted as they might be. I'm not implying anything."

"What is with all this *down on yonder farm* redneck talk, Rachel? Is that how you lecture your students?"

"Kindly indulge me, oh great man of contemporary American literature and post-Jimmy Carter language. But I'm higher than a

Georgia pine, and I seem to remember that you used to lapse into your street Spanish whenever you had a few shots too many of your favorite añejo. What was your favorite phrase? Something like *la puta madre que te parió!*"

"Yeah. Still comes in handy on the golf course when I miss a putt and don't want to say anything offensive in Turkish like *orospu çocuğu.*"

"And what does that mean, Mr. Sultan Ben Ja Meen?"

"Son of a bitch. That's a very bad, I mean very bad, thing to say in Turkey even though, obviously, golf balls don't have mothers."

"All right, all right. Stop digressing, Ben. Please continue, with or without passion, as the spirit moves you."

"Okay, Rachel. This is very weird for me. Holding the dubious distinction of being the only woman who ever cheated on me, you are missing from my life for so many years and now here you are, part of a rescue team I don't know how you got involved with. This has got to be the craziest, most unbelievable thing ever. I mean, I was under the impression that you are a university professor, but now you've got a hole in your lung which is causing you enough pain to be hitting that little morphine button like you're playing Whack-a-Mole, and like it or not, admit to it or not, you are judging me. I don't know how to deal with that."

"Well, deal with this, Ben. The way I see it, you've got three choices with respect to your alleged daughter. I've made a mental list while lying here like an old hound dog on the porch: (*a*) abandon Irina, perhaps to Kateryna, although that would be asking a lot from her, and she already has a child. That would be difficult financially, emotionally, etc. Plus, Ukrainians will never accept her, especially now, as she is a Russian."

Ben interrupted and raised a finger in the air to physically make his point. "Technically not a Russian. Moldovan."

"Whatever. She's not Ukrainian, that's for damn sure. Now where was I? Okay, (*b*) bring Irina to Istanbul to live with you. This will be very difficult because of language and school issues. Also, more importantly, anyone you are dating there will never accept this idea. It would be a constant reminder that you had an affair with some other woman."

This time, Ben raised his hand like a schoolboy seeking permission from the teacher to go to the restroom. "I'm not dating anyone at the moment."

Rachel ignored the brief arrhythmia and continued, "Or (*c*) get over this fantasy life and return to America with Irina, put Irina in a good school, and forge a new life. Visit all your friends everywhere with her as much as possible. In four years or less, she will graduate high school and go to university, and then you both can decide if she belongs in the US or Turkey or wherever."

"Huh," was all Ben could muster. Even over the past few hours, he hadn't thought this through as thoroughly as Rachel had in just the last few minutes. He had just assumed he would probably do *a* or *b*. "I don't think that I can just pick up and leave Istanbul, Rachel. I have a life there. I have work there. I have friends there. I must talk to them about this."

"Ya know, Ben, sometimes you are just as dumb and happy as a dead pig in the sunshine. You are oblivious and apparently don't have a clue about friendship or love. True, you have many good friends, and of that I'm sure you are aware. But what you don't seem to be able to get through that thick skull of yours is that friends like you have—Kateryna, Bamkiz, Jimmy, Donald, Howman, Johan—those kinds of friends are scarce as hens' teeth. These friends flew from all over the damn world to come to your aid. True, my first idea was to surprise you with a social reunion, but when we learned of your disappearance, we embarked on a mission, a mission to find our friend Ben. And your Turkish friends? Well, the true ones won't ever let you disappear from their lives any more than we did. Don't you grasp that you have true friends who love you beyond time? Damn, boy! Sometimes I believe that you're so stupid that if you had an idea, it would die of loneliness!" This last comment caused Ben to raise his eyebrows nearly above his hairline.

"I'm not as obtuse as you believe, Rachel. It's just that oftentimes when I've allowed people into my heart"—he looked directly at her—"they have burrowed inside, eaten it, then spit it out and walked away."

"Oh get over that, Ben. That was more than thirty-five years ago, for cryin' out loud. I've already confessed that it was the biggest mistake of my life. How do you think that makes me feel to hear that you've appropriated it for your own litany of personal insults? Not only do I dwell on it, I also attribute it to having deformed my life. I detest having to admit it, but I am a disappointed woman. I now know that I'll never have you, but it won't stop me thinking of what could have been. Or what would have been if I hadn't been such a fool. I would enjoy having a good man in my life. That goes without saying. And I understand that it can't...*shouldn't* be you. I acknowledge that and have come to terms with it. Besides, I have come to understand that this *need*, this *wanting* of mine may be nothing more than an archaic, socially-induced concept perpetrated by sexist, insecure men. So I hereby reject the need and will henceforth concentrate on what I want. Now how's that for clarity of mind, Mr. Ben Jacobson?" Rachel shifted on her pillows and continued, "However, I have found the confidence to go and make my way in the world with certainty. But this isn't about me now. It's about you and a young girl who needs a family, irrespective of her origins or motives. Pardon me for stating the obvious, but you need to make a decision that damned well better be the smart one."

"Okay."

"*Okay*? What are you? The damned One-Word Answer Man?"

"Okay as in you should know that I've never been able to purge you from my mind. That sounds corny as hell, but perhaps it's some kind of karmic connection—now I am dating myself—remember that sexually and spiritually dimorphous comparative religion prof we had at Duke in that course we so enjoyed about Tantric Buddhism."

"You're digressing, Ben."

"Right. It's because this is hard to say. I never forgot you. I kept you preserved in my mind as that same tall, skinny, fashion model-looking girl with the micro miniskirts, long brown hair, and enormous eyes. That fact that you were a few years older than I was, exciting."

"Are you intimating that I've changed?" Rachel sarcastically growled with a wink.

In no mood for jokes, Ben continued, "We've both changed. I was angry because you cheated on me with that hippie douchebag, who, I'm sure, was actually a nice guy. It was really just about my ego, and my thinking that everything was all about me. So you see, I have learned a thing or two over the past few years. And you can never understand how shocked I was to see you with that rescue team in Ukraine or how I felt when you were hit and lying on the ground. That was when my worlds collided and then were ripped apart. I had to stay with Irina, you see. Because she was the *now* world. You were my *then* world."

Rachel's eyes started to tear as she listened to Ben's monologue.

He continued, "It was like I couldn't cognitively accept your being there at that minute. Too many things were happening at once. This is what I believe a baby must feel like when it is delivered. Going from the familiar—despite the fact that the familiar isn't so great because it is limited to a small, wet space—to a large, open, noisy, unfamiliar, dangerous world. But I want you to know that now I understand and I am really, *really* overwhelmed by what you arranged for me here. Bringing everyone together for this reunion was an amazing idea, and to put it mildly, I'm so sorry that it didn't exactly work out the way you probably hoped—my being with my Turkish friends, this new kid in my life, you catching a bullet and ending up in this hospital in Kiev. So despite everything, Rachel, you did an outstanding thing. Perhaps the most outstanding thing that anyone has ever done for me, so consider yourself redeemed." He chuckled at his weak attempt at humor. He almost always laughed at his own jokes, even if no one else did. "You succeeded in connecting the almost unconnectable."

"And you also need to immediately connect with all those true friends you have out there, 'specially the ones here and in Istanbul, waitin' on you. So get on outta here, Ben, and let me rest in peace. Uh, that's not exactly what I meant to say. The drugs, you know. I'm not dead yet."

"Okay, Rachel. Thank you for your honesty despite its brutality. It's what I needed. I'm going back to Kateryna's house and then see if I can find a flight back to Istanbul tonight. I'm sure that Donald will come back here to handle your arrangements. I hope to see you soon in the States, all in one piece with the lungs of an Olympic runner like Usain Bolt and an opera star like Andrea Bocelli."

"Well, I don't know if I like being compared to a couple of guys, but I get your point. I'll see you then, Good Lord willing and the creek don't rise."

CHAPTER 44

Rachel and Donald

Present, Donald's G650ER jet

THE COPILOT PULLED the door down and secured it before rejoining Donald in the cockpit, where he was completing the preflight check. Rachel was reclining in her seat, with a belt lightly about her waist. She'd insisted on changing from her hospital gown into a loose-fitting, geometric-print sundress Karen Lassiter had given to her. The fact that Rachel had immediately signed a confidentiality agreement and liability waiver had apparently put Karen in an extremely generous state of mind. The short sleeves accommodated the IV line, which was connected to a plastic bag suspended from a hastily installed hook above. Kateryna had arranged for her manicurist to come to the hospital the previous afternoon after Ben had left and had sent her hair stylist in the morning to do a wash and blow-dry for Rachel. She'd also given Rachel a small brightly colored plastic bag of makeup from a store in the Globus shopping center near Maidan Square. But for the ugly wound in her chest with the thick bandage that surrounded her upper torso, Rachel felt almost presentable.

The seat that would normally have been in front of her had been removed and replaced with a large cushion that she arranged to suit her long legs. Making Rachel comfortable for the long trip was an exercise tempered with relativity, but nevertheless, every effort was made to keep things tolerable. They would first fly to Lisbon and, after refueling, continue on to Raleigh-Durham, where she would be met by an ambulance from the Duke University Medical Center. Donald had arranged for a surgical nurse recommended by Dr. Ludwig to come along on the plane from a private hospital in Switzerland that specialized in thoracic trauma. Rachel, still somewhat softened by pain meds, was quite comfortable, all things considered. She hoped that Donald would come out of the cockpit eventually and spend some time with her. The Swiss nurse had all the personality of a cadaver. She was competent and professional to be sure but possessed no bedside manner. She heard Donald's unique New York accent come through the speaker over her head, announcing their imminent takeoff.

The jet's rapid acceleration and the sharp incline of ascent pressed Rachel back into the seat, causing a momentary twinge of pain to the incision the doctors had made to enable them to cleanly close the wound and minimize scarring. Although she didn't need reminding as to why she was in her current circumstances, she kind of enjoyed it in a mildly masochistic kind of way. In her entire life, she'd never received so much attention. She wouldn't have even traded this for a positive article in the *New York Times Book Review*.

As they leveled out at thirty-eight thousand feet, Donald left the cockpit and came to her side. After shooing away the nurse from the adjacent seat, he articulated his six-foot-three-inch frame into something resembling an irregular nonagon in the narrow aisle of the aircraft to be closer to Rachel. "I don't think two people have ever gone through so much trouble to be alone," Donald said with only a minute trace of sarcasm.

"Is that what this is?" Rachel chuckled. "Kind of like a date?"

"If you wish. I certainly would like that. You know, there are all kinds of stories about couples having sex on planes, the Mile High Club and all that—"

"Donald, if that's what you want, I think that you've outdone yourself choosing perhaps the most inappropriate woman in the western hemisphere for that purpose. At least at this particular moment. Or are you so desperate that you have to arrange for the girl to be shot in the lung to soften her up? I mean, what kind of foreplay is that?"

"That was bad aim, Rachel. He was supposed to aim higher and just wing you in the shoulder. He paid dearly for that mistake, I'll remind you." They were both trying to remain expressionless. He leaned in to really see her face in the light coming through the window and could smell her lightly floral scent, like what he imagined the South to smell like on a warm summer's day. She was only two years younger than him and yet not a wrinkle on her soft skin, just the hint of crow's feet, more like hummingbird feet, at the corners of her eyes.

"Stop examining me, for Chrissake! First we are joking about your seduction technique and now you're acting like my dermatologist!" She hurriedly closed the window shade.

"Rachel, I can't get over you. You really don't have a clue, do you?"

"About what? About how ridiculous it was that a sixty-something-year-old woman thought she could just round up a gang of dissolute gentlemen—incongruity intended—and zip off to Istanbul and Ukraine and God knows where and resume a forty-year-old party like it never stopped?" She rolled her eyes and continued, "And that no one might get hurt? Which includes, by the by, both emotionally and physically. That everything would still be the same? That I would have such enduring allure as to find Ben in love with me the same as before when I unceremoniously dumped him for a complete idiot pseudointellectual hippie who never learned how to use deodorant?"

"That's not what I was thinking."

"What then, Don Quixote?" She did think he looked somewhat like the Cervantes character with his tall, rail-thin stature and aristocratic bearing.

"What I meant was that, ummm, you failed to notice that you actually did capture the hearts of everyone else of the male sex who was along for this ride. Certainly Jimmy, Bamkiz, and probably Howman, not to mention, most of all, me." Donald was feeling extremely uncomfortable at this point. He could pitch a deal to the toughest analyst or most demanding investor, but selling himself as a romantic interest was virtually impossible for him.

She knew that something might have been brewing with Jimmy but dismissed it because of their age difference. Donald was another kettle of fish entirely. Truth be told, she had been interested in Donald right from the get-go. She loved his funny intonation when he spoke—a tad affected, slightly New York skeptical, the raised eyebrow, the mustache always slightly askew, and the occasional "ummm" when he had at least twenty-five different thoughts simultaneously running through his exceptional mind. She especially appreciated his constant generosity and prodigious intelligence. She also liked the way he focused 100 percent of his attention on her whenever she spoke. Rachel didn't know whether to dial up or downplay the Southern accent when she spoke to him and instead found herself imitating his curious way of speaking. She wriggled in her seat at the thought of being a verbal chameleon.

"Do you know that when you are speaking with me you start to lose the Southern drawl," Donald inquired.

She blushed deeply. Busted. "You don't really know anything about me," she deflected, accent back in business.

"That's not entirely correct," Donald said. He knew from Ben that Rachel could have been a member of the Daughters of the American Revolution several times over if she had so chosen, yet she detested any organization that centered on from whom and where someone came rather than what they had personally accomplished. He knew that her forbears had been slave owners who had freed their workers a number of years before the Civil War had started, only to receive death threats from their neighbors. She knew that her great-grandfather had been a Northern-educated engineer who had built the town's water system and brought indoor plumbing into virtually every household within a twenty-mile radius. He knew that, once upon a time, she had been a crazy sexy ingenue who loved to fly up to New York with Ben and shop at Henri Bendel on Fifth Avenue and party at Studio 54. And he understood that once Ben was out of her life, she had never traveled farther north than Washington, DC, steeping herself in antiquated Southern ways, writing about famous

Southern authors and hiding, for the most part, in the little town where she had been born and raised that bore her family's name. It was a complete mystery to him why he should be so attracted to this woman.

"I understand that it must appear we are as different as chalk and cheese," Donald said. "But there is one fundamental thing we have in common, besides our obvious good looks and, ummm, extraordinarily high intelligence quotients, of course."

Rachel cocked her head. Was this some kind of a New York pickup line about to be delivered? "And pray tell, what might that be?"

"We are both of an age, unfulfilled for want of the right mate, or partner, or whatever euphemism for husband or wife you might prefer. And I mean we aren't bad looking. More accurately, I mean, you are great looking, and I'm still—"

"Vertical." She finished his sentence. She began cognitively and intellectually multitasking. Although originally it was Ben whom she wanted, she was beginning to understand that it was Donald she needed—a man capable of, and apparently ready to, fully commit to taking care of her.

"Yes. Vertical with a strong heartbeat." His mustache turned up at the corners, symmetrically this time. "But what I wanted to say to you was that, ummm, in the past I've always chosen the wrong kind of woman to be with. I was influenced by money, looks, similar social and religious backgrounds, political power, and business backgrounds. Always some common denominator on the superficial level, but never anything on the deeper emotional or spiritual level. So I was immediately attracted to you because"

"We have absolutely nothing in common," she finished his sentence again.

"I usually hate when people do that. Finish the other's sentence, I mean."

She ignored this. "In other words, you were intrigued by my utterly complete and overwhelming difference from you. Now that sounds like a healthy reason to begin a relationship. Sounds kind of egocentric to me, Donald."

He smiled at her drawl. "Well, at least we're both rather tall. And I've always liked hush puppies. Although the carbs are probably bad for me now."

"That's a good start," Rachel agreed. She couldn't help but notice that he was completely focused on her now. "You won't be kissin' the pillow, and I'll just have to learn how to fry up some low-carb puppies for y'all."

CHAPTER 45

Lale, Ben, and Irina

Present, Istanbul

TWO WEEKS HAD passed since Rachel had returned to the States with Donald. The other friends had likewise returned to their respective homes, vowing to keep in better and more constant touch with one another. Ben believed this would be the case as they had shared an experience that was not soon to be forgotten.

Lale, Ben, and Irina were sitting under a propane heater at a waterside table at Aşşk Kahve in the little town of Kuruçeşme alongside the Bosporus. Irina was looking down into the dark green water, pretending to be fascinated with the array of garbage and dead jellyfish that were bobbing so close to the seawall. Ben had his eyes closed and was trying to categorize the myriad of scents he inhaled: köfte and grilled fish from the adjacent tables, cigarette smoke from the countless Marlboro Lights burning around them, Lale's Chanel perfume, and something else he couldn't quite put his finger on, which, when he thought about it, was a rather strange expression since it would be difficult to put your finger on something as intangible as a smell.

Lale was being uncharacteristically quiet. She was looking intently at both Ben and Irina, and there was a palpable tension she was trying to avoid acknowledging. She waited for a small, noisy fishing boat to pass before breaking the silence. "I have been thinking about this muchly."

"I've been thinking a lot about this," Irina corrected her.

"Don't correct her English, honey," Ben instructed. "I like her flavor of English just the way it is."

"Flavor. *Tat*, we say in Turkish." Lale smiled at the girl. "Like your father is always asking for *tatlandırıcı*—taste sweetener—when a waiter doesn't know what Splenda is."

"I can imagine what you've been thinking about," Irina said to Lale. "About what to do with me. I don't fit in here. I don't fit in Kiev. The kids in Istanbul are different than I am. They just care about clothes and clubs and where they are going on holiday with their parents. They start out polite and speak in English to me, and then five seconds later they are back to speaking in fast Turkish and I don't know what they are saying. Probably something like what a loser this Russian girl is."

"Not true," Ben interjected. "That's just a cultural thing here. Once they are somewhat comfortable with you, they forget their manners and revert to Turkish. Happens to me all the time. And I know just enough of the language that if they were insulting me, I'd be kicking their asses, but it's never the case. They just forget that my Turkish is at a prekindergarten level."

"Well, if your Turkish is prekindergarten, mine is prenatal," Irina said, surprising them both with her vocabulary and mature sense of humor.

Lale was looking very sad. Always an emotional woman, she had learned to disguise her feelings around acquaintances but rarely hid them from family and close friends. "Ben, I have not been sleeping. I cannot do work or play bridge or even do my Instagram. I am not talking with my girlfriends or my mother or my kids. All I can think about is what to do. What is best for this beautiful, sweet girl *Yavrum*," she stressed, using the term for "my puppy" and stroking Irina's cheek. Ben and Irina sat silently waiting for her to continue. They both understood that this was the sound of the second shoe dropping. "I cannot do it. I just can *not* do it. I can *not* take on the responsibility of raising this wonderful girl. I have grown up two kids already and they have been out of the house for ten years, and I can *not* go through that again. You will think me selfish and ego centered—" She started crying silently.

Irina and Ben were silent, not surprised but shocked nevertheless that she had given this so much thought. She seemed to want to continue, so they kept quiet until she regained her composure sufficiently to go on.

"I am not wanting to throw you out of my life, Ben. You mean so much to me and your friendship means more than anything. Ever since I met you, there was one thing that I couldn't accept about you fully: that you always seem to be running away from your responsibilities. Everything you have told me about your life, you were going from one thing to another thing, one career to another career, one woman to another, one friend to another, one interest to a new one. No kids. That was a big warning sign for me, but I ignored it and came to understand that you were afraid and also honest with yourself and every woman that you wouldn't know how to be a father. You're being a godfather to Vlady only proves it."

Ben sat up straighter. "How do you mean, 'proves it'?"

"Because you are only good at being a *çakma baba*, a fake father. You see him for a few days, you spoil him, you teach him, you help support him, but you are not *there* for him. You leave that up to Kateryna. And maybe that's as it should be since he is not really your son. But I don't know. Either you are a parent or you are not in this world. At least that is what I believe."

"I'm not going to argue with you, Lale. As usual, you have me dead to rights."

"I don't understand dead to rights," Lale said, confused.

"I mean that you are correct in your assessment of me."

"So now you have met your *destinée*, Ben, with this youngster. And you must take some responsibility because there is no one else to do it. And what I'm saying is that I cannot help you this time." She drew several deep breaths. Between inhalations she, kept on, "You know you really stressed me out with going back and forth to Kiev for Vlady, but I put up with it because I love Kateryna and she was alone. Yet she is an adult who made a choice, and she is an amazing mother. As good as I am a mother, Ben. But you haven't been a father to anyone yet. So now this is your chance. Not just your chance, your obligation and opportunity to be accountable for your actions." She delivered this last part with great strength of conviction.

"And so that's it? You're saying that I just hit the road," Ben said quietly. "What about the biography of your father?"

Irina just listened intently, knowing that her immediate fate hung in the balance. This was very strange for her: to be talked about like she wasn't there, yet privy to such a critical aspect of her future. She completely understood Lale and was not at all angry with her. She believed in Ben and hoped that he would consider her wishes before making a decision that might affect both of them so momentously. She felt as light as a feather. She felt like all her physical attributes had vanished, as if she couldn't make a sound if she tried or a movement if she wanted. As if she didn't smell, couldn't be seen, couldn't be heard. Like a wraith.

"I didn't say that, and it is certainly not what I want. You will finish the book from there. You are almost finished anyway. If you will go to New York, I will see you often. I would be with you like now, but I do not know if that is the best place to bring her. Better Washington although I do not like it so much. I feel like it is a city of the dead. Or maybe even your old home Potomac in Maryland where you used to live with horses might be best. The schools, the countryside."

Ben could not think of anything to say, so he just kept quiet and let her finish expressing her thoughts.

"It is surprising to hear myself say this, Ben, but everything and everyone has changed during this past month. I think that for the first time I can remember, you are listening to me. I mean really listening. And for maybe the first time, I am speaking not just for myself, my own *egoism*, but for the three of us sitting here at this table." She glanced at Irina, who nodded in understanding. "Irina, you didn't know any of us before. We had our struggles, our problems with health and friends or people we thought were our friends but were not. Now everything I see in a different way. I see the reality of the goodness of your father's friends, and I only hope that he sees that too."

"I do. I most certainly do, Lale," Ben agreed.

Lale looked directly at him now. "These friends who came here from everywhere, they are so different from one another. But they all share a common bond—*you*. My heart was bursting with pride for you and your friends, but I also felt very jealous, very envious of you and these people. At first, I felt angry that this strange woman from the South came to see you, like she wanted you to fall in love with her again. That very much *nervoused* me, but what could I do? I was completely surprised by her. Then I understood that this wasn't like a threat to me. She was just another unrealistic, naive American. How could she think that there would still be any feelings left in you for her? *Aptal!* Stupid! This wasn't like the other women that I felt I always had to share you with in some way. Then I became much closer with Ipek. I came to understand why you liked her so much and how she was really such a good friend to you. Not a girlfriend like I was suspecting, but just a friend who was a girl who looked at you like an *Abi,* a big brother. And while I was back here and you and the others were in *Ukrayna*…Ukraine, Ipek and I grew to be very close friends, and she made me realize that I had everything all wrong. Most of my friends were booollshit, *çakma* people and most of your friends are real." Lale paused in her monologue to take a sip of tea. It had become cold and she signaled the waiter for a refill. "Do you understand that, Ben? These are real friends." He nodded in assent while she continued.

"In fact, Ipek and I spent a lot of time with Johan and Bamkiz when you were away with the others. I learned a lot about you, and we talked about how you had begun to change. They all remembered you as a very fun guy, but someone who just took everything and everyone for granted. I told them that I thought that you had changed since the cancer experience. Howman agreed with me on that as he shared the experience with you. Now I am waiting to see if you have grown from this experience." She took a deep breath. "I think that maybe you have."

Ben started to speak, but she interrupted him. "So just to finish before you say anything, I expect you to leave here with Irina, and I expect you to be a complete *benadam*, a good man, and raise this beautiful girl as your daughter. And for once, don't put yourself first."

Epilogue

One year later, Potomac, Maryland

OCCASIONALLY, AN EXQUISITE Indian summer visits Maryland in late October or early November. The temperature soars above seventy degrees, and despite an earlier frost, insects usually associated with July reappear and flowers blossom: asters, white turtleheads, cardinal flowers, and black-eyed Susans provided a colorful perimeter to the old stone and wood colonial house. What makes this micro season so special is that there is little, if any, humidity, and although the trees boast their peak colors usually associated with the imminent approach of winter, you feel like jumping in the pool and lying naked in the sun.

The sugar maples in his backyard had turned fiery orange red, and the poplars were golden yellow. The deep crimson leaves of a red maple had begun to carpet the ground, providing a sweet, loamy scent as they slowly decomposed while the lighter brown leaves of the post oaks that lined the rear of the property blew in the light wind across the deep green mat of ryegrass.

Howman, who no longer tolerated being called the Blitz, had recently taken up painting with water colors. He had his easel set up in the shade of an oak tree and was working on one of his character-istically unusual landscapes. Soft realism of a physical, natural scene with completely incongruent people inserted in a variety of irrele-vant sizes throughout was his current métier. In the present exam-

255

ple, he had replaced everyone with a historical, political, or celebrity counterpart. Ben was represented by Benjamin Franklin, Jimmy by Fred Astaire, Bamkiz was depicted as Christopher Columbus, and Kateryna was in the guise of Madonna holding Baby Jesus, who, of course, sported Vlady's face. Irina was front and center as Joan of Arc. Ben, on the other hand, appeared as a small, rotund figure in the background with arms upraised to a flock of blackbirds, in the guise of Alfred Hitchcock.

In an effort to look more artistic, Howman had recently grown a distinctly gray Van Dyke *beardlet*. However, when combined with the Washington Nationals baseball cap and red, white, and blue Capitals jersey he was wearing, the resulting impression was more of a typical DC sports fanatic than a hipster artist. But the colors were perfect for the season, and to his credit, he had foregone the Wizards accoutrements he often added to his wardrobe. Howman had always fit in as both the iconoclastic Everyman and conformist Nowhere Man—a human dichotomy. Sometimes he was a social chameleon blending in with any crowd and, at other times, an unforgiving rebel, appearing at black-tie events with jeans and a denim bow tie. Today, he was enjoying the quiet of the exurbs and having the opportunity to capture a peaceful scene he never wanted to forget. Most of the time, he was a quiet person, and throughout the events in Turkey and Ukraine, he had remained in the background, always willing to lend a hand when needed, expecting nothing in return, and forever being a positive force for the group. He was then as he was being now, at ease with himself and those around him.

The only discord emanated from the Bose outdoor speakers that Ben had installed around the perimeter of the stone patio. Irina had become a fan of vintage rap over the past few months and now Tupac Shakur's "Me against the World" was interrupting Ben's reverie and Howman's concentration.

The question is will I live? No one in the world loves me.
I'm headed for danger, don't trust strangers.
Put one in the chamber whenever I'm feelin' this anger.

Don't wanna make excuses 'cause this is how it is.
What's the use unless we're shootin' no one notices
the youth
It's just me against the world, baby.

Howman put down his brush in exasperation and walked over to the cooler chest and grabbed a beer, but Ben tried concentrating on the lyrics. They were full of alienation and anger and despair. Did Irina still think that it was her against the world? Hopefully, she just liked the repetitive beat and the way the spoken words became indistinguishable from the percussive sounds of the music. Ben sat suspended from a cage-like tree swing that he had hung from the lowest limb of a massive black oak. Irina and Vlady were happily struggling on the Pawleys Island hammock that was tied between two sugar maples about fifty feet away.

Vlady finally gave up on trying to push Irina out of the hammock and began cajoling Jimmy into a climbing contest on the black oak from which Ben was suspended. By climbing into Ben's lap, then reaching around to grab the wicker slats of the hanging chair, the little monkey managed to pull himself up the chain to the large branch. From there, it was an easy climb to over thirty feet above their heads. In a panic, Kateryna begged Jimmy to get him down as the little boy sat comfortably looking down at his mother with a mocking smile and swinging legs. Groaning a complaint as he emerged from the hanging chair, Ben gave Jimmy a leg up to the lowest branch, and within seconds, Jimmy had reached the boy.

"This is what I get for letting you take him to that climbing gym!" Kateryna shouted up to Jimmy. "The two of you are making me crazy."

"Come up here, Mama," Vlady called. "I can see everybody!"

Ben offered her his cupped hands for a boost, but she merely scowled at him. Although she had recently lost almost ten pounds and looked as fit as a tigress, she was neither interested in, nor capable of, climbing trees. She had begun to realize that ever since Jimmy had become a fixture in their lives, now she had two little boys to worry about.

Ben wondered what it was that compelled little boys to want to climb. He included himself and Jimmy in this category because, in many ways, he knew that they would never fully grow up. Not that he wanted to, but assuming the duties of fatherhood had at least tempered his risk-taking approach to life. Now he had responsibilities that he never could have imagined. When he had purchased the house, which architecturally bore a close resemblance to the one he had lived in when he had cancer many years before, there had been a dilapidated swing set and climbing wall in the yard. Considering it a hazard due its poor condition and since Irina was far too old to ever debase herself by using such a thing, he had taken it apart and sent it to the dump. But he had kept the little engraved wooden plaque that read "Life must be lived as play." He researched this and learned that it was someone's abridgment of Plato's quote: "We should live out our lives playing at certain pastimes."

Ben firmly believed in the philosophical underpinnings of this quote. Happiness from recreation was both fundamental and characteristic of a good life, a life in which a person fulfills human nature in a superlative way. Mankind possesses a set of purposes, which are typically human and are inherent to our very nature. The positive person is virtuous, meaning one has outstanding abilities and emotional tendencies that allow one to fulfill his or her common human ends. He understood well that *virtuous* didn't necessarily mean perfect, but rather trying to do the right thing under the circumstances. He was doing his best to follow that path now. He had called his friends together for a reunion of sorts. It was a dual celebration of Irina's birthday as well as a surprise engagement.

Kateryna, Jimmy, and Vlady had arrived from Kiev the previous night on one of Donald's aircraft that was deadheading back from a charter to Odessa. Thus far, they had avoided experiencing any symptoms of jet lag. Johan and Bamkiz were another matter entirely. They were stretched out on a valuable 1920s Tabriz that had been spread on top of the thick grass, exacerbating their condition with absurdly strong Long Island iced teas. Bamkiz had brought the large old carpet as a wedding gift for Rachel and Donald but temporarily appropriated it for ground cover. He maintained to everyone that this was all part of an *aging treatment*. He reminded Ben of the time they had driven down a street in Esfahan that had been covered with rugs that were in the process of being "antiqued." In comparison, this was a relatively mild treatment for a work of craftsmanship that would probably fetch upward of $45,000 in one of the oriental carpet galleries of lower Manhattan.

For two men who ran an adventure travel business, at the moment Johan and Bamkiz hardly looked the part. In fact, they looked downright dissolute after consuming the better part of a bottle of fifteen-year-old single-malt Scotch whiskey on the flight to Washington. Over the past six months, they had personally accompanied their guests on four trips to the Gulf of Guinea and successfully brought seven blue marlins over eight hundred pounds each to the boat for tag and release, along with innumerable elephant yellowfin tuna averaging three hundred pounds. This was par for the course for Johan, but Bamkiz was never at home on the water. He suffered intermittent bouts of seasickness, which could never be revealed to the clients. Conversely, Johan hated walking and stalking. He was a man of the salt and could sit or stand for hours on end in a rocking boat without any ill affect.

They also had taken two hunters in their sixties from Aspen on a two-week ibex and boar-hunting trip in the mountains of southern Turkey, followed by an illuminating three days with Ipek and Lale. During ten days of literally running up and down the Taurus Mountains with these ridiculously fit, gray-haired guys who were used to exercise at eight thousand feet above sea level, they encountered a group of starving Syrian refugees. Six families who had fled the depredations of ISIS managed to leave the refugee camp near the Turkish-Syrian border almost one year ago. They wandered far to the northwest, thinking that they could make it on their own to Ankara. Without maps or GPS, they had become hopelessly lost. Some were slightly injured with ankle sprains, and all were suffering from malnutrition and dysentery from a polluted river where they had consumed water in a sheepherding area below the mountains.

The meat from their boar and ibex kills had fed this group of families well, and Bamkiz had called in the heli for a medevac. After bringing the Syrians to an aid station in Adana, Turkey, the partners had gone in different directions for a month, Bamkiz on a walkabout in the Australian outback with a group of recovering prescription drug addicts, and Johan on a steelhead fishing trip in northern British Columbia with a group of business executives who could drink like the fish they were unsuccessfully trying to catch. Johan finally talked them into forgetting the shy, elusive steelhead and moving farther inland to throw some flies at the monster rainbow trout that inhabited those northern rivers. He then escorted identical twin brothers Matt and Steve Agassea and their girlfriends on a salmon and halibut fishing adventure off the coast of Langara Island. He had nearly been drowned when a two hundred-pound halibut had pulled him into the freezing cold water after one of the women had dropped her fishing rod overboard with the line wrapped around Johan's hand as he was trying to pull the fish over the gunwale. The big fish had pulled him eighty feet down before he could cut the line with the snap-blade knife he kept tied to his waist.

The pair reconnected in Mozambique to take a more intrepid group hunting for buffalo and sable. Although they enjoyed the good life of a tented safari at night, the days were spent beating through the brush to avoid surprising any lions. At the same time, they had to endure the constant stress of staring down 1,500-pound highly aggressive animals while the anal-retentive lawyers and investment bankers obsessed over their shooting positions. Each day they walked for miles, keeping the hunters a safe distance behind. This added to their anxiety because they were in constant apprehension of being shot by one of their clients who might mistake them for a big cat or other dangerous quarry. This condition was solved when Johan decided that the clients would only receive their ammunition directly from one of the bush guides after the game was sighted and everyone had moved away from the field of fire. Only while taking long shots at sable, hartebeest, waterbuck, and eland from high rocky outcrops were they able to relax and chat with the men who were paying so dearly for this wilderness experience.

Their customers were not only paying for a bucket-list level of hunting and fishing but also for the uniquely entertaining companionship of Johan and Bamkiz. In addition to the intellectualized

Abbot and Costello bantering of the two partners, other offerings were available. These weren't your standard high-dollar safaris and fishing expeditions. Often, they were requested to arrange for escorts (which Kateryna handled from Kiev), high-efficiency, encrypted satellite Wi-Fi so business deals would not be interrupted, and sporting events like the World Cup from Brazil could be viewed. The starting price for their adventures was $5,000 per person per day. Donald's jet charter company provided air transport at discounted rates for his friends, which greatly contributed to the bottom line.

This all involved incredibly complex logistics, which Kateryna provided through her competent administrative and managerial support but required a prodigious amount of energy from the two men. By mid-October, the pair figured that they had banked over $500,000 in profits but lost a combined total of seventy-five pounds. Such was how they arrived in Maryland, superbly fit for two middle-aged guys who previously never walked when they could drive but were now completely out of gas.

Irina had quietly come over to Ben's hanging chair and gently squeezed in next to him as Lale and Ipek's taxi pulled up in the driveway, followed by a chauffeured car with Rachel and Donald. "The guests of honor have arrived," she whispered to him.

"The guest of honor is already here," Ben winked back at her. They awkwardly slid out of the hanging chair and trotted up to their four guests. Everyone embraced and Ben and Lale clung to each other for a particularly long time. When they pulled apart, Ben could see tears in Lale's eyes.

"I don't know whether you should be mad at me or happy at me," she confessed.

"Happy," Ben answered, deciding not to correct her grammar. "Not mad at all. Why would you even think of such a thing? You and Ipek make a wonderful couple although I must admit, you caught me completely by surprise." He walked over to Rachel and Donald and helped them with their luggage, directing Vlady to rouse Bamkiz and Johan and asking Howman for some help.

As soon as Lale, Ipek, Rachel, and Donald had showered and changed into more comfortable clothes, everyone reconvened on the large stone patio for drinks and catching up. It was late afternoon, and despite the summerlike weather experienced for most of the day, as the sun began to set, the temperature invariably dropped. Bamkiz and Jimmy fired up the charcoal set inside an old oil drum that had been sawed in half to serve as a grill while Howman looked for some lighter, less intrusive music. He settled on "No Woman, No Cry" by Bob Marley and the Wailers.

Rachel took control of the cooking, running between the kitchen and the grill, working with Lale and Ipek to adorn a long table with baskets of freshly baked whole grain bread, pitchers of iced tea, and bowls of salad, sweet corn, and dirty rice. Donald grilled antelope steaks and salmon fillets that Johan had brought, occasionally grabbing Rachel for a consultation of the amorous kind.

Irina and Ben had returned to the hanging chair, this time snuggled together under an old Hudson's Bay blanket that he had received many years ago from his father. For a long time, neither spoke as they observed the human theater that played before them. There wasn't any need for them to talk now. They just watched their good friends, each with their own thoughts of how interesting life had been over the past eighteen months. Irina had grown accustomed to her new life and was prospering at her high school, successful with making friends as well as earning commendable grades. Ben had focused his entire being on her, easing the transition to American life and subordinating himself to her emotional needs as best he could. Now and for the foreseeable future, she was first in his life, and he was subordinated to her requirements. Rather than being an annoyance or inconvenience, she was giving him a quality of life he had never before experienced. This was the first time since leaving Istanbul that he had shared her with so many people his own age, and as they had been through such a formative experience together, this was nothing short of perfect. He looked down affectionately at Irina as she studied the mismatched but intimately connected group chatting on the patio.

Irina turned her face upward toward her father. "They are all like misfit angels, aren't they?" she said to him.

"Not quite C. S. Lewis," Ben replied, "but close enough."

About the Author

GARY S. LACHMAN is an itinerant adventurer and international lawyer who suffers from situational ADHD. He is the author of five prior works, including two murder mysteries, a science-fiction novella, a personal tale of cancer survival, and a master's degree textbook on international real estate, investment, development, and law in emerging markets. A US Coast Guard licensed captain, he is passionate about environmental issues, particularly clean rivers and seas and sustainable fisheries. He runs a deep-sea fishing charter boat operation in South Florida and British Columbia, Canada.

Lachman spent many years with the State Department, engaged in improving diplomatic facilities and intelligence community support in over forty countries around the globe. During this time, he added to the extraordinary cast of characters he considers true friends that he's amassed since childhood. He recently lived for several years in Istanbul, Turkey, enjoying an indulged life of private jets, lavish parties, and super yachts, only to return to his home port of Palm Beach, Florida, to hunt the mahi-mahi, sailfish, marlin, tuna, and wahoo that inhabit the azure waters of the Gulf Stream.